FOREVER SOUL TIES

2012

JAN

CH

Also by Vanessa Davis Griggs

Redeeming Waters

Ray of Hope

The Blessed Trinity Series

The Truth Is the Light

Goodness and Mercy

Practicing What You Preach

If Memory Serves

Strongholds

Blessed Trinity

Published by Kensington Publishing Corp.

FOREVER SOUL TIES

VANESSA DAVIS GRIGGS

Kensington Publishing Corp.
http://www.kensingtonbooks.com

Dedicated to
Joseph Lee Jr., Ruth Washington, Abraham Lee, James Daniel Lee,
Rachel Shockley, Mary Mack, and my beautiful mother,
Josephine Davis

Acknowledgments

I'm forever thankful to God for choosing me and calling me to this place I now am. I know that God truly is love! To my mother and father, Josephine and James Davis Jr.: thank you for loving us and for the sacrifices you've made on behalf of your family.

To my husband, Jeffery; my children Jeffery, Jeremy, and Johnathan; my grandchildren Asia and Ashlynn: each of you have truly blessed my life. Danette Dial, Terence Davis, Cameron Davis, Guy Griggs, Mark Davis, Arlinda Davis, Emmanuel Davis, Cumberlan Davis, and my nieces and nephews: we are family, and I'm grateful for every mountain God has brought us over. We know what an awesome God we serve!

My deepest thanks to my editor at Kensington/Dafina, Selena James, for your hard work and all that you do! Through my life's journey, I've been blessed to meet and know some really wonderful people (so many, I can't name them all here). People like: Bonita Chaney, Rosetta Moore, Vanessa L. Rice, Zelda Miles, Linda H. Jones, Shirley Walker, Stephanie Perry Moore, Thyosis Scott, Melva Jackson, Dr. Askhari Johnson Hodari, Alice Gordon, Tracy Windley, Alease Sims, Gregg Pelt, Laura McClure, Delta Sigma Theta Sorority Birmingham Alumnae Chapter, Pat Davis, Lashanda Harris, Dr. Norma McLauchlin, and the Lady Lifers of New Life Bible Church in Fayetteville, North Carolina.

Special thanks to Mary Monroe for blessing me with your kind words. You always make me smile. To Oprah Winfrey: thank you for not only telling but showing us that, "God can dream a bigger dream for you than you can ever dream for yourself."

I am, and will forever be, grateful to those of you who have been so supportive of what God has placed in my hands to do. Thank you for choosing my books and thanks for spreading the word to others. I truly love, appreciate, and thank God for each of you!

You can find me on the Web at:

www.VanessaDavisGriggs.com. I adore hearing from you!

Chapter 1

How much less man, that is a worm? and the son of man, which is a worm?

—Job 25:6

I am a sinner.

That's the first thing you need to know about me. Some might say a worm, although when it comes to worms, there are so many various types. The second thing you need to know is that those who brought me up and exposed the fact that I'd been caught in the act, "the very act" of adultery, weren't really after me. By this I mean: they were out to expose, to trick really, the thirty-three-year-old pastor who'd already effectively turned many of their lives and traditional beliefs upside down and on their sanctimonious heads.

So this wasn't *really* about me and the man I've loved since the very first day I laid eyes upon him, two months and fifteen days shy of me being fourteen years old. The afro-sporting, caramel-hued man of sixteen and a half who wore a grown-up hat (a fedora, I believe it was, although I didn't know the name of it at the time), cocked (as was also his head) ever so slightly to the side. He smiled at me. And his eyes . . . His eyes lassoed my heart before his bass voice ever even uttered the first sound that would completely rein me in to tie our hearts and forever knit our souls together.

Oh, I know you think that this is all an exaggeration. But the fact that I'm a little over fifty now proves my point. That tiny spark lit all those years ago was burning strong inside of a roaring fire some forty years later. What would *you* call it?

So if this is the case, you might ask, then why were he and I caught in adultery? Why is this not a celebration account of our blissful years of holy matrimony together?

Simple. I'm married and so is he. But we're not married to each other. In the past forty years our paths have crossed (on occasion) here and there. At one church program and, early on, one funeral of someone we both knew. And then there was the one surprise time at a department store (which I confess was weird and *quite* awkward for me). Especially since he had two of his (what would eventually become) three daughters with him, and I had my three daughters and a niece with me. He teasingly introduced me as "This would have been your mother." I believe he said *would* and not *should*. I'm pretty sure that's what he said: would, although I confess maybe I wasn't listening as closely as I could or should have. How was I to know he'd be saying something weighty like that? I mean, I was still in shock at running into him in the women's department at Rich's in the mall.

Then came the time, ten years ago, that changed everything. The time he called my business, The Painted Lady Flower Shop, not knowing he'd be reaching me.

When I saw his name and number on the caller ID, I confess I could barely breathe. I tried to decide whether I should answer it or just let it go to voice mail, knowing full well I would not return the call if it did and that there was no one else in my one-woman shop to do it. And if I did answer it, should I let him know it was me, or just be as I am with everyone and anyone else who calls?

Cool, calm, and in my most polished professional voice, I answered on the third ring. And as soon as he learned he was speaking to me, he veered away from what he'd originally called for. We did, however, eventually come back to it: he needed flowers . . . for his wife . . . of twenty years now. The woman he'd married and was still married to. The girlfriend, actually, he was dating when he and I first met. The one he'd continued dating after he'd stepped up and asked me to slow dance to a song that, *to this very day,* still takes me back to that night of him gazing into my eyes as I stood on the next to the last step in the basement at a house party.

"Flowers for your wife?" I said with as much excitement as I could muster. "Oh, that is wonderful!" I was happy for him; really I was. His ordering flowers had to mean things were going well for the two of them. After all, he was calling to order my most expensive arrangement of flowers for his wife—although I suppose it could just as well have meant they were having major problems and he was trying to find a way to fix things. That's the thing about flowers: giving them works in either case.

I explained I could have them delivered wherever he wanted. He wanted, instead, to come by the shop and pick them up. I told him I'd have them ready on the day and time he desired.

When he walked into my shop, older (in his midforties then) but still just as handsome (if not more so) and as debonair as I'd remembered him the last time our paths crossed almost ten years earlier, I wasn't ready. No, no, the flowers were ready and waiting. The best job I'd ever done (if I may say so myself).

I wasn't ready.

Not after my knees discovered it was him and cowardly buckled—completely betraying me by refusing to do their part in holding the rest of me up.

Chapter 2

He maketh wars to cease unto the end of the earth;
he breaketh the bow, and cutteth the spear in sun-
der; he burneth the chariot in the fire.

—Psalm 46:9

"I got you," he said as he quickly rushed over and caught me. I hurriedly righted myself and took a step away from him. He glanced down at my feet as though he was looking for the culprit of me almost falling. I looked down as well, as though I, too, was looking for a reason for my lost footing. "I'm all right," I said. "Thanks for the save."

He smiled, and in a warm, chocolaty-smooth voice said, "Butterfly." He shook his head as he bit down on his bottom lip, then said, "My beautiful little black butterfly."

I swiftly glanced down again. "My shoes. I guess I should have worn a different pair. These are a bit high, at least for this type of floor here. They're not broken in good . . . my shoes, that is . . . the soles of them . . . These shoes just happen to match. . . ."

"You haven't changed a bit," he said with a grin. "You're still that same funny, bubbly, wonderfully beautiful girl I met all those years ago when you were thirteen."

I touched my hair with its strands of silver. "That's not true; I'm much, *much* older now."

He continued to smile. "Which merely confirms that wine does *indeed* only get better with time." He stared into my eyes, then ticked his head twice.

"Well, Spears . . . Spear Carrier, let me get your order," I said, bringing us both back to reality.

He laughed. "Spears? Spear Carrier? No one calls me Spears *or* Spear Carrier anymore. Well, hardly anyone. Talk about a throwback."

I grinned. "Is that right?" I'd never called him Spears or Spear Carrier, not even back then. I'd always called him by his given name: Ethan Duane Roberts.

"That was *way* back in the day," he said. "Back when I was into javelin throwing. I *was* good though. I loved throwing a javelin." He made an imaginary throw. "I really thought I was going to make it to the Olympics: throwing, running, jumping . . . something."

"Well, I guess we all had big dreams back then."

He looked intensely at me. "Yeah. We did, didn't we? I was into sports big time. And you—"

"Had dreams of other things." I nodded. My way of ending where his statement was about to lead us. "Let me get your order." I walked into the back room and retrieved the flowers he'd ordered.

"My goodness! Those are gorgeous!" he said when I stepped back in carrying a crystal vase of flowers like it was a hard-earned trophy. "Absolutely . . . beautiful!"

I set them on the counter so he could get a better look at them. "Thank you, Mister Roberts," I said. "I'm glad you like them. I believe your wife will be impressed with you for purchasing these. This arrangement is my top-of-the-line offering."

"Oh, you think, huh?" His tone was dismissive.

"Is there something wrong with them? Something you don't like or that you need me to fix?" I asked. "I want my customers to be satisfied. So if—"

"Oh, there's nothing wrong with the flowers. In fact I've never seen anything so lovely . . . so magnificent, so gorgeous," he said before making an obvious show of gazing deeply into my eyes. "Well, almost never," he said with a mischievous grin.

"Are you sure you like them? Are you sure now?"

"Oh, I'm more than sure. And I'm more than satisfied. It's just my wife . . . Oh, forget it. I'm sure she's going to love them . . . *or not.*"

I started to pursue where he was going with that, but then realized it really wasn't my business. If he loved what I'd done, then my job was completed. I told him the total amount owed. He handed me a gold credit card. I processed it, had him sign, and that was that—the end of our transaction.

"Thanks," I said.

"My pleasure," he said.

As he carefully picked up the large vase of flowers, it occurred to me that he might have a time with them in the car. "Let me get a box for you to set the vase in so it won't tip over." I went to the back again and returned with a box adequate enough to handle the task.

"Thanks again," he said. "And I'm definitely going to send more business your way."

"I certainly will appreciate that. With the slight economic downturn, it's been hard out here for folks with their own businesses. No one's giving us much of a hand up. At least, not *here.*"

"Well, thanks again," he said as he headed toward the door.

I hurried to the door and opened it for him. "Oh, it was my pleasure. Do come back again . . . and soon," I said. And as quickly as those words left my mouth, I wished I hadn't said them. Not because I hadn't meant them; I say those exact same words to every single person who patronizes my business. In fact, it's part of my mission statement. *I will let my customers know it was a pleasure serving them. And I will always invite existing customers to patronize my business again.* But for some reason, saying those words to Ethan "Spears . . . Spear Carrier" Roberts had a totally different meaning. *Totally* different.

At least, they did for me.

Chapter 3

For all seek their own, not the things which are Jesus Christ's.

—Philippians 2:21

Two weeks later, Ethan called again and ordered the same type of flower arrangement as before. I couldn't help but smile. That had to mean the flowers worked. Once again, he wanted to pick them up. And once again, I told him they would be ready and waiting. Realizing from something I'd said that my business was a one-woman operation, he inquired what time I closed for lunch. I told him two p.m. since most people tended to visit or call during their lunch time anywhere between eleven a.m. and one thirty p.m. He said he'd be by to pick up the flowers before two.

So when I looked at my watch the day he was scheduled to be there and saw that it was five minutes before two, I began to wonder what might have happened to him. But being the owner, there was no hard and fast rule that said I had to take lunch at two on the dot. Honestly, I was just praying that nothing bad had transpired.

Ethan casually strolled through the door wearing a gorgeous forest green suit exactly two minutes before two o'clock.

"Hi," he said, as though he hadn't had me a little on pins and needles.

"Hi there," I said with a genuine smile, relieved that he was all right. "Let me get your order."

"Butterfly," he said, causing me to stop in midturn. "Have you eaten anything yet?"

I turned completely back toward him. "No. But I'm good. That's the great thing about being the boss; I'm in charge. And as the owner, I want to ensure that all of my customers are taken care of. Did you need something else? You're welcome to browse. I'm not in any hurry."

"No, I don't need anything else. It's just . . . well . . . I haven't had lunch yet. And I was wondering . . ." He seemed to be having a hard time finding the words he was looking for. "I mean to say . . . if you don't already have plans . . ." He let out a slightly audible sigh. "Would you like to go get a bite with me? Lunch, I mean . . . go get a bite of lunch with me. My treat."

"Oh, you don't have to do that."

"I know. I'd just like to sit and chat with you. If you don't mind. You know . . . catch up on what's been going on in your life," he said.

I frowned. "You know . . . I don't think that would be a good idea. I'm married; you're married. You know how that is."

He chuckled. I could tell it was forced. "Oh, it wouldn't be a *date* or anything like *that*. It would merely be two old acquaintances who both normally eat lunch separately . . . at least I assume you eat lunch or something that counts as lunch." He grinned. "It would simply be two people eating a bite of lunch together . . . while we talk. That's it. It doesn't even have to be a big lunch either. And if you're worried about being away from the shop for too long, we can go someplace near here. I don't know how long you usually take for lunch, but we can stick to your normal time." He tilted his head slightly. "Come on. Don't leave me hanging out here flapping in the wind. What's a bite amongst two old friends?"

"Well . . ."

"Come on. Don't make me have to get down on my knees and beg." He then smiled with those eyes that had a way of appearing, at times, to twinkle. His smile and those doggone gorgeous brown eyes, once again, began doing a job on me.

I smiled back, then shrugged. "Well, okay. I mean, it's only lunch . . . right?"

"There you go," he said with a single clap. "It's *only* lunch. Would you like to go somewhere close to here or would you prefer I pick the place?"

"There are only a few fast food joints near here, not any great eating places. Sadly, this area is becoming a ghost town. Oh, wait! There is this sweet little deli ten minutes up the road. I hope *they* haven't moved or closed shop."

"Then we can go there if that's where you'd like." He nodded, then promptly burst forth with another one of his full grins, displaying his still-perfect teeth just as I remembered them being when I was thirteen. "I'll wait for you in my car," he said.

"Oh, you mean we're going to ride together? Me and you? In the same car?"

"Well, it makes sense, don't you think? There's no reason for us to drive separate vehicles to the same destination. Besides, I still have to come back to get my flowers. We certainly wouldn't want them in the car in this late-August Southern heat wilting . . . drooping . . . dying . . . while we sit in an air-conditioned place . . . eating away."

"Yes . . . your flowers. You're right. They'll definitely fare better if we leave them here until you're ready to take them home or back to work with you."

"Actually, I'm off work now. Totally free. All yours, for the rest of the afternoon in fact."

That's when I should have given him his vase of flowers and politely escorted him right out of the front door.

I suppose that's why people say hindsight is twenty-twenty.

Chapter 4

For we know that the law is spiritual: but I am carnal, sold under sin.

—Romans 7:14

It was near the end of August, after most of the teens (who would have likely packed the place) had returned to school following their summer vacation when Ethan and I unceremoniously strolled into Daisy Queen's Deli. I concluded that was why the place was so empty, especially during this time of day. I loved Daisy Queen's Deli, whose style was much like the popular deli franchises of the day without patrons having to go through a line to place their orders. The other big difference was Daisy Queen's Deli's bread wasn't as thick as those franchises, making me feel better about eating a sandwich from there, knowing that I wasn't consuming a bucketload of carbs.

Besides, Daisy and Queen were entrepreneurs much like me. Queen and her mother, Daisy, started their business some ten years earlier, originally serving their customers in what most referred to as "a hole in the wall." It was a really tiny place. But Daisy had created a special sauce for her sandwiches and that secret sauce created its own buzz, quickly putting that hole in the wall on the map. Then there was that television show that traveled to towns in search of the best eating places. They'd heard about Daisy Queen's Deli, came and featured it on the show, and the rest—as people like to say—is history. Daisy Queen's Deli's business boomed so much after that segment aired that Daisy and her mother had no other choice *but* to expand to a bigger place.

Of course like many businesses around that time, as soon as they moved to another area that seemed to be booming, the economic bust came roaring in like a lion. Businesses began closing their doors, slowly at first, like prey singularly and inconspicuously being picked off so you didn't notice how much trouble many of the companies were in. There would be one empty space, then another, and before you knew it, an entire row of previously occupied buildings would be vacant with the exception of possibly one lone store trying desperately to hang in there. But people who shop don't like vacant areas. They prefer shopping where some life still appears.

The owners of the vacant buildings tried doing various things to keep the strip and inside malls going until things picked back up again. Things like giving one year of free rent to any business that either chose to stay or chose to open a business there.

That's how I was able to begin my lifelong dream of opening my own floral shop. It's hard to start a business, but even more so when you're black. It's difficult to obtain the needed financing. And most of our ancestors didn't have stashes of cash to be passed down to help sustain the next generations. So black people get financially creative. Just ask folks like Spike Lee and Robert Townsend. It's not as easy as folks think to secure a business loan (small or otherwise).

Noting that there wasn't anyone visibly working in the deli at the time, Ethan and I chose a table close to the window. I absolutely adore sunlight; I always have.

"A penny for your thoughts," Ethan said as we sat there in silence at first.

I smiled. "A penny? *A penny?* Is that all my thoughts are going for these days? You do know things have gone up considerably, don't you?"

He released a small chuckle. "Oh, believe me: I know how much things have gone up. All right. What's the going rate for thoughts these days?"

I waved him off. "I'm just playing with you." How silly was that! I can't believe I even formed my mouth to say that.

He leaned in a little. I still couldn't get over how handsome he continued to be at the age of forty-five. His skin was smooth, but a little more filled out than in his teen years. A touch of gray, just enough to appear strategically placed in one small area, gave him an air of distinction. I never thought I'd think gray could be so sexy, but it was. I wanted to touch it. Thank goodness I resisted the temptation.

"Whatever is on your mind must be pretty heavy," he said with a lift to his voice.

"What?" I flashed him a "cat that ate the canary" smile, hoping to throw him off.

"I just asked you what you're thinking and you're just sitting there with a big beautiful smile on your face."

"I was thinking . . . that we need to order." I looked around for someone to come and take our order. Actually, I was just trying to break away from Ethan's engaging eyes. His eyes were so hypnotizing, the last thing I needed was to get caught up in them. Been there, done that, got the T-shirt.

Ethan sat back against his chair. "Yeah, that's right. You do have to get back."

A young woman came in from the back room. I raised my hand and beckoned to her. She threw her hand up to let me know she would be over to us shortly.

"I'm sorry," the young woman, who looked to be in her late teens or early twenties, said when she reached our table. "But we don't take orders at the tables anymore. You have to go through the line now." She gestured toward the area resembling other franchises' setup. I hadn't paid it much attention when we came in.

"You don't? We do?" I said. "When did all of *this* happen?"

"No, ma'am. Yes, ma'am. Things changed about a month ago. You have to go through the line now and tell me what you want as I make your sandwich."

"Oh, okay," I said. Ethan quickly got up to assist me as I stood. That's when it hit me how long it had been since I'd been out to eat with a man. And with him helping me up like that, just how long it had been since I'd been around a gentle-man.

When it came to eating out (especially with my husband), that generally translated into one of us bringing food in. And as far as opening a door, helping me when I sat down, helping me up, that was something I read about in fairy tales or sweet romance novels; something that you happened to see when you saw other people out who were head-over-heels in love. My husband, Zeke, and I didn't even walk side by side when we were together. In fact, if you didn't know any better and you happened to see the two of us, you'd declare there was some rule that mandated me to walk so many paces behind him.

Of course, that wasn't the case. Almost a foot taller than me, my husband's stride just happened to be longer than mine. He walks slowly but can cover a lot more ground than I do with less of an effort. It looks like I'm trotting to keep up with him. And for whatever reason, he won't make an effort to ensure we're next to each other when we're together. Even when he's not taking long strides, he stays far enough away from being next to me that it would be hard for anyone to say we're a couple.

"So why did y'all change this?" I asked the young woman who was now taking our orders at the glass-covered counter.

"You know how it is." Her employee pin read FRANCESCA. "People are always trying to come up with ways to save money. This way, you don't have to have as many people working. Instead of someone taking your order, filling it, and bringing it out to you, you cut out all of those middle people."

"Are Daisy and Queen still running things?" I asked.

"Yes, ma'am. Neither of them is here right now though. Queen is my mama and Daisy is my grandmama. You know them?"

"I've met them both before."

"Yes, ma'am," Francesca said. She finished our order, placed our plain white tissue–wrapped sandwiches on a brown tray, handed us each a large cup to get our own drinks from the soda dispensing machine, then rang us up.

Ethan and I both got sweet tea. Daisy Queen's Deli's tea is the best around. In fact, one of the grocery chains reportedly tried getting her to package her tea to sell exclusively in their stores. I would definitely buy a gallon of Daisy Queen's tea if it was available like that.

Ethan said grace for us. It was really nice having a man even mention grace before eating, let alone to take the lead in doing it. My husband certainly didn't do that. And on the rare occasions when we had company and I asked him to, he merely looked at me and said, "You can do it." So generally I'd been the one who prayed.

"This is so good!" Ethan said, bringing me back to the food before us. "Wow! I mean *really* good." He bit into his turkey sandwich again before he'd finished the previous bite.

"I told you they have great food here." I bit into my tuna melt sandwich.

"Indeed you did. It's just: not everyone's taste is the same. How was I to know you would be so incredibly right?" He spoke with food still in his mouth.

"See, you should stop underestimating me."

"You would think I would have learned after all of these years." He grinned.

I was about to take another bite. I stopped and held my sandwich in midair. I knew what he was hinting about. When we were teens, he thought because he was from the city and I was from the country that I was some country girl who didn't know anything. He got burned more than a few times from that assumption.

"Are you thinking about the first time I came to see you?" he asked, scrunching down slightly as though he was trying to read my thoughts.

I smiled. "Not exactly," I said. Although that first time *was* in the bundle of times he'd grossly underestimated me. "But since you brought it up, that's yet a *perfect* example of another time you should have listened to *and* believed me."

"Yeah." He snickered. "I thought for sure I was going to get with you that day, *if* you know what I mean. But you shut a homeboy down quick! Just like a virus in a computer shuts down the whole operating system, you shut me *down*."

I laughed. "What do you know about computers and operating software?"

He primped his mouth, then simultaneously smoothed down each side of his perfectly trimmed mustache with his thumb and index finger. "Okay, you got me. I confess: I know nothing about computers, except that they're beginning to be heavily implemented at the plant where I work."

"And where exactly do you work? What do you do? Besides the well-publicized work we all have heard that you do."

"I work at a place called A&D. I've been there since I graduated from high school. Well, actually, I graduated high school, attended our local junior college here for one semester, decided that I really needed to *make* money as opposed to funneling it out. So I put in an application at the A&D plant and I've been there ever since, a little over twenty-two years now." He took a sip of his tea. "I'm like a supervisor, only not in management. I'm also a union steward. Upper management wants to promote me into management, but some of the folks in management are treated horribly. They don't get paid overtime most of the time because they are salaried. And should they end up getting fired, many times they're just gone without any recourse, other than filing a lawsuit. At least if one of us is unjustly fired, we have the union to back us up. So . . . what were you doing prior to owning your own business?" He bit into his sandwich and chewed as he focused a laser-beam gaze on me.

"I worked for the Social Security Administration. I was with them almost twenty years. Then an opportunity came along that allowed me the chance to follow my dreams. I left my job, started my floral shop, and haven't looked back, too much, anyway." I pretended to laugh.

He nodded. "So, did you take an early retirement or something?"

"Nope. Just left. No retirement, no nothing. Two years ago, I realized I was living for everyone *except* me. I married pretty early—"

"Yeah, I know. Not exactly my favorite memory."

I smiled. "What?"

"When you got married." He placed both arms up on the table and leaned in toward me. "I asked you not to get married. I asked you not to marry him."

I sat back against my padded seat. "You asked me not to marry him while you were still with your girlfriend. Yeah, that's right. You know: the girlfriend you ended up marrying yourself. The girlfriend you've been with since the first day I met you."

"What else did you expect for me to do after you up and married . . . what's his name again?"

"His name is Zeke."

He smiled. "Good old Zeke. Lucky man. I hope he knows how blessed he is to have snagged you."

"Apparently you didn't think I was such a prize. You had a chance . . ." I stopped. "You know what? It really doesn't matter. You married what's her face and I married Zeke."

He started laughing. "What's her face? That's cute."

"I don't know her name. I just know you must have loved her a lot. A *lot*."

"Don't you *even* go there. If you hadn't gotten married to what's his name, you and I probably would be together today."

"Don't even try it," I said. "We both know that you really didn't want to be with me."

"Why do you keep saying that? I told you the last time you said it that it wasn't true."

"You need to stop," I said.

"Stop what? I asked you not to marry him, did I not?" Ethan leaned in closer. "Did I *not* ask you to not marry him? Tell the truth."

"You asked me a few days before my wedding date."

"And you married him anyway." He flopped back against his seat.

I leaned in. "I married him anyway because I figured that you didn't want me enough to be with me totally, but you also didn't want me to have anyone of my own. Just how long did you think I was supposed to wait on you?"

"See," he said. "There you go again. If you hadn't gotten

married, you and I would have married. I honestly and truly believe that."

I let out a loud sigh and sat back against the seat.

"What's the sigh for?"

"It's for you saying stuff like this now. I really loved you. But I didn't want to be talking to someone else's guy. I wanted my own. If you wanted me, you should have chosen *me*. Instead, you wanted both of us."

He laughed. "I don't know why you keep saying stuff like that. I told you, I couldn't break up with her. She hadn't done anything for me to justify breaking up with her."

"So what was I supposed to be? Your backup, 'just in case'? Someone there ready and waiting when you and she *did* finally call it quits?" I shook my head. "Look, it doesn't matter now. You stayed with her, and I ended up marrying someone else. It's done now."

He leaned in, set both elbows on the table, and propped his chin on his fists as he looked at me for a few seconds. He then sat back straight. "I guess we messed up," he said. "You and I would be together right now if you hadn't married good old Zeke."

"Well, you know what? I didn't want to be number two with you when I could be number one with someone else."

"Will you stop saying that," he said. "You were not number two. You know how I felt about you."

"I know that I need to finish eating so I can get back to the shop. That much, I *do* know."

He nodded, then took the last bite of his sandwich.

Chapter 5

Ethan jumped out of the car to open the door for me when we arrived back at my shop. I started to open the door before he could get there, but I didn't want him to think I was pouting or retaliating for the discussion we'd had while eating.

As far as I was concerned, it was a settled matter. It was settled when I realized he was likely never going to stop going with the girl who was his girlfriend, long before I came on the scene. Not counting when I learned he'd also tried talking to another girl around the same time he was trying to talk to me. Admittedly, the other girl he was trying to talk to didn't bother me as much as his already having a steady girlfriend. It just wasn't my style to be with someone who had someone already. And fighting over a man was not something I *ever* cared about doing either. Not ever.

And *that* included my dear husband Zeke.

Ethan still needed to pick up the flowers he'd ordered, so he came along with me. I unlocked the front door to the shop and turned the alarm off. I then turned the notice on the door to indicate I was back and open for business.

"Let me get your flowers," I said, then promptly went to the back room to retrieve them.

I came back with the flowers, pleased with how this arrange-

ment had turned out, and set the vase down on the counter before him.

"Nice," he said. "Very nice."

"Thank you. I think so. But then, what else would you expect
me to say." I flashed him a satisfied smile.

"May I have a card for it?"

"Sure," I said. "You didn't tell me what to put on one, so I
didn't fix one. I'll be glad to prepare the card for you."

"Oh, I got it. All I need is a blank card so I can write what I
want."

I pulled out the various cards for him to choose the design
he wanted.

"Butterflies," he said as he picked up one of my two favorites.
"Perfect." He purred the word. "So . . . how much is my damage?" he asked, referring to what he owed for the flowers. I
gave him his bill. He pulled out a one-hundred-
dollar bill and handed it to me. He laughed a little as I held it a
few seconds. "Oh, and you can check to make sure it's not
counterfeit. I won't be offended."

I held it up in the air and looked at it, mostly to mess with
him. He laughed again as he shook his head a few times. I went
to the register and got his change. He wrote on the floral card,
then placed it into the plastic cardholder I'd placed in the
arrangement.

"Your change," I said as I counted the money out into his
hand.

He stuck the money in one of his coat pockets. "Thank you."
He took my right hand. "And thanks for going to lunch with
me today. I really enjoyed it."

"Yeah, it was nice. And thank you for buying."

He then leaned down before I knew what he was about to do,
and softly planted a kiss on my cheek. "I'll talk to you later."

"Yeah," I said, stunned that he'd just done what he did.

He picked up the vase of flowers and smiled. "You really like
these? You really think they're nice?" he asked of the arrangement. "Really?"

"Yes. Why? Is there something wrong? Something you don't like?"

He smiled. "Oh, no. I just wanted to be sure you liked them." He held the vase out to me. "Because *these* . . . are for you." He put the vase in my hands, then turned and walked away.

"What?" I said as I stood there with the flowers. "Come back here. What do you mean these are for me?"

He turned back around. "I mean . . . they're for you."

"What? You don't want them?" I tilted my head. "What are you saying?"

"What are *you* saying?" he asked. "That *you* don't want them?"

I shook my head. "That's not what I'm saying. It's just I'm not understanding what you're saying . . . what you're doing."

He came back and touched my hand. "These flowers . . . I bought for you."

"I can't accept these." I glanced down at the flowers. I'd done an *extra* special job with this arrangement. I'd put my best cut of flowers in there; put in more flowers than I even normally did. I looked back up at him with a quizzical look.

"Well, they're yours," was all he said. He nodded, smiled, then strolled with his signature, back-in-the-day swag out the door.

After he left, I looked at the card. It merely said, FOREVER.

Chapter 6

Upon this I awaked, and beheld; and my sleep was sweet unto me.

—Jeremiah 31:26

I opened my eyes and couldn't help but smile. The vase of flowers was there on my nightstand. I couldn't believe Ethan had done that. It certainly wasn't what I was expecting. I felt bad keeping the flowers; I know how special that arrangement had been when I made it, the extra love I'd put into it. I wanted his wife to be blown over by his gift, having no idea he was planning on giving that gift to me. I sat up and admired the flowers, hoping that people who received the flowers I made appreciated them the way I appreciated these.

Zeke began to stir. "Hey," he said, waking up. "You woke? Man, I'm tired."

I turned to look in his face. "Well, maybe if you didn't stay out so late, you would get enough sleep and you wouldn't be so tired in the mornings."

"Maybe if you could say something nice to me instead of nagging about everything I do, I'd stay at home more."

"Oh, so now you're trying to say that I'm the reason you stay out all night?" I folded my arms.

He let out a laugh as he cocked his head to one side. "So what did you do? Feel sorry for yourself and give yourself some flowers? Or is your little business not doing so well, just like I said it wouldn't, and you decided to bring those flowers home with you instead of throwing them away like you probably have to end up doing with most of your stock these days. I told you people don't buy enough flowers to justify anyone starting a florist shop, especially someone who had a good job already."

"Zeke, why can't you be supportive of anything I do?"

"I am supportive. I'm supportive of you getting up and fixing me some breakfast before I have to get up and go to work." He sat up straight, pressing his back against the mahogany headboard. He closed his eyes. "I'm hungry."

"Well, I cooked dinner last night. If you'd been here, you could have eaten then."

"You don't get home until almost seven each night."

"And that's a problem how?"

"That's a problem because I'm here bored out of my mind. You know that I'm hyper. I need to be doing something," Zeke said, his eyes fully opened now.

"Then why don't you cook? That will give you something to do and would help me out tremendously."

"Me? Cook?" He laughed. "Okay, apparently you've been smelling a bit too many fumes or something. You know it's a woman's job to cook for the family."

"And why is that? Who said it was a woman's job?"

Zeke looked at me. "My mother cooked for the six of us and she didn't complain or wouldn't have dared look to my father to cook. That's what strong women do. They hold it down."

I looked him up and down. "So are you trying to say I'm not a strong woman?"

"No, that's not what I'm saying." He let his head go back again. "Listen, all I asked was for you to get up and fix my breakfast so I can get out of here and deal with these folks on this construction site. If you don't want to cook me anything, then fine. I'll just stop at McDonald's or somewhere. Geez!"

"Oh, no." I got up. "I wouldn't dare want you to think I'm shirking any of my duties as a wife. You want breakfast? I'll fix you breakfast."

"Can you make me some eggs, grits, bacon, and toast? Oh, and make my eggs fried and not scrambled like you usually do. I like fried eggs."

I put my hands on my hips. "I'm sorry, but this is not Burger King. You can't have it your way."

"So, the flowers?" He nodded toward the vase. "You didn't answer my question about them." He then laughed one of his sinister laughs.

I considered telling him the truth: that someone had given them to me. But then it hit me: he wouldn't have believed me or even likely cared, so why bother.

"Your breakfast will be ready soon." I headed toward the bathroom.

"Just what I thought," he said with a slight chuckle. "But you need to be selling the flowers and not self-indulging. If you ask me, flowers are just a waste of money. That's my opinion. They don't live more than a week or two before you have to throw them out. That's why I've never wasted money buying you flowers. But if you can find enough suckers out there to buy them, then God bless you. We can certainly use the money."

I turned around and started toward his side of the bed. "Zeke—" I stopped. "You know what?" I tapped my hand twice on my hip where I'd placed it.

He grinned, loving that he always knew how to get me riled. "What?"

"Forget you," I said, spitting the words out and moving my head in sync with both words.

He laughed. "No problem. Just hurry up with my breakfast," he said. Then I heard him under his breath say, "Going to make me late for work. I shouldn't have to ask anyway."

I refused to take the bait this morning. This is how he and I begin every morning. He finds something to criticize about me and I'm left mad and upset while he laughs. Well, this morning I was determined not to let him take me down that path.

This morning, I awakened to a vase of beautiful flowers. For the first time in a long time, I slept well and I woke up to flowers that I didn't have to give to myself. And there was no way I was going to allow even Zeke to take any of my joy from me.

No way.

Chapter 7

See then that ye walk circumspectly, not as fools,
but as wise.

—Ephesians 5:15

It had been weeks since Ethan had given me the flowers. I hadn't heard from him anymore, which was fine. I didn't like the way I felt when I was around him. I mean I liked it, but it wasn't good for me. After all these years, he still caused a fluttering to take place inside my stomach. It was like a whole flock of butterflies was in there, all trying to take flight at once.

To keep in shape, I liked to walk. But since I'd started my business, I hadn't had a lot of time or opportunity to do it. I could feel the effects of me not being able to do it. I didn't have as much energy and I was putting on a few pounds. When I worked for the Social Security Administration, I walked during my lunchtime. And if I didn't walk then, I'd go to the park after I came home from work. My girls loved going to the park. They would play on the jungle gym, slide, and swing while I walked. Sometimes I would meet up with a friend and we'd talk while we walked. I didn't have a lot of those times though—walking with friends.

After I left Social Security, I would go to the park in the morning before my class on floral arrangement. Honestly, I've been working with flowers since I was first married. In the beginning, I did it as a hobby—just one more thing for Zeke to make fun about when it came to me. After our three children were born (and with my full work schedule outside the home as well as inside), I just let my desire fall by the wayside. Besides, buying flowers (especially the ones I loved) was expensive, and I couldn't grow all of the flowers the way I would have liked. Well, I could have, had Zeke been more cooperative about helping me. But he didn't want to dig or help me do anything.

There was just too much to do and not enough hours in one day to do it. My friend Danielle was quick to remind me that I wasn't superwoman, so I needed to let go of the cape and quit trying to draw an *S* on my chest, especially when both of my hands were tied behind my back.

Danielle had a way with words and making the point clear. She's one of my friends who didn't have a lot of time to walk with me, but she was a lot of fun to talk to whenever we did. Danielle had things going on in her own marriage. She believed her husband was cheating on her, although she couldn't prove it. And as much as I talked about Zeke, her husband treated her a lot worse than Zeke ever did me. Zeke knew better than to put me down in front of other people. He could say all he wanted when we were in the privacy of our home, but not when others were around. That's where I drew the line. He didn't have but one time to make that mistake with me, and he'd already used it.

It was a sunny morning in September, and I just wanted to walk. I'd started back walking a few weeks ago, after work when I closed. This particular morning, the flower shop wasn't busy. With the exception of a few funerals that generated several orders at one time, and three nice-size weddings, so far I was only receiving sporadic orders. Nothing, at least at this point, that would even *remotely* justify me hiring anyone to work for me.

I was thankful that I had the first year of rent free that came from me having signed a five-year lease for the building. There's no way I would have been able to keep the doors open had it not been for that blessing. My hope was that things would pick up soon. I knew that Valentine's Day and Mother's Day were two booming times for this type of business. I was just hoping I could hold on until those days rolled around and gave my company the boost it needed.

So I laced up my white tennis shoes—not the ones I normally

kept at work to work in when I was trying to be cute; the ones I'd bought specifically for walking. I felt I could be gone about thirty or forty minutes without anyone ever even missing me.

Just as I was about to leave to drive over to the park, the shop's phone rang. The caller ID read: A&D. My heart skipped a beat as I recalled that was where Ethan said he worked. Then again, it might not even be him. He *had* promised to send some business my way. Maybe this was just someone who worked there that he'd referred to me. I answered the phone, "The Painted Lady Flower Shop. How may I help you?"

"Hi," the male voice said with an obvious smile. My heart flipped; it was Ethan!

I quietly exhaled so he wouldn't be able to hear me do it. "Hi there," I said.

"Do you know who this is?" he asked.

"Of course I do."

"So what are you up to?"

"Oh, not much. It's kind of slow around here," I said. "I'm sure you know how things can be sometimes." I didn't want him to think I wasn't doing so great.

"Yeah, it's slow here today as well. In fact, they're letting some of us take off early. They allow us to do that when it's slow and they don't need as many workers. They save money that way."

"That's nice of them, especially if someone has something they want or need to do."

"Yeah. Listen, I was wondering if you'd like to do something today. With me, that is. You know, have a chance to talk some more." I could tell he was nervous.

"Well, actually, I was just about to go walking . . . at the park."

"Seriously? Are you serious?"

"Yeah," I said, frowning. "Why are you saying it like *that?*"

"Because I work out a lot and I would love to go walking with you."

I was a bit leery. That was a little *too* convenient for me. "I don't know."

"What? You don't know if we should walk together? Come on, you're being silly now, don't you think? You were going to go walking. I just so happen to have time off. What's the harm in the two of us walking together? I mean two old friends . . . walking in a public park together . . ."

I laughed. "You're good at doing that."

"Good at what?"

"You know: that 'two old friends' number you seem to give me."

"Well, we are friends, aren't we?"

"Yes, I guess so."

"And we are old, wouldn't you agree?" He chuckled. "Hold up. I don't mean old in the sense of *old*."

"But you're right. We are both older now."

"Older, but not old. You and I can still hold our own. And honestly, you don't look like you've aged a bit."

He made me smile. "Two old friends, huh?"

"Yes. Two old friends, walking in the park, getting our exercise on, getting our hearts pumping."

I'm sure when he said that about our hearts, he was talking about the one that pumps and circulates blood. But when it came to me and him, it was obvious (to me anyway) that the other sense of our hearts—love—was more in jeopardy of being pumped. I know I knew it; I'm sure he must have, too.

"Come on. Let's do this," he said. "Tell me which park you're going to and I'll meet you there."

"Okay," I said. But since he was planning to be there, I decided it was best we meet in a park other than the one I normally patronized. I thought about a park I'd seen when I was passing through another area. It was close enough, maybe an extra five minutes away. When I mentioned the park's name, he knew exactly where it was.

"Are you leaving right now?" he asked.

"Yeah."

"Then I'll see you shortly," he said.

And as soon as I hung up, I felt I'd made another huge mistake in saying yes to Ethan . . . *yet* again. But for reasons I can't fully explain, when it came to Ethan, it was just hard for me to say no.

Chapter 8

Redeeming the time, because the days are evil.
—Ephesians 5:16

"Wow, when you go walking, you're really serious," Ethan said when he came up to me. He gave me the once-over. "I mean, you don't play."

I had changed out of my work clothes into a purple with gold trim jogging suit. Had I not been meeting Ethan, I would have done what I normally do and just worn my clothes. It's just that, given what I remembered about Ethan from our earlier days, I figured he was likely a serious walker. And if he was, he was coming to the park to really work out. The last thing I needed was to sweat out my clothes and have to walk around in smelly clothes for the rest of the day. And the way my life goes, this would probably be the day when a bunch of folks decided to come into the shop to buy flowers, just because I'd sweated my clothes out.

"What were you expecting?" I said, playing it off. "I knew you would most likely *bring* it. I decided this was the least I could do to keep up."

"Oh, so you thought I was going to bring it, huh?"

"Yes." I gave him my own once-over, mainly to return the favor he'd just done to me. Although I must say that he looked exceptionally good in his black jogging pants and that black (rather tight-fitting) spandex top. "It looks like I was right," I said. "I can see that you came dressed to do some *serious* damage on this track."

"I told you that I work out. I have to. It's important that I keep my body in shape in order for me to do what I do." He began to do warm-up exercises.

I looked at the things he was doing—stretches and lunges. "So you do all of that before you walk, just *to* walk?"

"Yes. You need to loosen and warm up your muscles before you begin. It keeps injuries down during a workout." He started doing more leg lunges.

I did a few of the things he was doing just so I wouldn't look like such a rookie. But I wasn't planning on doing anything more than walking, possibly jogging a few yards, then back to my normal walking again. "Well, feel free to do what you normally do," I said. "Don't let me slow you down."

He smiled, then bounced a few times. "Oh, come on. Let me see how well you can keep up with me. I promise: I'll take it easy on you."

"Oh, you'll take it easy on me, huh?"

"Yeah. Besides, it will allow us to talk while we do it."

"Talk? While we're running or whatever it is you plan on doing?"

"Yes . . . talk. Talking is a good way to gauge how well you're doing. We should be able to do what we do and still hold a decent amount of conversation."

"All right," I said with a smirk. "But I reserve the right to quit when my body tells me it's done."

He bounced a few more times as he shook his body loose. I was not about to do all of that. I will confess: he did look good when *he* did it. With me, I didn't think it would so much.

We began to walk, which was great since that's what I'd come to the park to do.

"So . . . tell me about your family?" he said as he looked at me while maintaining a comfortable stride.

"I have three daughters."

"Yeah. I remember them from that time I saw you in Rich's

some years back. So what are their names and how old are they now?"

"My oldest is Zanetta. She's twenty-two, serving in the Air Force."

"Wow, the Air Force!"

"Yes. She's always been fascinated with planes, ever since she was a little girl. She's always wanted to fly. So in spite of what her father and I argued against when she told us her intentions to enlist in the military, she was determined she was going to join the Air Force."

"So are you okay now with her being in the Air Force? Wow . . . military. You know, she could have learned to fly through other means."

"I know. But she was also interested in the money she'd earn for college by being in the military," I said. "So I'm okay with what she's doing. She's living her life the way she wants. Then there's my middle daughter who turned twenty last month. Her name is Zion. And Zion decided after she graduated from high school that she wanted to do missionary work. So she's off right now helping people in Haiti. And last, but certainly not least, is my youngest daughter, Zynique, who's seventeen, a senior in high school. Zynique has decided she's going to own a dance studio after she graduates from high school. I suspect it will be a few years before *that* happens. The girl loves to dance! And she's good at it, too. So despite her father's and my insistence that she should still go to college and *then* start her own company, she's interning with a woman who has her own studio. Zynique has *concluded* that she's learning just as much of what she needs to know from Madame Perry—that's the lady who owns the dance studio—if not more, being hands on with her."

"An interesting set of children you have," Ethan said as he suddenly broke out into a jog.

Without even thinking about it, I jogged right along with him. "Yes, they are. But I'm proud of them. I had planned on working at Social Security to help them with their college expenses, but as it happens, none of them appear to need me for that. In fact, my children are the reason I decided to leave Social Security and start my own company." I was breathing harder now, a real indication of how out of shape I really was. But then it hit me how far we'd jogged without taking a break, and I was feeling pumped about that, although I knew my body would likely pay for this later tonight.

Ethan glanced over at me and began to slow things back to a walk. I couldn't help but wonder if I'd looked physically distressed and whether, had he been jogging alone, he would have even stopped at that point.

"So you're saying that your children were the reason you left that great-paying job with all of those great benefits? Everybody knows that people who work for the government have terrific jobs."

"Yeah." I was attempting to talk while at the same time trying to catch my breath. "You see . . . they were each . . . following their . . . dreams. . . ."

"And you realized that you'd put your dreams on hold," Ethan said, tremendously helping me out by completing my sentence for me.

"Precisely," I said.

"I've been there. But couldn't you have waited and started the business after you retired or did it while you were working at Social Security? That way you could have still gotten a check while earning your retirement benefits." He glanced over at me with a quick smile. "You know how we do."

I pressed my hand into my right side as I continued to walk. I could feel slight pain there, but I wasn't going to wimp out and tell Ethan I needed to stop, not at this point. Besides, what's that saying? No pain, no gain.

"Yeah, I could have stayed," I said. "But I started noticing that more and more people I personally knew were dying all around me. Most of them were in their early fifties and sixties, and there they were dying. So I started thinking: Who's to say I'll be around when it's time for *me* to retire? Who's to say I'll be in good health when that time arrives? Who's to say that financially, even, I'd be any better off by the time I'm old enough and have enough service to retire to do it?"

"All good points."

I let my hand dangle down at my side as I picked up the pace to keep up with Ethan. "Besides," I said, still speaking as I walked. "This opportunity seemed to have landed in my lap. I had been praying about starting my own business, and it was like God lined everything up just for me. And I'm sure you know that when God says it's time, you have to move on it. You can't stand in a place of indecision. You have to jump on it right then, or the cloud will still be moving and you'll find your-self totally left behind."

"Redeeming the time," Ethan said.

"What?"

"Redeeming the time. You know: redeeming the time is mak-ing the most of every opportunity, even when it looks like you arrived late for the event," he said. "It's doing several things at once in order to catch up. Sort of like what you and I are doing right now. We're walking while at the same time talking and catching up on lost time."

"Yeah. Okay. Redeeming the time."

Ethan broke out into a jog again. I started to jog with him, but, a few steps into it, I decided I didn't want to. So I contin-ued to walk. He looked back at me, grinned, then began to run full out.

I laughed. "Show-off," I yelled after him. But he was too far gone to likely have even heard me.

Chapter 9

Wherefore be ye not unwise, but understanding what the will of the Lord is.

—Ephesians 5:17

I'd walked three miles in a few seconds under fifty-two minutes. I had to admit: walking with Ethan had caused my time to be better than at any other time, at least in my adult lifetime. He held his index finger high in the air, letting me know that he was going to do one more lap . . . finish up one more mile, making a total of six miles for him. He started running at full speed again. I was now sitting at a picnic table, merely a spectator. As I watched him, I couldn't help but notice that, even with him being well over forty, the look of his body and the condition of his body were both impressive. There was absolutely no denying these facts.

After performing his cooling-down routine (something else I never bothered to do), he came over to the table and sat across from me.

"What are you grinning about?" I asked as he sat there staring intensely at me with a full grin on his face.

"Oh, nothing. I'm just"—he cocked his head a little—"what is the correct word I'm looking for? Impressed. Yeah, I'm impressed."

"Is that right? And what exactly are you impressed about? The fact that you ran laps around me . . . literally. I mean you did two miles for every one that I did."

"But you held your own," Ethan said with several nods. "I'm

scared of you. A few more sessions with me and you'll be running me into the ground."

"A few more sessions with you?" I released a hearty laugh. "In your dreams! In . . . your . . . dreams."

"Oh, now, we don't want to talk about my dreams. I know you don't want to hear about my dreams lately." He wiped the pouring-down sweat from his face with a blue hand towel.

I knew that was an opening for me to take, but I refused to walk through that door. I remained quiet.

"Do you have any water in your car?" he asked.

"As a matter of fact, I do," I said.

"Well, would you mind sharing with a brother?"

"Okay, hold up. Do you mean to tell *me* that you came here, ran full out like that, and you didn't bring any water with you?"

He ticked his head and smiled, wiping his face again with the towel. "I suppose that's exactly what I'm telling you."

"Well, that's an unwise thing to do. You shouldn't be running like that, knowing you're going to need some water afterward, and not have any on hand."

He coughed a few times. "I know. So are you going to share your water with me or not?"

I stood up. "I guess I'll share. I'd hate to be like those people Jesus used in that parable He told. You know, the parable about those folks who passed by the wounded man lying on the side of the road, essentially leaving him to die."

"Yeah, that's right," Ethan said as he stood up. "Be a Good Samaritan and help me out."

"I'll go get it and bring it back," I said.

"It's okay. I'll walk with you to your car and get it."

"Yeah, I guess that would be good." I looked at my watch. I'd been gone for over an hour now. "I do need to get back to the shop. Although I doubt anyone has called or come by. Things have been really slow these days." After I said it, I felt I shouldn't have said that to him. He was a customer. Besides, it may have sounded like I was asking him to help me . . . to send me some business, which I absolutely wasn't doing. I just felt so at home whenever I was with Ethan. He's always had that effect on me.

He'd once admitted it was mutual. Years back, when we were talking as a young couple, he used to say I was "like Converse tennis shoes—a perfect fit."

We reached my car. I unlocked it and got in to get the bottle of water I'd brought with me. He gestured for me to unlock the other side, which I did. He got in and sat in the passenger's seat.

"What are you doing?" I said, in a teasing tone.

"Waiting on you to get my water."

"I told you I was getting it." I found the bottle of water and handed it to him.

He immediately twisted off the cap and drank half of it, without even taking a breathing break.

"Good grief!" I said. "How do you do that?"

He lowered the bottle and removed it from his mouth. "Do what?"

"Drink so much water at one time."

"I'm thirsty. That was a good workout today, a *really* good workout. What can I say? You inspire me."

"So what are you trying to tell me?" I asked. "That you don't normally work out like that?"

"Oh, I do. But you make a man want to push himself a little harder, to go a little farther." He suddenly cast his eyes down. Seconds later, he looked into my eyes.

And it was at that point, as I really looked into his eyes, it was as though a light inside of him had been dimmed to its lowest settings, almost turned completely off. And he wasn't pretending either to garner my sympathy. I don't think he even knew I could see it. Ethan was hurting. And it appeared to be a deep hurt.

Instinctively, I reached over and touched his hand. *Big mistake.* He seized my hand and squeezed it. "I'm tired," he said. "I'm seriously thinking about quitting everything."

"Everything? What do you mean by everything?"

"My marriage, for one. I'm actually thinking about getting a divorce. My wife and I are so far apart it's not even funny. I'm thinking about divorcing her and going somewhere like Colorado or California. I'm also considering taking a break from the church. I don't mean I'll stop going to church, just stop doing what I do ministry-wise."

"Oh, now, things can't be *that* bad. Can they?"

"Oh"—he sang the word—"but it is." He looked down as though he was ashamed of the words coming from his mouth. I could see he needed someone to listen to him, hear him out. "I'm just tired. I'm tired. I've tried to make things work at home and at church, for so long, at some point you just get tired of trying." He looked at me. "Do you know what I'm saying?"

Yeah, I knew what he was saying. But I wasn't going to hijack his pity party and make it mine. "You know, Ethan, we all go through tough times. You just have to keep praying and find a way to make things better. And I believe things are going to get better."

"I've tried. I'm telling you: everything I know to do, I've done it and then some. The only reasons I haven't left yet, and the only thing that's been keeping me from leaving right now, today, are my girls. I just can't leave them. They need me. They do. I'm the one who actually takes care of them."

"I'm sure you do a lot for them, but don't you think you may be being a bit hard on your wife?"

He made a grunting sound. "Hard? Okay, let's see what you think, and you let me know if I'm being too hard on her. My wife goes to work—that's when she decides she wants to work, but that's another subject for another time. When she comes home from work, usually I've cooked dinner and have food ready and on the table."

"Hold up." I raised my hand as though I were a human stop sign. "You cook?"

"Yes, I cook."

I raised my hand again. "Hold up. *And* you have food ready when *she* gets home? Supper is done and waiting when your wife comes home?"

He tilted his head to the side and tried, without success, not to smile. "Yes."

"You have to excuse me for staying on this a minute, but you're a rarity, that's for sure. It's hard to find a man who will cook every now and then, let alone cook almost every day *and* have food ready when his wife comes home."

He shook his head. "I know. But if I don't cook, then my girls don't get a decent meal. Okay, it's like this. My wife is supposed to get off work at five. Her job is fifteen miles from our house. Given that traffic can be heavy during that time, it still shouldn't take her but thirty . . . maybe forty-five minutes, no more than an hour, even on a bad day, to get home. Almost every single night, she never steps foot in the house before six-fifty-five. She then waltzes in, speaks to the girls, gets a plate, dishes out the food I've fixed for her, changes her clothes, and back *out* the door she goes again."

"You're kidding me, right? I know you're kidding."

"Nope. I'm not kidding. If I'm lying, I'm flying."

"Well, in defense of your wife, I will say that women need to get out every now and then."

"My wife does this pretty much every single night."

"She sounds a lot like my husband." I said it before I could stop myself.

"Your husband does that, too?"

"Yes." I tried to play it down. "But he's a man. That's what men do. Right? My husband comes home and, back when all of our girls were young and still at home, he would spend a little time with them, eat, then leave to 'get with his boys.' "

"First off, I honestly can't believe your husband would leave anything as wonderful as you at home to go be with a bunch of hard legs." Ethan primped his mouth and shook his head. "No way."

"Well, he did. And he still does. At least, that's what he used to do or that's what he used to *say* that he was doing. These days, he goes to the horse or dog track, the bingo hall, the casino some hours away, I don't know. In any event, he's been leaving me like this since two days after we said our wedding vows." I forced a smile, hoping to not let Ethan know just how much this topic really hurt. "But . . . back to you. So tell me:

what are your daughters' names and how old are they now?" I said to change the conversation to a lighter, more pleasant topic.

"I have three daughters."

"Three? When I saw you at Rich's that time, you only had two."

"Yeah, we had another daughter a little after that. My oldest daughter's name is Ashley. She's seventeen, a senior in high school this year, and she wants to be a nurse. Phoenix Arissa is fifteen and a sophomore. And there's my baby girl, Jacquetta, who will turn eight on November twenty-eighth."

"Wow, my youngest daughter was born on November twenty-eight. That's something. Listening to you, it's evident you're absolutely crazy about them."

"I am. I love those girls so much. I love being a father, which is why I don't want to leave my wife. I'm sure she'll want full custody of them, just to spite me and to make their lives miserable, even though she doesn't spend much time with them now. I'm the one who takes them to their dance lessons, karate lessons, picks them up from various after-school activities and practices when they participate in sports. I try to attend all of their functions, which can be hard when you have as much on your plate as I do." He laughed. "In fact, when they were little, I was the one who did their hair for them."

"No," I said. "You can comb and plait hair?"

"Yes." He smiled. "I can plait and braid hair. And when Ashley participated in that event to be a debutante, I was the one traveling everywhere when she and I were trying to find a long white gown and the white gloves she would need. The dress couldn't be ivory, pearl, or champagne. We *had* to find a white one. It was hard, but we found one. And let's not forget the pearls. Can't forget the pearls. She had to have pearls as well. Phoenix Arissa is heavy into ballet these days. They're practicing for a presentation of the *Nutcracker*. I'm the one who makes sure she gets to her rehearsals, even when her mother is home 'resting' from being out late Friday night and into early Saturday morning."

"Just curious, but why do you call your middle daughter

Phoenix Arissa instead of just Phoenix or Arissa even, which are both beautiful names I might add?"

"Oh, she was the one who decided that's what she wanted to be called." Ethan let out a chuckle. "When she was a little girl, after we taught her her full name, she liked saying Phoenix Arissa. Later, if you merely called her Phoenix, she'd say, 'You said it wrong! It's Phoenix Arissa.' So, we started calling her Phoenix Arissa. To this day, that's what she still insists on being called. It's what she wants."

I smiled. "It sounds like you have a great relationship with her."

"I do with all of them." He turned his body squarely to face me. "You see, I believe that if men would show their daughters the way they *should* be treated, they'll have higher standards of how they'll stand to be treated when it's *not* daddy. Then when some guy steps to them, if they're not being treated the way they were treated by their fathers, dude will have to step off and step back. I don't want my daughters ever feeling like they missed out on anything from me—attempting to find it in some knucklehead who, in all fairness to some of these boys that don't have fathers or a good man in their lives, were never taught or shown how to treat a woman right."

"Yeah, that's what I have been most concerned about with our daughters. Their father was hardly ever around. I pray every day that they don't end up with some guy who treats them badly and they feel they're just supposed to accept it."

"You mean like you do?"

I pulled back. "What do you mean 'like I do'?"

"Sounds to me like you let your husband treat you badly," Ethan said.

"No. Not really. He doesn't hit me. He will fuss, but not much. Now don't get me wrong, he's not always the nicest person. And he'll tell you that I fuss enough for the both of us. He's a relatively calm, cool guy. I fuss, and he systematically stands there not saying much, which only makes me furious and fuss that much more."

Ethan let out a chuckle. "Yeah. And why do you women do that?"

"Do what?"

"Fuss even harder when we don't say anything back to you?"

"Why don't y'all say something when we're fussing?" I said. "What we're really saying when we fuss is: let me know that I really matter to you and show that you actually care. That's it." I threw both my hands up and out and held them like I was a statue for a few seconds before putting them down.

"And what we're thinking at that moment is: don't say anything to set her off any more than she already is. Just be quiet and pray that she runs out of steam soon."

"Well, I don't look at what my husband is doing to me as mistreating me." I reflected over that thought for a few seconds. "Nope. He really doesn't *mistreat* me."

"Okay. If you say so," Ethan said. "But if you were *my* wife, I can assure you I wouldn't be going anywhere where you weren't. And if I had to be separated from you, you'd better believe I couldn't wait to get back to you. Why go somewhere else when everything you want and desire is already right there with you?"

"Yeah, you say that now because you're not married to me," I said. "But you and I both know that it's a different story when people are married. All of that 'Baby, I love you' stuff goes right out the window when you start leaving dirty clothes all over the floor like you have a maid to pick up after you. There's a dishwasher now, as opposed to when you may have first started out, and you're acting like your hands don't work to open it up and put your own dirty dishes inside. I then start fussing. . . ."

He held his hands up in surrender. "Okay, okay. It's me, here. I didn't do it."

I smiled. "Sorry. Here we were talking about you and your things, and I'm going off on my own little tangent about my home."

"Well, I hope you know that I'm always here if you ever want to talk or merely unload . . . get something off of *your* chest."

"No. I don't think that would be a good idea," I said. "Not a good idea."

"And why is that?"

I turned and stared at him. "Soul ties," I said.

He turned up his nose. "Soul ties?"

"Yeah. Look, Ethan. I'm going to be straight with you. I understand how things work. If I start telling you things and you start telling me things, before you know anything, we're sowing into each other's lives. And when you do that, you create and, I dare say, tighten ties with each other. Soul ties are strong. They go deeper than what can be seen on the surface." I shook my head slowly as I thought about it. "You and I need to be careful, that's all I'm saying. But I truly am concerned about what and how you're feeling right now. So have you talked with your wife about how you feel? Have you told her any of these things you just told me?"

"Yes, I have talked to her and I've talked to her, all to no avail. And I'm just tired now. I don't know if any of this matters anymore. My marriage, my job, what I'm doing for the Lord. Does it matter?" He appeared exasperated.

"Okay, now wait, wait, wait," I said, and again, without thinking, I placed my hand on his. "What you're doing for the Lord is important work. Souls are being led to the Lord because of what you do. Do you understand? People are being introduced to Christ because of you. So you can't be serious about even *thinking* about quitting the work that you're doing."

"How am I supposed to help somebody else when my own house is not right? Huh?" Ethan said. "How can I tell someone else how to make their marriage stronger when I can't even manage to keep my own wife at home? And I've prayed for so long, but it doesn't seem like God is listening. I'm just being real right now. Yes, I know scriptures. I *know* them; I can quote them. I know all of the right things to say. I do. But sometimes . . ." He stopped and made a fist, then hit his thigh with it.

"I know. I *know.* I've been there myself, believe me. But you can't quit now. You can't. You know this is just the devil trying to take you out. You're doing too much for the Kingdom of God for you to even *think* about going out like this. The harvest is plentiful and the laborers are just too few." I shook my head.

"Look, I'm not quitting on God. I'm just tired. Do you have

any idea what it feels like to have to put on a happy face almost every time you step out of your house? Every single day of your life, you have to fake happiness."

Yes, as a matter of fact I do know.

"And who can I tell how I'm feeling? Certainly not anyone at church. Nobody wants to see me as being weak or having problems. My friends really don't want to hear me talking about how bad I feel about things. Not the friends in *my* life. Most of them are in the same boat or worse. So where or who else do I turn to except God? But when I talk to Him, I'm left wondering if He even cares. I'm just being real with you. I'm being totally honest."

I took his hand again and squeezed it. "And that's fine, Ethan. You can be real with me. You can be as raw and as honest with how you feel as you need to be. I don't mind. And I won't judge you for what you say." Everybody needs a safe place they can go and be open and true in how they're feeling.

He looked at me and tilted his head slightly before smiling, then gave me a quick nod. "Well, you need to get back to your shop. I've kept you long enough."

"Yeah," I said. "I've been gone much longer than I'd originally intended."

"Well, I'm grateful and appreciate the time we were able to spend today."

"Me, too," I said.

And without any warning, he leaned over and kissed me. Not a peck, but a real kiss. When he finished, I was frowning for two reasons. One: that he'd kissed me. And the other?

That I'd let him.

Chapter 10

*Who shall separate us from the love of Christ? shall
tribulation, or distress, or persecution, or famine, or
nakedness, or peril, or sword?*

— Romans 8:35

Later that night, as I sat in a chair alone in my bedroom with
the television turned to a show I wasn't even watching, I replayed the events of the day.

As normal, I'd gone to the flower shop, arriving a little before eight a.m. The shop's advertised hours were nine to five,
mainly because the area wasn't as safe as it used to be, and because there wasn't a real reason to remain open past five. When
I first opened my doors for business during the middle of May,
the advertised operating hours were from nine a.m. until seven
p.m. But no one ever called or came by after four o'clock. So at
the beginning of September, I made the decision to change the
shop's closing time to five.

On this day, I'd closed the shop and gone to the park to walk
as I'd done a few times already. Ethan called just as I was on my
way out of the door. I'd agreed to let him walk with me, not that
I could have really stopped him. After all, it is a public park.
Anyone can come and walk if they so choose. So Ethan came.

We walked and we talked. Honestly, it was a great workout. I
mean, people pay to be worked out like that. He'd asked for
water. And I just so happened to have a bottle of water in my
car. What was I supposed to do? He'd worked out much harder
than I had. He needed that water. Sort of reminded me of Jesus
and that woman from Samaria—the woman at the well that

Jesus busted about her husbands. The woman who had come to draw water from a well that Jesus truthfully had no business even being at when He said to her, "Give me to drink."

No. That wasn't a good example. Jesus was doing a good thing. He was on His job, doing the work of Him who had sent Him. He was doing the work of His Father in Heaven. *Ethan* . . . Ethan was just out walking and running for exercise sake.

Still, he needed some water. And I had some in my car. I'd gone to get it. In fact, I did offer to bring it back to him. But instead, he followed me to my car. He'd gotten inside my car . . . sat there in the seat next to me. No big deal. We talked. He opened up. His words touched me. He wasn't playing a game. He just needed someone to talk to; he needed a friend. And we were friends. Well, maybe not friends in the sense of the word "friends." But I can't lie: I care about what happens to him. I care about what he's going through. He needed someone to encourage him. After all, he's doing a great work for the Kingdom of God. This much I know.

And like the prophet Nehemiah in the Bible, Ethan had to know that he was doing a good work and he couldn't come down. That's all Satan was trying to do; he was trying to get Ethan to come down off the wall. I decided to stand with Ethan to let him know that he couldn't come down off the wall. He had to stay on the wall and keep doing God's work. That's all today was about. I was trying to do my part by encouraging him the best way that I knew how.

But then . . . then something happened.

Something changed during the conversation. And he leaned over and kissed me. Okay, so he just got caught up in the moment. That was all that was. His emotions merely got the best of him. That would be okay, except for what he said after he'd finished kissing me. That's what has me wrestling with everything as I sit here with nothing but my thoughts to play with.

"I . . . have wanted to do that for *so* long," Ethan had said.

He'd wanted to kiss me for a long time? How long? How long had he been thinking about kissing me? Was it since he called the flower shop that first day and got me? Since he ordered that second set of flowers and gave them to me? Since he saw me at the park today?

Or was it even farther back than that? Like that time I saw him at that funeral a few years after we were both married to other people. Or maybe it was that day we ran into each other in the mall at Rich's?

How long had Ethan been thinking about doing that? How long had he thought about kissing me?

And if it was before he called my flower shop that day to order a bouquet of flowers for his wife, had he really only *happened* to call? Or did he already know that was my place of business? Did he know I was the owner of The Painted Lady Flower Shop? Had he called on purpose just so he could find a way to see me again? Was I the unsuspecting subject of a well-orchestrated setup?

How long had Ethan Roberts thought about kissing me? But more important now: how long would it take for me to get over him having kissed me?

How long?

Chapter 11

But exhort one another daily, while it is called TODAY;
lest any of you be hardened through the deceitful-
ness of sin.

—Hebrews 3:13

E than called me at the flower shop the following day.
"Listen, I wanted to let you know how much you blessed me yesterday," he said immediately after I finished my professional answering spiel.

I picked up a cut yellow gladiolus by its stem. "I didn't do anything special."

"Oh, trust me: you did a lot more than you'll ever know."

"If you say so. I'm just glad I was able to be of some help." I paused to give him an opportunity to be more specific on what was better now since the last time we spoke. *Had he gone home and things were better with his wife? Had he decided what he was doing in ministry was indeed too important to turn his back on? Was he deep-sixing that whole idea of leaving here to live somewhere all the way across country?*

"I can't talk long," he said. "I'm on my break and wanted to call you and say hello. And to let you know how much you blessed me yesterday. Hopefully, we can do that again soon." He said the word "soon" as though it were more of a question than a statement.

"Sure. I suppose," I said. "I like to walk."

"Great. Admittedly though, it will be almost impossible for me to get off of work and walk in the morning time the way I was able to yesterday."

"Me, too. I can only go like that when things are slow here at the shop. I'm expecting business to pick up any time now. And when that happens, I definitely won't be taking off during the morning hours to go walking. Not like I've been able to do lately."

"Maybe you and I can go in the afternoon? I normally get off work at two when we're not working overtime, which occasionally we do."

"If you get off work at two, what time do you have to be there?" I said, then quickly realizing the invasiveness of the question, I added, "Just out of curiosity."

He laughed. "It's fine. I don't mind you asking things like that. In fact, you can ask me anything you want. When it comes to you, I have nothing to hide. I have to be at work bright and early at five in the morning, and I generally get off at two in the afternoon; one-thirty if I only take a thirty-minute lunch break."

"Five to two, that's an odd shift."

"Sort of. But it works for the company. We have lots of eighteen-wheelers that come in during the morning hours that must be loaded early. Personally, I like getting off work that early in the afternoon. It gives me time to get things done before everyone else gets off. And I can do things like pick up my daughters from after-school activities or take them to their doctor's and dentist's appointments, stuff like that."

"Yeah, but you have to get up so early in order to get to work on time."

"I do. But I'm used to it. I've been doing it for years now."

"Well . . . maybe we *can* walk sometimes. It will be fine. We'll see how our schedules go, and if it works, it works."

"Great," he said. "Then I'll just check in with you on occasion to see if you're interested. And if you are, we'll go. If you're busy or can't go, then we'll just try for another time."

He definitely had me thinking now. It *would* be nice having someone to walk with. But agreeing to go with Ethan would now leave me wondering whether I should go when I can or wait and see if he's going to call. I guess it wouldn't hurt if I ended up walking twice in a day. On the other hand, if I didn't walk because I was waiting on his call, then that would be a day of missed walking. More than likely, I wouldn't be doing much walking during the early part of the day, opting for the afternoon. If he was going to walk, I'm sure he'd call and let me know—

"Excuse me, what did you say?" I asked, suddenly aware that while I was working this out in my head, he was talking.

"My fifteen-minute break is almost up so I was saying that I need to get off the phone. But I had to call and let you know how much you helped me yesterday, and how much I enjoyed spending that time with you, short as it was. Believe me: I needed that more than you'll ever know."

"So does this mean that you're going to fight the good fight of faith *yet* another day?" I said with a smile in my voice.

"Yes, I'm going to fight the good fight of faith *yet* another day. Oh, and I did talk to my wife last night after she came home."

"That's good. So how did it go? That's if you don't mind my asking."

"It went . . . pretty well; I must say that it did. We both expressed things we needed to say to each other. She assured me that she was going to *try* and do more with our girls. We both agreed to try and do better by each other."

"That's great! I told you the two of you just needed to talk."

"Yes, you did. But it's not like she and I haven't had this talk before. And it's not like she hasn't said she was going to *try* and do better before. The word *try* is what bothers me the most. I don't believe in try. I believe either you do or you don't. But that's another discussion for another time. As for me and my wife, we'll just have to see how things go. Time has a way of telling that which is untold."

"Ooh, I like that. 'Time has a way of telling that which is untold.' I'll have to remember that and use it sometime. Seriously though: I'm glad to hear that things may be heading in a better direction for you. I really am."

Ethan chuckled. "I've got to get off this phone, but I have to tell you this real quick. She even said something about the flowers I gave her."

"You mean the ones you bought her back in August? The ones you got from my shop?"

"Yep. Those," he said. "Last night, she finally thanked me for them."

"Hold up," I said. "You're kidding, right?"

"No. I'm as serious as a heart attack."

"You mean to tell me that she didn't say anything about the flowers when you gave them to her a month ago?"

"She didn't say one word. Didn't mumble, didn't grunt, didn't open her mouth," Ethan said. "When I gave them to her, she shrugged, then set the vase down on the table in the den where we stood."

"Wow," I said, trying to contain my true astonishment in hearing this. "So you didn't know whether she liked them or not."

"Well, from her reaction when I gave them to her, I would have said she couldn't have cared less. But"—he said with a lift in his voice—"last night, my darling wife told me, 'Thanks for the flowers.' At first I was thinking she'd received some flowers yesterday at work and thought I'd sent them. So I asked, 'What flowers?' To which she proceeded to say, 'The ones you brought home to me. You know: the ones you bought me a few weeks ago. They were real nice.' Almost floored me. I couldn't believe it."

"*You* can't believe it? I can't believe *that*. Those flowers were gorgeous, if I may say so myself. And for you to have bought them for no special reason or occasion, that's something in itself. At least, you didn't indicate it was for a special day."

"No, it wasn't for a special day. Maybe *that* was the problem. Maybe she thought I'd done something I was trying to make up for or something like that. But I wasn't. She's the one who goes out every night."

"I'm just glad you seem to be in a better place today than you were yesterday. So no more talk about leaving the state or anything else. Not your marriage. Not your home. And definitely not your girls or ministry. Okay?"

"No more talk about anything, especially now, because I

really have to get off this phone before I end up late from my break," he said.

"Okay. Well, thanks for the update. I'm glad things may be turning around for you. I really am," I said.

He laughed. "As I indicated earlier: time will tell. But in the meantime, I wanted to thank you for your ear and your encouragement. And thanks so much for being there when I needed someone to vent to. You have no idea how much that means to someone like me. I'll talk to you later," he said. "All right?"

"All right," I said. "Bye."

He hung up as I stood there holding the phone in one hand and that same gladiolus in the other—happy that he and his wife were on the right track. My only wish was that I could say something to my own husband and get through to him. Because no matter how many times Zeke and I have talked, he has yet to once acknowledge that there's a problem. He *definitely* has never said he was going to try to do better.

I've told him how I feel about him leaving me at home every night. But the most I've ever gotten from him? Instead of him leaving the way he used to without saying that he was going, he now will say "I'll be back" as he's going out the door.

Ethan, thinking enough to call me and let me know I had been a blessing to him just by listening, *absolutely* made my day.

It made my day!

Chapter 12

In those days they shall say no more, The fathers have eaten a sour grape, and the children's teeth are set on edge.

—Jeremiah 31:29

It had been two weeks since Ethan had called with his praise progress report. I was definitely praying for him and his family while zealously praying for me and mine. It didn't seem to matter. Zeke wasn't staying home any more now than he had been before my personal concentrated prayer service began. But at least he wasn't walking around like he'd eaten a batch of sour grapes.

I'd heard from Zanetta—Zane as her new friends were now calling her. I didn't really care for that spin on her name, mostly because I'd taken such great care in naming her in the first place. Actually, I'd given great consideration when I named all three of our children. Me being so in love with Zeke in the beginning, I wanted our firstborn to be named after him. So when our first child ended up not being a boy, I held to it as closely as I could by naming her Zanetta.

The name Zanetta was different. I'd taken the name Annetta (which happened to be my best friend's name in high school), added a letter, and dropped one to come up with Zanetta. By Zeke's name starting with a Z, the name Zanetta turned out to be a perfect way to tie the two of them together. Dropping one of the n's in Annetta made sense and it looked much better that way. Who could have foreseen that in doing this, some other folks would decide to be creative and drop the "t-t-a" entirely and start calling her Zane?

Zanetta played it off whenever I had something to say about it. She claimed they called her Zane because of how zany she could be. I will admit that Zanetta is definitely one who knows how to make you laugh. You wouldn't know that by looking at her. She always looks so serious. But she can have you splitting your sides. That's just one more thing I was missing with her being gone: there was no one around to make me laugh the way she could.

But she was doing well in the United States Air Force, traveling all around the world, all at the behest and expense of the military. My firstborn was living her dreams. So when she called and told me essentially that she'd gotten serious with this young man and was thinking about getting married, I thought she was merely making another one of her jokes. It took some doing, but she was eventually able to convince me that she was *indeed* serious.

Hallelujah!

You'd have to know Zanetta to understand why this was such a big deal. Zanetta has always been so laser-focused on her dreams and goals. Since she was in middle school, if a boy tried to talk to her, she just wasn't interested, not at all. Not if it meant it would get in the way of her reaching her goal. In school, her goal was to make straight As and stay on the A-honor roll. It didn't take her long to discover that talking to boys somehow took away from her studying time, and she wasn't having that. Not in middle school, not in high school, and to my chagrin, apparently not while serving in the military.

Being a straight-A student, she could have easily juggled hanging out with friends (girls and boys), going out every now and then. But Zanetta was self-motivated and she wasn't going to let anything or anyone get in the way of her achieving a set goal. She'd received academic as well as sports scholarships that totaled more than enough money for her to go to college and be a doctor if she'd chosen to, something I had highly encouraged her to look at as a career. I mean, she had the grades, she had the drive, she had the discipline, and here were folks handing her all the finances she would need without her having to pay anything back (unlike those taking out student loans). Her front-end sacrifices had already earned it for her. I could just see it: *My daughter the doctor. Doctor Zanetta.*

"Do you have any idea how many people you'll be able to bless as a doctor?" I had said to her when she and I were discussing what she'd like to do after high school.

But Zanetta didn't want to be a doctor. She wanted to be a pilot. She wanted to fly planes. And apparently, not just any old planes, but fighter jets. She'd been saying things like this since she was old enough to talk. In fact, I used to get under Zeke's skin by telling him that instead of her first word being "Daddy," it was "jet," or more to the way she pronounced it "det." Zeke accused me of lying, but I promise you, she was saying "jet." If she was watching television and a plane appeared on the screen, it didn't matter what she was doing, she would giggle and jump up and down while pointing at the TV, speaking what Zeke called "zibber-jabber." And when she was old enough to tell us what she wanted for Christmas, there was always at least one plane on her list.

They say when children are young they usually let you know by their actions or they'll tell you what they want to be when they grow up. It's just many parents don't always pay close enough attention. I suppose I shouldn't have been shocked when she told us that she was joining the Air Force and planned to fly their planes.

My second child, Zion, has always been somewhat tempered and quiet. As a baby, she watched people, but was content to play by herself if she had to. I used to feel bad because it appeared she was alone a lot, possibly mistreated. If she tried to play with Zanetta and her older sister wouldn't play with her, Zion would, without any drama or fanfare, merely get something she liked, and off she'd go by herself. It didn't seem to faze or bother her as much as it bothered me. I suppose that's the case, since she never complained or said anything otherwise, at least not to me.

I'd chosen the name Zion because of my sudden love of reading scriptures. Our Sunday school class had decided we were going to read through the Bible in one year. So I read my Bible every single day during the time I was pregnant with her. Originally, I thought it was going to be hard. But since there wasn't a set time I had to read (as long as it was before I closed my eyes for the night), I would read at least one of the suggested sections we were given on "How to read the Bible in a year" a day.

Sometimes I would read when I first woke up. Sometimes I would read while at work during my breaks. When I got home from work, the only time I would have most of the time, was right before I went to sleep. The biggest problem with bedtime and reading the Bible is that it seemed to put me to sleep that much quicker.

But I had loved the name Zion. During that time, it even appeared to be a sign from God. I would randomly open the Bible, and there was the name Zion. Right before she was born I was reading scriptures talking about Zion. And it didn't hurt that Zion began with a *Z*, a perfect name for our second girl. Since I'd named our first child using the letter Z, I decided to name the second one with a Z as well.

And of all things, Zion grew up and decided she wanted to be a missionary. I don't know *how* that happened. I believe I was more upset about it than her father. And one would think he would have been since he's not even that much of a church-goer.

Zeke laughed at me as I fussed to him about her plans to join a missionary group, essentially likening it to her "becoming a nun."

"No, it's not," he said. "Lots of missionaries marry. Nuns don't, unless you count their marriage to Jesus."

Zeke was right. People who did missionary work did get married. I think that was what was bugging me more than anything: the idea that so far, two of my daughters were seemingly avoiding men and relationships altogether, and the fact that I might not ever become a grandmother if they did. Not that I wanted to be a grandmother anytime soon (not saying that I would have minded, either, in the proper marital context). But I did want to believe that *somewhere* down the road, I'd get to hear a little one call me "Grandma," "Grandmother," "Granny," "Nana," "Mee-mee," "Mee-maw," or something along that line.

Zeke shut me down from that grandmother talk when he cleverly said, "You'd better be careful what you wish for. You do know we still have our baby girl. And she *definitely* is not shying away from boys. She just might make you a grandmother before you know it."

At that point, I directed my energies into making sure that our youngest child wasn't working to make us grandparents anytime soon—accident or no accident.

My baby.

Of course, after you've named the first two children using the same letter, you have to keep it going. Otherwise, there will be that one child who questions why he or she was the odd child out. The problem with this was that our third child was another girl, and I was running out of nice names that began with the letter Z. I'd almost decided to go with the name Zabrina when a visiting preacher spoke a "Word" over me and the child I was carrying. He said the child was going to be unique. For some reason, I couldn't get that word out of my head: Unique.

Well, as also could have been predicted, when the baby came, Zeke was nowhere to be found. By that I mean: neither I nor anyone else could find him. Keep in mind that this was before everybody owned their own cell phones. And granted the baby *did* come two weeks before her projected due date. And she'd chosen, of all times, to make her entrance at night, during the time when her father was normally gone (as opposed to her two older sisters who came, one in the afternoon, and the other at four o'clock in the morning).

Zeke had come home as usual around one that morning and found me gone. I didn't even leave him the courtesy of a note as to where I was going. I'd called my friend and neighbor up the street, Kelly Posey. She'd been the one to take me to the hospital, first dropping off my two girls at her house, then staying with me through the whole birthing thing, which didn't even take long enough for me to take off my coat and shoes before the nurse said, "I caught her." My having waited around, hoping and praying that Zeke would come home before the baby came, and I almost didn't make it to the hospital in time.

Kelly told me later that Zeke had called her house when he came home and discovered I wasn't there. She laughed as she said, "Do you know that fool husband of yours had the nerve to ask my husband when he called if you and I were out partying somewhere. My husband said he couldn't believe he'd called *our* house saying mess like that. Here you are nine months pregnant, and he thinks you and I are out getting our party on at some club."

Kelly told him I'd given birth when she carried the girls home so they could get ready for school. He arrived at the hospital that morning a little before eight, I guess after Kelly dropped the children off and they were safely at the bus stop.

Kelly had been absolutely wonderful. She'd stayed with me until three that morning and was up early enough to take my children home. Kelly laughed at how Zanetta, as young as she was at the time, was the driving force in ensuring that she didn't mess up her perfect attendance record at school. Zanetta made sure Kelly got up in time to get her home so she could get ready for school. Kelly tried to tell her she could legitimately be off from school after having a new baby sister born during the morning hours. Zanetta almost started to cry because she wanted to go to school.

I hadn't been surprised Zeke had said something crazy like that. He didn't like the fact that I had any friends at all. Here he was gone every night of the week, but he didn't want me going anywhere, except to work and church functions. And even church stuff got him going. He thought my church attendance was extreme. But to have a friend to talk with, to do things with—Zeke did everything he could to keep that from happening. He's the main reason my friend Danielle and I are no longer best friends.

If I wanted to go somewhere, he wouldn't stay home and keep the girls. If there was somewhere I had to be, I had to either take the girls with me or find a babysitter. And the few times that Kelly and I did go out, he clowned so, it wasn't even funny.

The first time Kelly and I went out, Zeke came home, found I wasn't there, and started drinking as he waited on my return. When I walked through the door, he started with his drunken talk, asking me who I'd slept with while I was gone. I didn't even bother dignifying his crazy talk with an answer. When that didn't work, he started crying, saying he had lost me and he didn't know how he was going to go on without me. If it hadn't been so pitiful, it would have been funny.

The next time I went out with Kelly (keep in mind that I probably went somewhere fun maybe twice in two years), he decided to stay home that night and wait for me to come back. I couldn't believe him. He wouldn't stay home with me when I was at home. He wouldn't stay home and keep *our* children for me to go somewhere. He wouldn't stay home from his normal routine to even take me out. But this particular time when I go out, he stays home and waits for me. *It was crazy!*

As before, when I walked in the door, he'd been drinking. He must have decided to approach things from a different angle this time around because he really attacked me for having been gone so long. He called me names because I'd "chosen" to leave our children instead of being a decent mother and staying home the way a good mother should. He then got in his car, drove off, called me from a pay phone, and proceeded to say, "Did you have fun with your lesbian friend?"

I slammed the phone down, hung up in his face.

I knew Zeke was trying to isolate me. *Why? Now that* was the question that I really couldn't answer. But then, Kelly's husband didn't like that she and I were friends much, either. Oh, he pretended to like me. And whenever I'd stop at their house and he was there, he was always polite and cordial to me. But I could tell he would have preferred I not be there at all, ever.

Kelly and I both concluded that our husbands were trying to control us. And the two of us having a friend outside of them just didn't work in their favor. Controllers know that if a person has someone to talk to outside of them, the person they are trying to control just might find the courage to make things better for themselves.

Kelly and I finally came to the conclusion that neither her husband nor mine truly wanted things to be better. Not for us.

But all of that was the past. And for whatever reason, today when Zeke woke up, he wasn't as nasty as he normally was. Today, he'd even smiled and said, "Good morning."

Ironically, something like that starts messing with your mind, starts you to wonder what exactly might he be up to.

What?

Chapter 13

Christmastime turned out to be busy for The Painted Lady Flower Shop. I was *too* excited about that! Forget how much we needed the money (and we really *did* need the money), it boosted my confidence tremendously. I was starting to question whether I'd done the right thing in leaving my job to do something as "irresponsible" (that's how Zeke refers to it when he thinks I'm not around to hear him) as to pursue my dreams. After all, I wasn't footloose and fancy-free like my daughters; I had responsibilities with my name on them. Zeke's lack of support had only added to my frustration.

He never seemed to have a positive word for me or what I was doing. Never. He didn't call me a loser outright. But I picked up on the words *not* said . . . the invisible words in between what *was* said. Zeke definitely resented that I'd left my great-paying job (a job that had taken some of the pressure off of him) with wonderful benefits (that included dental insurance), to pursue what he'd referred to as "the unknown."

So when the phone at the shop started ringing off the hook with people placing orders for floral arrangements and plants such as poinsettias for Christmas, I couldn't do anything but thank God.

And if all of this wasn't enough, I was given the gift of another surprise: all three of our daughters were home for Christmas. With all of this, you'd think this would have been a great Christmas.

Well, you'd be wrong.

Zanetta had informed us she was coming home, so we were expecting her. But Zion's visit was a complete surprise. Zanetta and Zion arrived within two days of each other. (I would later learn that Zanetta had been the one to talk Zion into coming.)

Zanetta looked good in her uniform, but she always looked good in blue. Zion had lost a lot of weight. She looked great as well. Zynique was over-the-moon ecstatic to see her two sisters. It had been over a year since either of them was last home.

"Zanetta, you look *so* good!" I said as we sat in the den. She was wearing a white and gold velour jogging suit. *Very classy.* There we were all together again: me, Zanetta, Zion, and Zynique just like old times. As usual, Zeke was gone. I thought for sure with all of his girls being here (and it being the holiday season), he would have foregone his nightly routine to spend time at home. Well, I *thought* wrong!

"Zion, have you been getting enough to eat over there in Haiti? Are they feeding you guys?" I asked.

"Why, Mother?" Zion said. She began to swing the top leg of her crossed legs, a sign I'd inadvertently touched a nerve.

I smiled. "I didn't mean anything by it. It's just you've lost a lot of weight. You look like you've lost two to three dress sizes."

"You would think you'd be happy about that," Zion said rather snippily.

I frowned. "Why would you think I'd be happy about you losing weight?"

"Oh, you know how you are." Zion tilted her head to one side. "You're always on us about something. If we eat too much, you think we need to cut back so we won't gain a lot of weight. If we lose weight, you think we must be doing something we're not supposed to be doing. I guess we can never win with you."

I knew exactly what Zion was referring to. When she was fourteen, I thought she might possibly be doing drugs. The signs were all there. She was slimming down way too fast and her behavior had become erratic. Her normally honor-roll, A–B grades were slipping to Cs and there was even one D. She was starting to get smart with me . . . talking back to me, something she never did and something she knew I didn't tolerate— not in *my* house.

I'd told her quickly, "Your little friends may have New Age mothers with New Age ways of thinking and disciplining. But I won't stand for a child, especially not one of mine, talking to grown people like they're equals."

Don't get me wrong: I believe in respecting children. I always gave my girls respect. I would hear them out completely; I always gave them a fair hearing. But when one of them would try to raise-up on me . . . that just wasn't going to fly. Not when you're eating my food and sleeping under the roof and in a bed I was providing. Yes, I believe it was my place to provide for them. And I love them more than life itself. But still . . .

"Well, Zion," I said, coming back to the discussion at hand. "I didn't mean anything by it. I was merely making an observation. That was all. You just look a bit thin to me. And I happen to know that where you are, doing the work that you do, you may have to do without," I said. "That was all I meant by it. You look good though."

Zion stopped swinging her leg. "Trust me: We're doing a lot better than many of the Haitians over there. It's a lot of work. But it's rewarding work."

I reached over, placed my hand on her knee, then playfully shook it. "Honey, I didn't mean anything by it. Really I didn't." Zion's hardened face softened a bit.

"At least you get to do what you want," Zynique said. "Mother won't let me do any fun things. It's all about my grades with her."

"Now, that's not true, Zynique," I said, turning toward my youngest daughter, who now appeared to be turning on me. "I let you spend time with Madame Perry. Do I not?"

"Yes. But you only do that because you started that flower shop and you want to get rid of me until you get home from the shop."

"Get rid of you?" I said puzzled. "What are you talking about?"

"I'm eighteen now and you're afraid I'm going to have some

boy over here while you're still at work. So you let me go over there to be sure I'm not here alone doing things you wouldn't approve of," Zynique said.

"Wow," I said. "Wow. And all the time I thought I was being flexible by letting you spend that time with Madame Perry. You were the one that asked . . . begged, if we want to be truthful about it, did you not?"

"Yes. But I've been asking you for the past two, almost three years, and you didn't say I could do it until this year, after you opened up your shop." Zynique folded her arms and made a huffing sound when she finished.

"I see. So you think I'm letting you go there because I want to pawn you off on someone while I do my thing? Is that right?"

"Absolutely."

"Well, Zynique. If you want to know the truth: I didn't say yes before because I didn't think a fifteen-year-old, even a sixteen-year-old needed to be working. That's what parents are for. Your father and I believe that we're the ones who are supposed to work and provide for our children. At least, until you're grown. After that—"

"We're on our own," Zynique said, finishing my sentence.

"Right. But if you must know: I went against my own personal judgment to let you work with Madame Perry because it seems like you really have your heart set on owning your own dance studio. I didn't want to be the one standing in the way of you or your dreams." I felt a tear begin to sting my eyes. "I thought I was doing something for you. I see now that apparently I can't win for losing."

Zanetta jumped in. "Mother, what you don't get is that all we ever saw from you was the disciplinary side. Since I've been in the Air Force, I get it. But when we were growing up, it just looked—to us, anyway—like you were the one always on us about *something*. You were the one who rode our backs. Dad was the one who seemed to understand better about how we felt and what we were going through."

"Dad is wonderful!" Zynique said, chiming in. "He gives me money when I ask him for it without giving me the third degree." Zynique looked at me with a look that felt judgmental. "Dad will let me go places without being all up in my business. Dad is not as uptight about things—at least, not like you are, Mother."

I nodded. Not because I agreed, but because I knew I couldn't say what I really wanted to say. At this point, it was best to just hold my tongue. What I wanted to say was: *Yes, it's easy for your daddy to be the cool one. He's not taking care of too many responsibilities. He's not here with you, Zynique, and he wasn't here for your sisters either. If you need any further proof, take a look around. He's not here right now! This is just the place where he stores his clothes, eats, and takes his baths. Everything fell and still falls on my shoulders. If I don't do it, things don't get done.*

I wanted to hang out with you girls the way he was able to, all of you, so you would possibly like me as a friend. But you didn't need me as your friend; you needed me as a mother. You, all of you, needed someone who would look out for you, someone who cared enough to make tough decisions and do things in your best interests—even if that decision meant or means you'll not talk to me or be upset with me. You needed and need someone who will push you to do your best, not because it makes me look good. But because I know you have it in you.

You need someone who would lay down her life for you, if the situation ever called for it. That's what you need and that's what your sisters needed. And I've been that. I am that! And more.

"Mother did a great job," Zanetta said, interrupting my internal dialogue. She looked over at me. "You did, Mother." She came over and grabbed my hand and squeezed it. "You did. I understand just how much. More than you'll ever know. I understand it all so much better now." She turned to her little sister. "And believe me, Zynique, you may not appreciate it now, but when you get older, you're also going to see things much clearer. I appreciate all that our mother did for me . . . for us."

"Zanetta's right," Zion said, then smiled at me, before hugging me. "Mother loves us. If I know nothing else, I know this. And Mother is going to do what she thinks is right and best." Zion gazed intensely into my eyes. "I'm sorry I was so sensitive about that comment. It's not you. I just have a lot on my mind. I was wrong to have lashed out at you like I did. Forgive me."

I nodded, smiled, then with both hands wiped away the tears that had somehow managed to sneak their way down to my face.

Chapter 14

I wisdom dwell with prudence, and find out knowledge of witty inventions.

—Proverbs 8:12

The month of February turned out to be another booming occasion for the shop. Coming up to Valentine's Day was crazy! I even got Zynique and her best friend Iesha to work for me after school and on the weekend leading up to the day when so many wanted to let their sweethearts know just how much they're loved. I'd hired a driver to deliver all of the flowers scheduled for delivery (as opposed to me delivering them myself). If nothing, I was a true realist: there was no way I could do everything.

Zynique and Iesha both turned out to be gifted in arranging flowers. If Zynique's heart wasn't so set on a dance studio, I could absolutely see her taking over my floral business.

Compared to the way things were jumping the week of February fourteen, it was church-mouse quiet at the shop when March came in. But because I'd ordered so much extra to ensure there was enough on hand for the Valentine's Day surge, I decided to create a few other floral specials that, to my delight, excitedly caused people to come in to the shop or call. There was hope that I was finally starting to figure out how to make this business work. *If nothing special is going on, create your own special.* I liked this saying so much I began using it for my shop's slogan.

Around the middle of March, one of the days when it was

molasses slow at the shop, I decided to lock up and go walking in the park. Admittedly, I missed my walking partner. I hadn't heard from Ethan since November when he'd called and wished me Happy Thanksgiving. He didn't say how things were going at home and I didn't ask. I could only pray that my previous advice to him about talking more to his wife, letting her in on his feelings, was paying off and helping them get their marriage back in sync.

The Lord knows *somebody's* marriage should be working, since mine apparently wasn't. It looked like the more I told Zeke how I felt, the more he rubbed salt in my wounds by either continuing to do what he now knew bothered or hurt me the most, or by finding even worse ways to try and do me in.

Still, I knew how much Ethan wanted (I dare say needed) things to go well at home and with his marriage. That's the kind of man he was. I'd absolutely heard his heart when we talked that day in my car back in September. He genuinely desired a better marriage despite that slipup of a kiss he'd planted on me.

So I prayed that things would get better for him . . . for all of them, if nothing else but for his girls. He loved those girls and his time with them. I saw it in his eyes, heard it in his voice, each time he spoke of them. I only wished Zeke had been or would be now, with Zynique, a fraction of what Ethan was with his girls. When at all possible, girls need their fathers in their lives. Ethan had said it best back in September. They need their fathers to step up and show them what it is or how it should be, to be loved by a real man so they don't have to search for it later in all the wrong places.

I caught myself. I needed to stop pining over Ethan and his problems.

So I closed the shop with my preprinted notice turned from OPEN to BE BACK AT with the simulated clock that allowed me to select a time. I went to the park where I normally go, not the one that Ethan and I had gone to back in September. This park was much smaller, but it got the job done I needed.

I loved being able to walk around the track, talking to God

under a beautiful indigo blue sky. It was like our special time together, just me and God. There were never many people at this park, especially during the morning hours when the school-age children were in school. It was also still a bit chilly outside, which was another reason folks weren't so anxious to be out there.

"Lord," I said as I began walking. "I thank You for Your many blessings. Thank You for waking me up this morning, clothed in my right mind. Thank You for everything being well with my family. And Lord, I thank You for forgiving me of my sins. You are so worthy to be praised. Thank You for the business You've given me. Thank You that it's beginning to thrive and it's going to take off like a rocket soon, in Jesus' name. I thank You that everywhere my feet tread belongs to me. I'm speaking life over my situations. I speak life over my health. I speak life over my family. I speak life over my husband. I speak life over our finances. Lord, I thank You for witty inventions and ideas, because I recognize that every good and every perfect gift comes from You.

"I succeed only because You know the plans that You have for me. Plans to prosper me. Plans to bless me and not hurt me. Lord, please touch my heart so that I can love the way *You* would have me to love. Direct my steps so that I will walk in the path You've ordained for me. And bless our pastor. Keep him as he does Your work. Bless me as I continue to spread the Good News of Your Son, Jesus, and all He has done to secure our salvation to those who don't know or haven't honestly accepted Him, starting in my own house, with my own husband. Let whatever my hands find to do be true ministry for Your Kingdom.

"And Lord . . . I know this might not sound right coming from me and given the situation, but please bless Ethan. I'm sure he has a lot on him right now. Temptation is all around and the spirit of discouragement waits to overtake him. Lord, You know his heart. You know his desires. Strengthen him and strengthen his marriage. Give him the desires of his heart as he continues to serve You. He is blessing so many. He's bringing

Your word to folks who might otherwise never hear it. Please . . ."
I looked up at the sky. "I ask these blessings in Your Son Jesus'
name. Amen."

I walked a few more laps around the track, purposely plant-
ing my feet down hard as I spoke scriptures that I desired to
manifest.

Just as I finished and was walking back to my car, I saw him—
Ethan getting out of his.

He saw me and started walking my way. Without thinking, I
sucked in a deep breath. And just that quickly, I forgot how to
exhale it out.

Chapter 15

We give thanks to God always for you all, making mention of you in our prayers.

—1 Thessalonians 1:2

"What are you doing here?" Ethan asked as he was about ten feet away; close enough for me to hear him, without him having to speak too loudly.

"I *could* ask you the same thing," I said, tilting my head ever so slightly as he came to a stop, an arm's length away from me.

"Well, since I asked first, I think the mannerly thing would be for you to answer my question."

"Mannerly, huh? Okay then. I was walking. Which now begs the question: are you following me?"

He laughed. "No, I'm not *following* you."

"Really now. And you expect me to believe that you just *happened* to show up at the same park where I *happened* to be, completely by coincidence?"

"I guess you'll have to believe it since it's the truth." Ethan then began to bounce up and down, the way he does when he's warming up.

"Well, if you *were* following me, then you're too late. I'm finished with my walk and I'm on my way back to the shop."

He grabbed one side of the top of his head with the opposite hand and tugged it ever so slightly a few times, then switched and did the other side. "So did you have a good workout?"

"Yes, I did. I'm taking it slow; I don't want to overdo it or anything. I just started back walking a few days ago, getting back into the groove and routine of it after not doing it these past few months. This is only my third time out here. I'm sure you know how that goes."

"Absolutely." He began doing lunges, first to the right side, then the left, before bending down to touch his toes.

"Well . . . have a good one," I said, feeling as though I was bothering him.

He stood up and began to bounce again. "Will do. I'm on vacation . . . church revival this whole week. I came here to work out. Have to keep in shape if I want to keep doing what I do."

I nodded, then opened my car door.

"Hey!" he said. I turned back toward him. "You're praying for me, aren't you?"

I smiled. "Yes."

"Yeah," he said, nodding with a smile. "I can tell. I can feel it." He began to nod more slowly before stopping completely. "Thank you."

I gave one quick nod of my head, got in my car, and watched him in my rearview mirror as he jogged toward the track.

As much as I was glad that our bumping into each other at the park wasn't anything more than sheer coincidence, I couldn't help but be a *little* disappointed that he hadn't had more to say to me.

Just a little.

Chapter 16

And the fruit of righteousness is sown in peace of them that make peace.

—James 3:18

The period coming up to Mother's Day had turned out to be another booming stretch for the flower shop. I was feeling pretty good about the business now. Zeke was the way he always was, although something wasn't quite right with him physically. I could tell he was definitely in pain. But he kept up his normal seven-day routine.

Zynique graduated from high school at the end of May.

"I'm so proud of you," I said as I snapped a picture, first of her with her father, then one with two of her friends.

"Oh, Mom!" she said, then turned to her father. "Daddy, take a picture of me and Mother." She came over and grabbed the camera out of my hand and handed it to Zeke before coming and standing next to me.

Zeke flipped, rotated, and turned the digital camera around in his hands several times. "I don't know how to use this thing," Zeke said, showing his exasperation.

"Just point it our way and look at the back," I said. "You'll see us on the screen and all you need to do when you get the shot you want is press the button at the top."

"What button?" He examined the camera. "This one here?" He pointed the camera at us. "I don't know how to do this." He held the camera up and looked at it again.

"Zeke, just point the camera at us and shoot. It's not that hard."

"It might not be hard for you and the young folks, but I told you I don't know how to do this." He pointed the camera the correct way this time.

"Would you like for me to take it for you?" Darlene asked Zeke.

"Yes, why don't you do it?" Zeke happily handed the camera to Darlene.

"Daddy!" Zynique said. "You didn't even try."

"I'm doing good to even be here," Zeke said. "But you're my baby girl, and you know there's nothing that would have made me miss being here, nothing in the world."

I couldn't help but want to add (but I didn't): *Nothing after you missed being there when she was born, among other things.*

"Daddy, you're the best!" Zynique said as she put her arms around my waist and waited as Darlene captured the shot. "Come on, Daddy. Come take a picture with me and Mom."

Zeke sauntered over with a righteous swag, grinning like all get out. Zynique stood between her father and me. Darlene snapped three pictures, then showed the digitized photos to Zynique.

"Oh, Daddy, you look so good! Mom, you look like you're mad."

"Well, I'm not. I'm happy. I'm happy because you, my sweet little baby girl, graduated."

Zynique grinned as she hugged me. "I'm going to a party after I leave here."

"But I have something planned for you at the house. I bought a graduation cake and everything. I have all these re-freshments. I invited folks from church, a few family members, and friends that couldn't be here because of the limited num-ber of guests you were allowed to attend for this—"

"Baby, let the girl go to the party with her friends," Zeke said to me. "Why on earth would you think she'd want to hang out with a bunch of old folks when she can hang out with folks her own age?"

"See, Mom. Daddy understands. He *always* understands."

"Zynique, you're welcome to invite your friends to our house," I said as I continued to plead my case. "I have plenty. I can even order in pizzas, if you want."

"But she doesn't want to come to our house for a party," Zeke said. "She just told you that she wants to have fun with her own friends at *their* party. So let the girl have her day. It *is* her day you know."

"Of course," I said, now smiling at Zynique even though it took all I could to muster it. "Sure. Whatever I bought will certainly keep. I'll just put it up and maybe we can celebrate as a family tomorrow. I'll just call everybody now and postpone it."

"Thank you, Mommy!" Zynique said. "Thanks, Daddy!" She kissed her father, then me. "I'm going now. But thanks for everything you two have done to help get me to this place. I'm finished with school! It's finally over!"

"I'll see you later, baby," I said to Zynique. "Don't forget your curfew."

"Mom! I'm an adult now. I should be able to stay out as late as I want, especially on a night like this. We were planning on eating breakfast together at IHOP in the morning."

"You're still living in our house, and I expect you home by your normal curfew," I said, still trying to smile so I wouldn't appear to be the party popper (not pooper, popper) of the bunch.

"Honey, let the child have an extra hour or two," Zeke said. "They're celebrating a milestone here. She's worked hard to get to this place."

I turned squarely to him so I could look him in the eye when I spoke and he would know I didn't need him opposing me on this, not at this juncture. "Zeke, Zynique needs to be home at her normal curfew."

Zeke wriggled his nose, nodded, then turned to Zynique. "Well, baby girl. Your mother says you need to be home at your regular curfew time."

"Yeah," Zynique said. "And Mother *always* has the final word." Zynique flashed a smile, then turned and left with Darlene.

Chapter 17

For we ourselves also were sometimes foolish, dis-
obedient, deceived, serving divers lusts and plea-
sures, living in malice and envy, hateful, and hating
one another.

—Titus 3:3

"See, Zeke. That's exactly what I'm talking about," I said as he drove us home from the graduation ceremony. "You do stuff like that all the time."

"Do what?"

"Undermine me. You've done this with our children since day one."

"You be tripping," Zeke said, glancing between me and the winding dark road.

"I'm not tripping. And I wish you'd quit saying that as your comeback every time I say something that you don't like."

"But you do be tripping. So what exactly are we arguing about tonight?"

"I'm not arguing. I'm just stating a fact. It's always been like that. I tell the girls one thing, and you come along, being Mister Good Guy, saying the complete opposite, saying what you know they want to hear, just so you can make me look bad."

"Okay, I think you're being a bit paranoid here. I don't do things just to make you look bad. I can't help it if our daughters feel and have always felt a stronger bond with me than with you."

I let out an audible huff as I frowned, although in the darkness, I'm sure he couldn't see the frown. "What?" I said.

"That's really what you're upset about. You're put out that

our children feel closer to me than you. It hurts that they relate to me better than they relate to you."

I started laughing. "Oh, that's funny! That is *fun*-ny."

"Laugh all you want, but that's really what has your girdle in a wad."

"No," I said, "it's not. And for your information, I don't wear a girdle. What's bugging me is how you've never really and truly been there for your daughters, not one of them. If you really want to dance with the truth, you've actually been MIA most of their lives."

"Okay, now see how crazy you sound. You know I've been at our house since day one, and I've never left you, not once. Not even when I should have, with your little confrontational self."

"You don't *live* there, Zeke. It's merely a place where you stop on your way to . . ." I turned and looked at him but it was too dark for me to see his face. "Where exactly is it that you go practically every night?"

"Out," he said.

"Yes, that's what you tell me. But where precisely is *out?* Give me an address, a location."

An approaching car cast a beam of light through our windshield, allowing me to see Zeke's face. "Here and there," he said, glancing over at me.

"See, that's what I mean. I don't know if 'here and there' means with this woman or that." I stared at him, hoping that despite the darkness, he would be able to feel my eyes boring a hole through him.

He laughed. "Okay, so I see you're going over to the other side again. That's all you do—look for something to fuss about. And that's exactly why I go somewhere other than my own house almost every night so I can get away: so I won't have to listen to you and ridiculous mess like this."

"Oh, you're full of it! You just use that as an excuse to keep doing what you do. What is it? You don't think I know that you have a girlfriend on the side?"

"All righty then. So now I have a girlfriend on the side?"

I could tell he had once again glanced over at me by the way his words seemed to slap me on the left side of my face. "Zeke,

I'm not a fool. And I'm not stupid by any means, even if on occasion I sometimes play one at home. I may not have ever called you on it, but you can't tell me that you've never cheated on me."

Zeke pulled into our driveway and pressed the button to raise the garage door. "You just have to find a way, don't you, baby? I don't care what you have to do; you always have to find a way. You're never satisfied until you push one of my buttons."

"I'm not your baby. So stop calling me baby!"

Zeke pulled the car into the garage and turned off the engine. "Okay, fine," he said calmly. "You don't want to be called baby, I won't call you baby." He opened his car door and stepped out.

I opened my car door and jumped out. "Don't you walk away from me while I'm talking." He kept walking. I hurried to catch him. "Do you think I don't know that you leave here so you can be with some other woman? Just because I never said anything to you about it, doesn't mean I didn't know."

Zeke turned around and stared at me, then chortled. "Why in heaven's name would I *ever* leave someone like you to be with another woman?" There was a certain sarcasm that came with his question that wasn't truly a question. "Huh?"

I began to nod profusely. "That's what you always do. I bring up something serious, and you treat it like it's a joke. Well, Zeke, while our daughters may think you're a really 'swell' person, I know better. Of course they think you're wonderful. You never disciplined them. You never dealt with the hard stuff. All you had to do was come home for a little while and be Mister Joy."

He let out a short laugh. "Mister Joy?"

"Yeah. You know: you'd come in and play with them. Make them laugh, then you're out of here. Everything bad to be dealt with was left on me to handle. They don't have any bad memories with you, Zeke, mostly because you weren't around long enough to give them any."

"Because I never spanked them, is that what this is all about? Oh, I know: you're still disturbed because to this very day, Zion won't let go of that time she got in trouble with you and I turned out to be the reasonable one between the two of us."

"Zion loved you! All Zion wanted was your love and attention. But you didn't even have time to give her that. So of course, she acted out. She was crying out for your attention. But you were too busy to see that. So when she had to be reined back in, whose shoulders was it left on? Mine! And that wasn't fair. I told you what that child needed, but you were too busy trying to get to some other woman's place to care!"

"Okay, so now you're saying it's my fault that Zion is doing missionary work? Is that what you're saying? It's my fault Zanetta joined the military so she could get as far away from us as possible? Is that what you're saying, my dear wife?"

"No, Zeke! I'm saying that Zion wanted to know she mattered to you and you never gave her that. Zanetta got a little bit of attention from you, but that was because she was your first child. Although, if we want to be real about all of this: even that attention only lasted a good hot second."

"And Zynique?" Zeke said. "What damage have I done to Zynique?"

I sighed. "Zeke, you're not hearing me. You haven't been here for any of us, Zynique included. I'm tired, Zeke. I'm tired."

"You're probably tired because of that stupid business you started. I don't know where your head was when you decided to quit your job and do something asinine like open a *flower* shop. Now you're stressed out because things aren't going all rosy the way you thought they would, so you want to take it out on me." He started toward the stairs that lead to our bedroom.

"No, Zeke," I said, following behind him. "That's an entirely different argument."

He stopped halfway up the staircase and turned back toward me. "So help me out here: which argument are we having right now? Are we arguing about our daughters? Are we arguing about my parenting? Are we arguing about me and my supposed affairs? Or are we arguing about your misjudgments that you somehow would like to pin on me?" He turned back around and continued until he reached our bedroom and went to the closet. Locating the maroon shirt I'd expressly bought him to wear (that he didn't) to Zynique's graduation, Zeke slipped it off the wooden hanger and quickly brushed past me as he stepped out of the closet.

I watched him as he hastily took off the dark blue shirt he wore, yanked tags off the new shirt, and put the maroon shirt on. "What are you doing?" I asked.

"What does it look like I'm doing? I'm changing my shirt," he said.

"For what?" I glanced at the clock on my nightstand. "It's almost nine o'clock."

He nimbly buttoned the last two buttons, then checked himself in the dresser mirror. "Because I want to wear it."

"You want to wear that eighty-dollar shirt I bought to bed? It's not a pajama top."

"Don't be silly. Of course I'm not wearing it to bed. I'm wearing it out."

"You're wearing it *out?*" My voice escalated. "We just came from being *out,*" I said.

He put on some cologne. "Well, if you think I'm going to stay here and listen to you accuse me of being a lousy father, husband, and man . . . a man you claim is cheating . . . has cheated on you—I can't even keep up at this point. But if you think I'm going to stay here and be subjected to this, then you have another *think* coming."

"You're not slick," I said. "I know *exactly* what you're doing."

"And what is that, dear wife?" He primped his mouth. "What am I doing?"

"You're trying to manufacture a reason so you can leave tonight and make it out to be my fault."

Zeke laughed. "You're good, I tell you." He cocked his hand like a gun and pointed his index finger directly at my face. "You are *good!*"

"So what is it? Did you tell her you would be over there after graduation and now you're running late? Is that it? Can't she be without you for one night?" I began to primp my mouth as I nodded. "Is that why you were all for Zynique going with her friends? You didn't want her throwing a monkey wrench into your plans tonight?"

Zeke leaned over to kiss me. I jerked back.

"You're tripping," he said. "So you know what? I *am* going to leave while you calm down."

I stomped my foot. "No, you're not going to leave! You're going to stay right here, and you and I are going to talk. We're going to figure out what's going on with us, and we're going to come up with a plan to fix it. Because, Zeke, I'm tired. I am tired. And I'm not happy. I've put up with this for over twenty years now. And I'm telling you that I'm tired of it."

He nodded. "Okay. So you want to talk?"

"Yes," I said. "I want us to work on this sham of a marriage we have. I want things to be the way they're supposed to be with a happily married couple."

He belted out a quick short laugh. "I've told you about reading romance books and watching those romantic shows. Baby, they're not real. Those folks are all made up. The life they're portraying on the pages and on screen, not real."

"I don't read romance novels. I'm too busy to read much of anything these days unless it's related to business. I'm talking about having a marriage like married couples are supposed to."

"Oh," he said. "You're talking about like your pastor? Your pastor who's fooling around on his wife, even as we speak. The one that everybody and his brother knows that it's going on. But just because the man can 'preach' no one wants to acknowledge it's going on. And every Sunday and Wednesday, y'all flock down to the 'church house' to hear him tell you how to live a life that *he's* not even trying to live. You and your little friends do more work at church and for that man than it seems you *ever* do for your own house and husbands."

"First of all, you can't believe everything you hear," I said about our pastor and his alleged affair, although I knew it was true. Our pastor has hit on me so many times, I had threatened to lay holy hands on him if he didn't stop.

"Oh, I'm pretty sure what's being said about your pastor is true." The way Zeke said it made me think he had some type of verifiable knowledge. "And his wife," Zeke continued, "might be a little thick, but homegirl—or should I say it the way she insists on everybody saying it?—'First Lady' doesn't let that stop her from getting around, if you know what I mean. So I'm sure you can't mean married like them. Let's see now: there's your friend Kelly and her husband—major cracks in their marriage. I'm talking major, major cracks."

I didn't need him telling me anything about Kelly. I knew what kind of a marriage she was in. As I've often said: as bad as Zeke was, he was *nothing* compared to Kelly's husband.

Zeke tried to sneak a glance at his watch without me seeing him. "So why do you keep looking at your watch?" I asked. "Am I keeping you from somewhere? Am I making you late? Do you need to call her and explain that you're dealing with something important tonight with your *wife?* Maybe you should call whomever and let them know you're not going to make it tonight."

"You know what? I'm not going to stand here for this. You said you wanted to talk, I was here. But all you want to do is belittle me and talk about what I do wrong. Well, what about you?"

"What about *me?*"

"You think living with you is a piece of cake?" He chuckled, I'm sure for effect. "Do you think being married to you is a walk in the park?"

"Zeke, I know I have my flaws. I never said I was perfect. And I'm not asking you to be perfect. I'm just asking you to meet me halfway. That's all. If there's something that I do that you want to talk about, then let's talk about it. Now is as good a time as any to put everything on the table. Either you want me and you want our marriage to work or you don't. I'm trying to do all I know how. But this can't be one-sided. It's not fair when it is."

"Look." He held up both hands. "You're right. You are *so* right. I'm confessing right here, right now. I've *not* been the best father. Yes, I should have been home a little more. I've not been the best husband although I really am better than 90 percent of husbands out there. No matter where I might go, at least I come home to you. And I didn't leave you with three children to have to raise all alone."

I pulled back and frowned. "You think the only way a man can leave a woman to raise children alone is by walking out on her completely? Have you been listening to anything I've been saying? You would come home, play with the children for a hot minute, eat, then leave. That was almost every single day of the week. I was the one here dealing with them and their home-work. I was the one left taking care of them."

"Come on, now. Let's be real. You were always the smart one. I couldn't have helped them with homework if I *had* to. You know that I barely graduated my own self. And now with all of this newfangled math and junk, I wouldn't have been much help to the children. I would have just gotten in the way and you know it."

"There you go again," I said. "I'm trying to tell you. Even if you didn't know how to do something, just being here would have made all the difference in the world. Children care about you, not always what you have and what you can do."

He nodded. "You're right. You're right. I'm a jerk. I'm a fail-ure as a parent."

I sighed. "You're not a failure, Zeke. Our girls love you. So that means something. It means a lot. All I've ever tried to get you to see is that you can always be better. *I* can always be better. As a couple, *we* can always be better."

"You're absolutely right." He smiled, then nodded. The phone rang. I looked, then started toward it to answer it. "I got it," he said, uncharacteristically rushing to beat me to it. "You go and change."

"No, I'll get it," I said, really determined to answer it now. When I did, the person (a woman) said she'd dialed the wrong number.

"Who was it?" Zeke asked, something else he rarely ever did.

"A woman . . . said she must have dialed the wrong number." I began to nod. "It was probably your girlfriend calling to see where you were." I was actually half-teasing.

"See, there you go again. Every time we seem to be making progress, you have to go say something crazy. You know what, I'm tired of this. Maybe if you have a little time to yourself to think about all of this, you'll stop the craziness." He walked out of the bedroom into the hall.

I ran behind him. "Zeke, where are you going? Zeke, don't you leave here! I mean it! I know what you're doing! I'm not stupid, Zeke! I know what you're doing here! You're not leaving because of me—"

As I made my way down the stairs trying to catch him, I heard the door to the garage open, then slam. And before I could get to the garage, he had cranked his car and was backing out.

Chapter 18

Humble yourselves in the sight of the Lord, and he shall lift you up.

—James 4:10

After Zeke stormed out, I walked the floor for a little while. And before I knew anything, I was *on* the floor on my knees, praying and crying. Not because he'd left the way he had. Not because I thought he was most likely having an affair. If he was, I was not the kind of woman that would be checking around trying to find out, that's for sure. And it was not part of my nature to fight another woman over some man, either. Zeke knew that. I'd already told him, years ago, that if he ever wanted to be with someone else, he was always welcome to get his stuff and leave. He could go live with whomever he pleased. I'm not going to beg a man to stay with me.

But Zeke wasn't going to do that. Zeke knew what a good woman he had in me. He wasn't going to walk away from me. The man was just greedy. Knowing him, he would want to keep the both of us. And since I don't really know how many women he may have been with, I can't say how serious he's been about anyone else, other than me. I only know how long he's been with me.

I wasn't going to ride around to see if I could find his car parked at someone's house or outside an apartment building or hotel. I wasn't going to put a tape recorder under our bed or tap the phone to record his conversations. I wasn't going to rifle through his things trying to find out whether he had someone else or not and if someone, who that person was. I wasn't going to do it. I wasn't going to.

I just wasn't.

Now my friend Shelia was totally different. She'd done all of those things and more. And even when she found proof that her husband was cheating on her, to the point where she learned her husband had fathered a child with one of his other women, she still stayed with him. Talking about "But I *love* him. I don't want to live without him. I just know, if we try, we can make this work. God can heal our marriage."

Okay. They say love covers a multitude of sins. Shelia was proving that out.

So I asked her, "What was the point in finding out he was cheating on you if you weren't going to do anything about it?"

"I just wanted to know," Shelia said. "I needed to know. That way I knew how to proceed." She sighed and looked at me as though *I* was the enemy. "This is spiritual warfare," she said. "The devil is trying to destroy godly marriages, and I'm not going to let him win."

"So you're proceeding by letting your husband stay there with you while it sounds like he's still seeing her? I don't get it. How is that defeating the devil?"

"Jermaine is trying to break it off with her," Shelia said of her husband. "But that woman is a psycho!"

"Well, if she's truly a psycho, it would seem to me that Jermaine would be running as fast as he can to get away from her."

"He wants to get out, believe me, he does. But you know they have that child together now," Shelia said. "You know how that can be. It's not the child's fault his mother is crazy and has no morals other than to sleep with another woman's husband. And the child is such a cute little boy. You know I have four girls and you know how much Jermaine always wanted a son. I believe this is going to work. I'm praying it's going to work. I just need you to touch and agree with me that it does." She held out her hand for me to touch it.

I just shook my head. "Shelia, you know: sometimes there's crazy that even a pill can't fix."

"I know, right?" she said with a lift in her voice, apparently not realizing I'd totally left her hand hanging out to dry.

I think she actually may have thought what I said about crazy and a pill that I was talking *exclusively* about Jermaine's other woman. I didn't even try and explain *that* one to her. She was my friend and I would be there when she needed me. *Hel-lo!*

Back to my own troubles. I was there on the floor by the couch praying. Praying helps me *so* much. I know a lot of people think that praying really doesn't change things all that much. Some folks say that you pray and oftentimes the problem is still staring you in the face when you get finished. But it really does help . . . me at least. I'd calmed down greatly; a perfect peace surrounded me when I was finished.

I showered and changed into my nightgown. As I crawled into the bed, I glanced at the clock on my nightstand. It was way past Zynique's curfew and she hadn't come home yet. She hadn't called, unless she'd called while I was in the shower. I checked the caller ID. Someone had called five minutes after ten. It was a blocked number. I was trying to think how I'd missed hearing the phone ring during that time. I hadn't gotten into the shower until after midnight.

It most likely happened when I went outside right after Zeke drove away. I'd gone outside for a minute just because I couldn't believe he'd been that blatantly bold as to walk out on me like that. Usually when we're arguing, he stays around until I've exhausted my words. He had to know I wasn't buying this *coincidence* theory: him trying to get out of the house, the phone ringing, a woman just *happening* to call the wrong number, and then he takes off—in a made-up huff of course, all because of me.

When we first got married he did that stuff, making it like it was always my fault. I *did* think it was my fault back then. I'd profoundly and sincerely apologize for things I didn't even cause. Yes, he most certainly did get me in the beginning of our marriage. But with age comes wisdom, at least for some it does. When I figured out what he was doing, I was done letting him manipulate me. He hadn't completely stopped what he was doing; he was merely attempting to hone his craft.

Zynique and Zeke came in the house at almost the same time. Zeke pulled into the garage and Zynique came through the front door five minutes after he turned off his car. I'm certain they saw each other. They couldn't have helped but.

I wanted to get up and confront them both. And had they arrived at separate times, I probably would have. But I didn't want to fuss with Zynique about breaking curfew when I really wanted to let Zeke have it for walking out on me like he had. I didn't want Zynique to have to hear me yelling at her father (as I'm sure she was tired of hearing) about what had just taken place on the night she was celebrating her monumental accomplishment.

Besides, had I said anything to Zynique, Zeke would have just taken up for her, once again painting me as the bad guy. And if I had said anything to Zeke, then Zynique would have felt justified in the assessment she'd made about me when she was twelve. "Nobody likes you! You're mean. And I feel sorry for Daddy! You're the reason he doesn't ever want to be at home. It's all because of you!"

That had really cut me to the bone, all the way to the white of the bone. Not because she was right. It was because she felt that way. She felt I was mean. That I made life so difficult that the only adult in the household, who had a right to stand up to me, couldn't take being around me.

So I decided to leave the two of them alone. And when Zeke came into the bedroom and said that he knew I wasn't asleep and that we should talk, I "played possum" (pretended to be asleep) and didn't say a word.

He crawled into the bed and tried to invade my side of it. I scooted over until I was practically on the edge. When he continued to scoot in my direction, I got up and went to Zanetta's old bedroom. Only thing: I couldn't go to sleep. So I stared at the ceiling and once again decided to just pray.

"Lord, I need some help down here. I don't think I can take

much more of this. I don't. Please, Lord, be a lifter of my spirits. Please . . ."

One thing about the devil is he has a way of figuring out the
weak points in our lives. Not because he's God, who happens to
be omniscient, omnipotent, and omnipresent. But because
that crafty little devil and his little imps listen in on the words
that we speak and they observe our every action. The devil can
pinpoint precisely the area where we're the most vulnerable
and, most times, we're the ones who end up letting him know
just where that area is.

Well, he must have been watching and listening to me and
my conversations. He definitely knew all of my weaknesses, at
least at this point in the game.

And the root of it could pretty much be traced right back to
my own home!

Chapter 19

*The aged women likewise, that they be in behavior
as becometh holiness, not false accusers, not given
to much wine, teachers of good things.*

—Titus 2:3

Zynique was having the time of her life working full-time with Madame Perry. In doing this, Zynique had become a blessing to Madame Perry. At least, that's what Madame Perry told me when she came into the flower shop right before closing time to place an order for a spray of flowers.

"Your baby certainly is a blessing," she said as soon as she cleared the doorway. A petite woman who immediately made you think of royalty when you first saw her by the sheer way in which she carried herself, Madame Perry dressed just as impeccably.

"Madame Perry," I said with excitement in my voice as I hugged her, both shocked and surprised to see her. "How nice of you to come by!"

"I've been meaning to stop by your shop for the longest time, my dear." She made a grand show of looking around, nodding her approval as she did so. "It's unfortunate that my first foray into your place would be due to the loss of a dear, sweet friend. You do have a charming place here, quite lovely."

"Why, thank you." I did a quick glance of the area closest to me.

"Yes, yes. I'm sure you've had a time with the initial start-up. So many things pop up that you don't plan for. At least, that was my experience. It is the nature of the beast, my dear, in owning a business. You think things are going to go one way, and before you know it, you're thrown a curveball." She smiled as she sat down at the table I'd set up only recently when I learned people didn't always want to stand at the counter as they decided what they might want.

"So you say you've lost a friend? I'm so sorry to hear that," I said, sitting down across from her.

"Thank you"—she patted my hand—"but no need to be sorry. My friend—Ruby was her name—lived a full life. Oh yes. Ruby certainly lived her life. And I will sorely miss her. But as she said to me when I visited her right before she transitioned to the other side, 'We know that this is not our home. We're merely pilgrims passing through. I'm getting ready to go back home now. I got my ticket and I'm going home.' But still, when you reach my age, you find yourself becoming more and more alone as family and friends continue leaving you. One by one, they go."

"Oh, but Madame Perry, the young people love you so much. They positively *adore* you! You'll never be alone."

She nodded. "Yes, I've been blessed with young folks surrounding me, making me feel so loved. But there's nothing like those who understand exactly what you're going through. That's what I'm going to miss most about dear Ruby. We both knew the struggles it took for us to get to where we were. We didn't forget those who are coming after us. But now, when I want to phone my friend, she'll no longer be on the other end to take my call." Madame Perry smiled. "That's why I thank God for Jesus. I'll forever have a friend on the other end. Jesus will be there with me until the end. I'm His and He's mine. That's what I told Zynique just the other day. That child of yours is a true blessing."

"Well, I appreciate you for having allowed her to work with you and you sharing your knowledge with her. She loves you so much. In fact, you're the reason she wants to open her own dance studio someday."

"Having knowledge is great." Madame Perry opened the book on the table that contained pictures of various sprays and floral arrangements. "But if you can't share what you have and what you know with others, what good does it do you to keep it? It ends up being buried with you."

"That's true," I said. "But from what Zynique tells me, you go beyond sharing. You're her mentor you know. She wants to be just like you."

"Well"—Madame Perry said as she gracefully flipped pages without ever looking at them—"I'm pouring everything I have in me into that daughter of yours. I want her to succeed beyond all expectations and imagination. But I'll tell you, just like I told her: we don't need another me. The idea is not for her to copy me. We need a more original of her—uniquely Zynique." Madame Perry laughed. "That little woman is going to make me look like an amateur when she gets all of this down pat. She's a natural-born dancer and a natural-born leader. And I truly believe she's going to become an awesome business-woman who'll make us all proud one of these days. You mark my words. In fact: you can write down that I declared it on *this* day." She lightly tapped the table with her index finger like she was sending a message in Morse code.

I nodded. There was definitely something special about Madame Perry. "Well, I'm just glad my baby has someone like you who's been willing to open her heart and help her in reaching her dreams."

Madame Perry nodded a few times, turned a few more pages, then closed the book. "Why don't you just fix some-thing really special for my friend?" she said. "I trust your judg-ment."

"I can do that." I then took down the information for her order, the price range she wanted, the full name of the de-ceased, when and to what funeral home the spray should be de-livered. She stood, nodded as though she was giving me her blessing, and left.

The shop's phone rang. It was Ethan, calling from his home number.

"What's wrong?" I said, hearing panic permeating throughout his voice.

"It's my daughter!" Ethan said. "I need you to pray! Oh, my Lord in Heaven! It's my baby girl! I need you to pray!"

Chapter 20

A double-minded man is unstable in all his ways.
—James 1:8

"What happened, Ethan? Tell me what's going on so I'll know what I need to be praying for," I said.

He took a few breaths. "I'm sorry. I'm sorry," he said.

"It's okay. Now tell me what's going on."

"I can't talk but a minute. But I had to call you. I know you've been praying for us. And I know you can get a prayer through. My daughter . . . Jacquetta is missing."

"What? When? How?"

"Long story short: her mother was supposed to pick her up from school."

"Your children are still in school?"

"Yes, this was their last day. They had to make up all of those snow days we had this year, so the school had to add more days at the end of the school year. Most of the children didn't even bother going to school today, but Jacquetta wanted to go. That girl loves school. Normally, she would ride the bus home, but today she wanted to stay and help her teacher take things down and put things away, something like that. Her mother told her she would pick her up. I told Denise I would get her since I normally get off at two, but Denise insisted she would do it. Said she was taking off work early anyway today. I guess I should have asked her why she was taking off, but you know what? None of that matters now. What matters is that she told my baby girl that she would be at the school to pick her up at two, and she wasn't."

"What do you mean 'she wasn't'?"

"I mean she forgot! Denise forgot to go by the school and pick Jacquetta up." I instantly heard the change of tone in his voice. "As usual, she had more important things to do. So she forgot that she'd told our daughter she'd pick her up. She'd told Jacquetta to be outside waiting for her no later than two."

"Wait a minute," I said. "Why would a teacher let her be out there by herself? I don't get that part. Even if—"

"The teacher told the police that Jacquetta said her mother was waiting outside. She thought Denise was out there already. Now Jacquetta's missing, and no one knows where she is. Phoenix Arissa believes Jacquetta likely tried to walk home. The police have searched the road from the school to our house. There's no sign of her. Nothing. Somebody probably saw her and snatched her up—"

"Stop that!" I said. "Do you hear me? I want you to stop that right now! You of all people know that death and life is in the power of the tongue. Don't you *dare* say another negative word on this matter, do you hear me?"

"You're right, you're right." He made a growling sound. "But I'm almost out of my mind at this point. Do you have any idea the thoughts that are running through my mind right now? Do you?"

"I have a pretty good idea. I want you to listen to me. I'm going to be praying like you won't believe. But you have *got* to set your thoughts on God and what He is doing right now and don't let your mind wander over there where the devil would like for you to go."

"You're right. You're right. Well, I'm going to get off this phone. But I just had to call you. I needed you to know what was going on. And I needed you to be praying with us. But I'm going to tell you: if some sicko has hurt or done anything to my little girl—"

"Ethan, don't go there," I said calmly, putting a stop to even allowing him to finish speaking that thought. "I just told you: you can't think in that direction. You need to use every ounce of your energy on God, His Word, and in Him showing His power through this situation. I believe that God has angels protecting her right now. God will deliver your daughter back to you and your family safe and sound. I believe that. But you must stay focused on God's Word right now. You must be diligent in His Word. You know what the Bible says about a double-minded man."

"I know. That's James 1:8, 'A double-minded man is unstable in all his ways.' I know the scriptures. But when it comes to something like this, there's a difference in what you know in your head and what's going on in your heart. I'm not going to lie to you: I'm scared right now."

"Ethan, God has not given you—"

" 'The spirit of fear,' " he said, finishing the scripture from Second Timothy 1:7. "I know, I know. I'm just being real with you now. That's why I called you. I knew you would keep my head on straight. I'm okay. Really, I'm okay. Thanks for reminding me that I have got to walk the talk. This is merely a test in a testimony. In the end, God will make a message out of this mess." He sighed. I could tell he was truly pressing now. "Well, I'm hanging up now."

"Okay. And you know I'm praying. I know God is going to bring your baby back home safely and unharmed to you. I know that in my heart, and I'm confessing it with my mouth. I thank God that it's done right now, in the name of Jesus! I thank You, God, that it's done! I thank You, God, for peace right now in this situation, Thank You for a peace that surpasses all understanding. I thank You for being a keeper of your Word. I thank You, God, for the promises of Psalm 91:3 *and* 4. 'Surely he shall deliver thee from the snare of the fowler, and from the noisome pestilence. He shall cover thee with his feathers, and under his wings shalt thou trust. . . .' "

"Thank You, Lord!" Ethan said. "Thank You for Your promise of Psalm 91:7. I pray that scripture over Jacquetta right now, in Jesus' name! 'A thousand shall fall at thy side, and ten thousand at thy right hand; but it shall not come nigh thee.' I thank You, Lord. Protect my child, right now. Protect *Your* child, right now. Bring our daughter safely home to us. Thank You, Lord. Thank You, Lord."

"These blessings we ask and we thank You for in advance, in Jesus' precious name, amen," I said, finishing the prayer.

"Thank you," Ethan said. "Thank you *so* very, very much." I could hear the tears in his voice as his voice cracked.

"If you can, will you keep me posted? And know that I'll be waiting to hear the glorious praise report of her speedy and safe return."

"Yeah," he said. "Yeah."

"Let me give you my home number," I said. "Just in case you need to call me there."

"Are you sure it's okay?"

"Yeah. I want to know the minute your daughter comes home."

"Yeah," he said, and I heard the smile and a slight uplift in his voice. "I'm sure it will be soon, too."

"Now *that's* what I'm talking about," I said. "Faith will move mountains. You just have to believe, then act like it's already so."

I gave him my home phone number and hung up. Going back into my office, I closed the door and prayed.

Chapter 21

In the day that thou stoodest on the other side, in the day that the strangers carried away captive his forces, and foreigners entered into his gates, and cast lots upon Jerusalem, even thou wast as one of them.

—Obadiah 1:11

After I got home, I continued to pray for Ethan's daughter's safe return. I could only imagine what he must be feeling. I wouldn't allow him to go there because I knew how important the words we speak can be. While at home, I was reminded of Daniel and how he had fasted and prayed for twenty-one days, expecting God to answer his prayer. On the surface, it looked like God wasn't listening or didn't care. After all, days then weeks had passed without any sign that God was doing anything.

But Daniel didn't let that stop him. He kept on praying, kept on believing, kept on speaking as though God was doing it. I went and got my Bible off the table in the den so I could read and encourage myself with God's Word. I turned to the book of Daniel, chapter 10, verses 10–13, and began reading the words out loud.

"And, behold, a hand touched me, which set me upon my knees and upon the palms of my hands. And he said unto me, O Daniel, a man greatly beloved, understand the words that I speak unto thee, and stand upright: for unto thee am I now sent. And when he had spoken this word unto me, I stood trembling. Then said he unto me, Fear not, Daniel: for from the first day that thou didst set thine heart to understand, and to chasten thyself before thy God, thy words were heard. . . ."

I stopped to reflect. *From the* first *day that thou didst set thine heart to understand, and to chasten thyself before thy God, thy* words *were* heard. *Thy words were* heard. *Wow . . . what an awesome God we serve.*

I continued to read. ". . . thy words were heard, and I am come for thy words. But the prince of the kingdom of Persia withstood me one and twenty days: but, lo, Michael, one of the chief princes, came to help me; and I remained there with the kings of Persia."

I closed the Bible. And just as I did, my phone began to ring. I looked at the caller ID and, seeing that it was Ethan, I quickly answered it, trying to hide any anxiousness I might have had.

"She's home!" he said as soon as I said hello. And I was thankful he hadn't prolonged letting me know with the normal answering etiquettes.

"Praise God!" I said.

"God is worthy to be praised! Yes, He is! Jacquetta is all right! She's all right! She's all right! A father of one of her little classmates happened to be driving down the road and saw her walking. He stopped, found out who she was, picked her up, and ended up taking her home with him."

"What?"

"I know, I know. And I definitely plan to have a talk with her about that. Since they were little, we've stressed to our children to be careful of strangers. I guess we need to take that talk a little farther to beyond strangers, especially since strangers aren't the only enemy."

"So why didn't he bring her home? Why didn't he call and let anybody know where she was? Wait a minute, he didn't—"

"No, he didn't do anything. It turns out, he's a really good guy. He took her to his house and told Jacquetta to call and let someone know where she was. Of course, she got with her little school friend, they got to playing . . . and I'm sure you, better than anyone, know how the rest goes."

"Oh, yeah. I know all *too* well."

"There was an Amber Alert out on her. Somehow, thank God, there was a tip that came in of someone seeing a red Mercedes picking up a young girl that fit Jacquetta's description. I don't know completely how everything came about, but they went to this man's house and . . . there was my daughter, safe and sound."

"But you would think he would have called one of you himself. He should have known you can't rely on children to do things like that, especially since he picked her up from the road the way he did."

"Well, I can assure you, should he ever do anything like that again, he himself will certainly be calling the next time," Ethan chuckled. "I just don't plan on there ever being a next time with my child." He released a sigh. "Listen, I'm not going to be long. I just wanted to let you know that God has heard and answered our prayers. That my daughter is back home safe—hallelujah—and sound. And to tell you how much I appreciate you for helping me hold it together earlier. Because honestly: I was coming a bit unglued."

"Well, you picked up the pieces and pulled yourself back together rather well. That's all that matters. And God did His thing and brought your little girl back to you. God showed up and showed out."

"Yes, He did! And I hope I haven't put you in a bad spot by calling you at home like this," he said.

"No. It's fine. Normally, I'm the one who answers this phone. Our girls have pretty much had their own line since they were old enough to talk on the phone. So my only daughter still at home never touches this one. But I wanted you to have the number. I knew your daughter was going to be all right, and I wanted to hear as soon as you knew something." I half laughed from the joy of this blessed outcome. "I would have been a little upset had I been forced to wait until who knows when to learn of this glorious news."

"Yeah."

"But if you should happen to call here again in the future, you *might* want to make sure it's me before you get going," I said, half teasing, half serious.

"I promise. This was a one-time thing. I just wanted to blurt the news out as quickly as I could. It sounded like it was you, but you're right: next time, I'll make sure it's you before I proceed. Well, I'm going now. Bye. Oh! And thanks again!" He was so happy.

After I hung up, it was only then that it hit me: he said *next time*.

Chapter 22

*For we have not a high priest which cannot be
touched with the feeling of our infirmities; but was
in all points tempted like as we are, yet without sin.*
                                        —Hebrews 4:15

A week later, Ethan called me at the flower shop.

"Are you busy right now?" Ethan said after he knew it was
me.

"No. In fact, I was just about to close up. Why? Do you need
to order something?"

"No. But I would like to see you. I was thinking if you were
free for dinner, I know this really nice restaurant I'd like to take
you to . . . you know, to thank you for being so supportive last
week."

I shook my head even though he couldn't see me. "Oh no.
That's not necessary at all. I'm just glad I could be of some
help. Your daughter being safely back at home is enough
thank-you for me."

"Oh, you were more than just *some* help. You got me back focused; reminded me that I was in spiritual warfare and that our
weapons are not carnal but mighty through God. There were
lots of folks with things to say on that day last week. Not many
of them were slapping me back into a place of faith, not the way
you did."

"Well," I said, with a controlled sigh, "it was my pleasure to
give whatever help I could. I'm just glad everything turned out
the way that it did."

"You and me both," Ethan said. "So let me take you to dinner as my way of saying thank you."

"As I just said, that's really not necessary. That's what friends are for, right?"

"Yes, that's what friends are for." He paused a second. "All right. Since you won't let me take you to dinner, may I at least stop by and bring you something?"

"Oh, Ethan—"

"You know: you're the hardest person I've ever seen when it comes to graciously receiving blessings. You're good at giving them; now when are you going to learn to accept? I hope you know that you're blocking my blessings right now."

"Is that right?" But his words did sort of slap me around a little bit. I hadn't thought about it, but he was absolutely right. I didn't like people doing things for me.

"So if you're going to be at the shop a little longer, I'll stop by and drop off what I have for you."

"E-than." I slightly sang his name. "Really, you don't owe me anything." Although in truth, I *was* curious about what he had.

"May I *please* come by?" He released a loud sigh. "Okay, let me try it this way. Will you still be at the shop twenty more minutes?"

"I'll be here," I said, looking at the clock on the wall and seeing that even if I wasn't going to be waiting on him, I'd still be around, if doing nothing more than putting things away.

Ethan arrived at my shop twenty minutes on the dot carrying a large brown bag in his hand. Although clothed quite casually, he was still dressed to the nines. As I locked the shop's door back, I quickly brushed my hair down with my hand. I stood there in my silver flat shoes wearing a one-hundred-percent polyester, wash-and-wear, black with thin red stripes, sailor-looking pantsuit. My head looked like someone who'd finished a day of buffing hardwood floors, and not with an electric buffer, either, but with a rag and on my hands and knees, as my mama would say.

Ethan stared at me, then let loose one of his signature grins. "Hi," he said.

"Hi." I brushed the side of my hair again and prayed my hair looked better than the last time I'd seen it in the mirror.

"You look fine," he said, as though he knew exactly what I was thinking.

I waved him off. "Oh, please. We both know better than that."

"Thank you for allowing me to come by so late. I'm sure you're anxious to get home." His deep baritone voice was smooth and so easy on the eardrums.

"Well, I won't very well stay in business long if I close my doors when people might be interested in coming in."

He stepped a little closer to me. "I wanted to properly thank you and to let you know how much I truly appreciate you."

"You've already thanked me. I'm serious. Saying it was *more* than enough."

He flashed me a sheepish grin. "Well, you'll have to forgive me, but I wanted to do a little more. I'm disappointed that you wouldn't allow me to take you to dinner. Nevertheless, this . . . is for you." He held out the bag to me by its twisted rope handles.

I glanced at the bag. "Ethan—"

He presented the brown bag to me again. "Please take it."

So I took it and, with a rather cheesy grin and sugar in my voice, said, "Thank you."

"You can't thank me until you've looked inside to see what it is. It could be something you don't want to thank me for. With me, you never know."

"You want me to open it right now?"

"That would be nice. I would like to know whether or not you like it."

I walked over to the table and set the bag on it. I peeked inside, almost afraid of what was in there.

He laughed. "It's not going to bite you. It's not alive."

"Yeah, well . . . when it comes to you, one can never be sure."

I pulled out a nice-sized, gold-colored box. "Oh my," I said. "No, you didn't? Is this a cake?"

"I did . . . and it is. Is it okay?"

I looked for a picture on the box; there wasn't one. He pulled out a paper with a picture of the cake on it and handed it to me. "Is it really a chocolate mousse torte cake?" I said. "Wow, this looks like it will *seriously* do damage to somebody."

"Oh, it's rich now, that's for sure. I had one like it once. One of the higher-ups at the company had one at her Christmas party last year. As soon as I saw it, I immediately thought of you."

"Really now. You thought of me?" I looked at the picture of the cake again, then back at him. "And why, exactly, is that?"

"Woman, please! The way you love chocolate. At least, you used to love it. Well, this is the platinum standard when it comes to chocolate."

"Platinum, huh? Okay, let's see what's all in here." I found where it described the chocolate mousse torte and began to read it out loud. " 'Two chocolate layers filled with luscious chocolate whipped cream mousse.' Ooh, my . . . sinful. 'Covered with milk chocolate frosting and dark chocolate glaze . . . garnished with fudge rosettes and dark chocolate shaving topped off with a Belgian chocolate plaque.' Wow, I think I just put on five pounds merely reading this. You're really trying to tempt me, aren't you? You really are."

"Oh, and that chocolate plaque that's on top?" Ethan said.

"Yeah?"

"It says, 'Thank you.' At least, that's what I told them I wanted when I ordered it."

"You really *are* trying to tempt me. Sinful indeed!" I teased. "So you ordered this? You mean to tell me you didn't walk into a store and just pick it up off a shelf?"

"Me, just walk into a store and merely pick up something for *you?* Oh no. I couldn't just saunter into any old store and merely pick you up something. No, that would never do. For you—only the best, no matter how far away it must be shipped," Ethan said with a fake, exaggerated British accent.

I laughed. "Now you're trying to make me sound like I'm some kind of a diva or something."

"A diva? You? Oh no, you're definitely not a diva." He shook his head.

"I don't know whether I should take that as a compliment or an insult."

"It's undeniably a compliment. You're the most down-to-earth person I know."

"Then maybe you *don't* know me as well as you think you do anymore."

"Fair enough. But the person I knew years ago, and the person I went to lunch with that time, not counting the person I've walked with in the park a few times, is *not* a diva."

"Okay, so where did you get the cake?" I said, then quickly recalled how many times I'd chastened my girls for doing something just like that. "The reason I'm asking is in case I fall head over heels in love with it and I want another one."

"You can just let me know and I'll gladly order you another one," Ethan said, grinning.

"And make you my pusher man?" I shook my head. "Nope. I think it would be best that I get the information and, if I want more, I order the next one myself. You know: cut out the middle man."

"All right then." He rubbed his freshly shaved chin. "I ordered it from a place called Bake Me A Wish! and an exclamation point is actually included at the end. I'm serious; there's an exclamation point at the end of the company's name. They give five percent to a fund where they will send cakes to our troops."

"Impressive. So you just call them and place an order?"

"Yes. You call. They'll tell you what all they have to choose from. And trust me: you may find that you'll have a hard time deciding. I believe they have a Web site, but you've probably already guessed by now that I'm computer challenged, to say the least. The woman who took my order almost talked me into going with the Triple Chocolate Enrobed Brownie for you. But

I knew for certain that the torte was delicious. So I decided to play it safe and go with what I knew."

"Ethan . . . playing it safe? Now that's an interesting concept." I then realized I was possibly teetering on flirting with him, so I decided to pull back a tad. "You're right. I just might be in trouble now that you've introduced me to this company. I bet they charge a pretty penny for this, huh?" I said.

"Oh now, they're definitely not cheap. But they're not *too* expensive. Shipping is what will get you. The company uses overnight shipping to ensure that what they ship is fresh when it arrives. And as soon as it came, I brought it to you."

"You really went to a lot of trouble, didn't you?"

He smiled. "You don't even know the half of it. They shipped it UPS, so I had to make sure I was home when it arrived."

"I understand that it's food, but why did you have to make sure you were home?"

"Because if my wife had even the slightest *hint* that this torte was in town, it would never have made it over here."

"You didn't buy one for your family?" I shook my head. "That's not right."

"That thing cost too much to buy two of them at the same time," he said, then started chuckling.

I picked up the box and held it out to him. "Look, you take this back home with you. Really."

"Nope."

"Yes! Ethan, I want you to take this home to your family." I held it out again. "Take it and give it to your wife."

"No," he said refusing to take the box. "I ordered it specifically for you, and that's where it's going to stay—with you. So end of discussion."

"Well, what if I tell you that it's going to be a problem for me to take it home and explain it to my husband?"

"Woman, please!" He snickered. "You need to try that one on somebody who doesn't know any better. If your husband asks you where it came from, just tell him the truth: a satisfied customer bought it and dropped it off at the shop. There's nothing false in that statement."

"So you're not going to take it back?" I said, taking a step closer to him as I tried to push the box into his hand (without hurting the cake, of course).

He shook his head. "I bought it for you and it will remain with you. It's my gift to you. You told me that you liked it, so you're going to keep it."

"What if I tell you I don't like it?"

"Then you wouldn't be telling the truth. And one thing that I do know about you is that you don't lie. You are one of the most truthful people I've ever known."

I smiled that he knew that about me. "You're right; I don't lie. At least, I try my best not to. Anybody will tell you that I'll either tell you the truth or I'll keep my mouth shut."

"I know that. I bought the cake for you"—he further closed the distance between us—"you like the cake, at least you like what you know about it so far"—he carefully took the cake out of my hand and set it on the table—"so you, my dearest among friends, are stuck with it." He took my hand and held it up as though he was about to bring it to his lips.

I nippily pulled my hand from him. "Okay," I said. "But only because you're insisting." I stepped closer to the other side of the table, making it a safe barrier between us. "Would you care for a slice of my torte?"

"I would. But since you declined my dinner offer, which was supposed to be part of my thank-you package with the cake being dessert, I guess I should pass."

"You could take your slice home with you, since you seem to be one of those fanatics who won't eat dessert before you eat *real* food."

He looked at me, pretending he was insulted, then nodded as he flashed a warm, quick smile. "Yeah, I guess I'm just old school like that. But . . ." He came around to the side of the table where I stood. I would have run, but that would have looked too much like children playing a game of tag or something. So I stood my ground. Ethan was now standing in front of me, too close for comfort. My heart was beating so loud, I thought for sure he could hear it.

He blinked his eyes several times as he bit down on his bottom lip. "I *have* been known to indulge in dessert before dinner . . . when the dessert was too tempting to hold off from," he said.

I swallowed hard. I know he heard *that*. "Ethan—"

And before I could say another word, he leaned down and kissed me.

Chapter 23

Seeing then that we have a great high priest, that is passed unto the heavens, Jesus the Son of God, let us hold fast our profession.

—Hebrews 4:14

"Ethan, don't," I said, shaking a little after pulling away from his embrace.

Ethan lovingly stared into my eyes. "You are so beautiful and so wonderful. You're really the one I should have married. Then we'd be together now . . . in our own home . . . possibly with fourteen children."

I laughed. "Fourteen, huh?"

He grinned. "Yeah. Fourteen . . . at least."

I shook my head. "I don't know about fourteen children. That's about ten more than I ever wanted."

"You would have wanted *our* fourteen, you know you would have. And I would have been right there with you, helping with each one of them. So this isn't some macho male thing going on. You know: 'Me Tarzan; you Jane.' "

I wriggled my nose. "So you're saying that your ultimate goal wouldn't have been to keep me barefoot and pregnant . . . me, regulated to the kitchen and the bedroom . . . you and I, during certain times, swinging from the chandelier?"

He put both of his arms around me as he gazed deeply into my eyes. "The kitchen? No. But I'm not going to lie: the bedroom and that swinging from the chandelier thing would have *definitely* been tops on our marriage list. At least, they would have been tops on mine. And I'm sure you know what the Bible says about marriage and the bed being undefiled."

"Yeah." I tried to pull away, but he wasn't having it. "You know: I find it rather interesting that you're throwing the Bible into this conversation when you and I are essentially committing adultery."

"We're committing adultery?" He frowned and leaned back a little. "And exactly how do you come to that conclusion? No sex has transpired between us. We're not sneaking around to some hotel or anything like that. You honestly think what we're doing constitutes committing adultery . . . us having an affair?"

"Ethan, you know what this is—me and you . . . what's going on right here, right now. You know this would count as adultery . . . having an affair . . . whatever you call cheating on a spouse."

Ethan tightened his arms that were still securely locked around me, pulling me closer as I tried to lean back from him. "You're talking about that Jimmy Carter thing, aren't you?"

I laughed. "Jimmy Carter thing?"

"Yeah. You remember that time Jimmy Carter said he'd committed adultery because he'd looked at another woman other than his wife with lust. So that meant he'd committed adultery in his heart. Of course, he was referring to a scripture that states whatever you do in your heart was the same as having done the actual act itself. Personally, I don't think good old Jimmy should have confessed that one, not out loud. By that standard, most of the men I know could be found guilty of committing adultery. There he was the president of the United States, confessing to something that he didn't even get any of the real benefits from. At least if you're going to be convicted of something, you should get something out of it." He hunched his shoulders. "Maybe that's just me."

"Yeah, of course you would say that."

He rocked me a few times. "Do you have any idea how much I've missed you?" He was totally changing the trajectory of the conversation back to us again.

"You missed me? You . . . missed . . . *me?*"

"Yes," Ethan said, standing perfectly still now. "And full disclosure: I like being with you. I want you, I do."

I sharply broke away from his embrace. All of this was getting a little *too* deep for me. It was one thing to be playing around the shallow edges of the adultery waters; quite another thing to be about to dive, headfirst, into the deep end of the adultery ocean.

"Ethan, you and I can be friends. We can talk when you want to. But we're not going to go there. We're not. Okay, let me put it this way: *I'm* not going there. Years ago, you and I had our chance to be together and we blew it." I looked him squarely in his eyes, before shoving my hand on my hip. "Well, to be perfectly honest: *you* blew it. Because I definitely wanted to be with you, but I wasn't the one in control of things—you were."

"Yeah, but you were the one who got married first," he said smugly.

"I got married because I wasn't going to sit around waiting for you to decide that you wanted something completely and singularly with me. You were too busy trying to keep me and your girlfriend at the same time. That got old real quick; and I deserved better than that. So, yes, I did find someone and yes, we got married."

"Yeah. You definitely showed me that I wasn't the only guy out there," Ethan said with a quick nod. "You found someone else and the two of you married. So what was I supposed to do at that point?" He sat down at the table. "I admit: maybe I did mess up by trying to talk to both of you at the same time. But what do you expect? I was young and stupid at that age. And Denise hadn't done anything for me to legitimately break up with her. What was I supposed to do?"

I sat down. "So you thought it was fair to me to make me the 'other woman,' essentially wait in the wings for my glorious opportunity to become your number one, once she messed up?"

He began to chuckle. "Yeah. I hear you. I just told you that I messed up. How was I to know what a huge mistake I was making in letting you slip through my fingers and out of my life? I was selfish. I didn't think about how you were feeling about the arrangement. And now, I suppose you can say I'm paying the price."

"Well, for sure it's too late to go back and change anything. What's done is done."

"It might be too late to go back, but it's never too late to start from where we are and go forward." Ethan grabbed my hands and hurriedly brought them up to his lips as he gently planted a kiss on my knuckles. We locked gazes. "I want you," he said. "I honestly and truly *want* you."

I was fighting hard; I'm not going to lie. Because I wanted him, too. I inhaled, then exhaled slowly as I silently counted to ten. "Ethan, it's not going to happen." I slowly shook my head as I spoke. "It's not going to happen."

"Why not? I'm opening up my heart to you. I'm being truthful with you . . . telling you that I truly want you. Hear my heart." He took my hand and placed it over his beating heart. I closed my eyes as I felt the thumping that seemed to instantaneously synchronize with the rhythm of my heart.

"It's taking everything I have within me right now not to whisk you off of your feet and carry you away," he said.

"Ethan, I know you. You're a good man . . . a godly man. Sure, your body may be telling you at this minute that it wants the two of us to be together—"

"Oh, my body didn't just start this conversation during this hour. It's been building for a long time. Trust when I say: it's been a long time coming. Do you remember that first day I met you? It was at a house party. Well, that day is essentially burned into my memory bank and in my heart. Let me put it this way: I could end up with Alzheimer's and I would *still* never forget you and that night I first saw you."

"Ethan, you really need to stop. This is wrong. And it does neither of us any good to stroll down this dead-end lane. We have separate lives now. That's the way it is. And we both know that you're never going to leave your wife. . . ." I said it as though it was a statement, but it really was an open question he was free to argue against, if he so chose.

"You're right. I can't leave my wife now, at least not right now. There are too many moving parts that would come to a screeching halt were she and I to divorce at this point. But mostly, I have to be there for my girls. True the older ones are close to being on their own, so if I left now, it wouldn't affect them as much. But my baby girl needs me. I can't leave her primarily in the care of a woman who is so focused on herself and her own desires that she doesn't have time to cook, wash clothes, or basically look after a child who still needs a parent present in her life." He stood and paced back and forth a few times.

He stopped and turned back toward me. "You remember when my daughter was missing last week? Well, Denise claims she'd gone to get her hair and nails done and that it totally slipped her mind that she was supposed to pick up Jacquetta. Tell me: how do you forget that your daughter's at the school waiting on you? How do you forget something like that? Huh? And it's not like they decided this a week in advance and she'd just forgotten when the date arrived. They'd talked about it the night before. And Jacquetta said she even reminded Denise before she left for school that morning."

"I'm sure you probably don't want to hear my opinion. But honestly, I don't think your wife forgot because of her hair and nails appointment. I think she likely has a man on the side. I'm not trying to be messy or get all in your business. But from all that you've shared with me about what's going on with her and the two of you, that's precisely what it sounds like to me. She likely got caught up with that guy and the time just slipped away before she knew it."

"Well, regardless of what Denise may or may not be doing and with whom, I just need to ensure that I'm around to take care of my daughters, especially the youngest."

"So that's going to be what? Another nine . . . ten years before she graduates from high school that you're going to need to be there?"

"Yeah. But I'm willing to make that sacrifice if that's what it takes to ensure my daughter has what she needs. Because if my wife and I divorce, Denise will certainly be granted the majority custody. The court won't give me custody even if I am the bet-

ter parent and I want custody. I'm a guy and Denise is the
mother. Unless I show that she's unfit, she'll get primary custody. And you can believe it's not that my wife would really want
custody. She knows I'm the one who takes care of them. She
would do it just to spite me. She would do it to get the child
support, which I honestly don't have a problem with paying or
her getting. But she would do it mainly to hurt me and to deny
me my fatherly rights, forgetting how much she'd be hurting
our daughters."

"That's a dilemma for sure," I said. "Then there's the
church."

"Yes, there's the church. But that's not forefront in my mind.
Church folks divorce all the time these days. It doesn't carry
the stigma the way it used to. The people who might have a
problem with it will get over it soon enough and move on,"
Ethan said. "My children are my greatest concern. And knowing Denise, she would likely have all kinds of people, men and
women, hanging around the house. I don't want that kind of a
life for my daughters. I don't. There's too much going on for
me to be a part of putting my children possibly in harm's way."

"I hear you with that one," I said. "I always said that if Zeke
and I didn't stay together and I found myself in the position of
having to date again while having girls in my house, I'd seriously think about putting off dating until my girls were grown.
And even then, you still have to be careful. Some of these men
are so bold that they'll try and hit on your grown daughters.
I'm not telling you what I've heard; I'm telling you what I
know."

"I hope you know I would never do anything like that.
Never," Ethan said, as he shook his head.

"I know that. I wasn't talking about somebody like you."

"I only have eyes for their mother," he said. "Although, I will
confess: your mother was hot!"

"My *mother?*"

"Yes. Your mother. Back when I would come to see you, I
thought your mother was fine."

"Ewww! That's gross! You thought my mother was fine?"

"Yes. What can I say? My father told me that if I wanted to

know what the girl was going to look like when she got older, check out the mother. I checked out your mother and she was both cute *and* fine."

"That's some sick stuff right there," I teased. "Now I'll have to work the rest of the night just to get that image out of my head. You were checking out my mother? *You* were checking out *my* mother. My *mother!*" I laughed.

"I wasn't planning on moving on it," Ethan said. "But I'm laying everything out on the table here. I don't want you feeling like I'm keeping anything from you."

"Well, if you had tried to hit on my mother, my daddy would have laid *you* out on the table." I laughed again.

Ethan moved in closer. "Let's get together . . . me and you. What do you say?"

"I say that as your friend, I'm going to save you from yourself. Because Ethan, I know you. I know how much you love God. And I know that if you and I cross the line, you're going to feel guilty. Then you're going to beat yourself up. And before you know anything, you're going to be standing before the church congregation crying your eyes out saying something like, 'I have sinned against God and against you.' So, I'm going to help you. I'm going to walk away from the edge, and I'm going to pull you back from the edge along with me."

"I won't regret it. I'm telling you. I've thought about this. I still love you, and I want to be with you."

I started pushing him toward the front door. "Thank you very much for the cake," I said. "And thank you for stopping by. Now you be careful on your way home and drive safely." I unlocked the door.

"I don't want to go," he said, turning and looking me in my eyes.

"Well, you don't have to go home, but you do have to leave here," I said.

He laughed, then softly tapped me on my nose. "You know: that's what I love so much about you. You honestly and truly care about me. You really do."

"Yes," I said in a serious tone. "I do."

"And you're funny, too," he said. "I love someone with a

sense of humor. I love to laugh. I don't get to laugh much these days. Everything and everybody is so serious. So thank you. And thanks for being the sunshine I need in my life, even if it's only for a little time. You are truly a blessing."

"Sure." I opened the door, gave him a shove, and watched him as he reluctantly walked away.

And only God knew that in my heart, I, too, had already committed adultery.

In my heart.

Chapter 24

Let us therefore come boldly unto the throne of grace, that we may obtain mercy, and find grace to help in time of need.

—Hebrews 4:16

When I arrived home from the shop, no one was there. I set the cake on the counter and began to search the refrigerator for something to eat.

As usual, Zeke had already come and gone. It was obvious he'd eaten—his dishes were exactly where he'd left them. That's what aggravated me so much about him. He wouldn't lift one finger to ever cook anything, not even a piece of toast. He expected me to cook, which was fine, but he would never even attempt to clean up when I finished, not ever. He wouldn't wash a dish. Wouldn't load the dishwasher with his dirty dishes. Wouldn't even put the leftovers in the refrigerator. According to him, "That's what women are for."

I had tried to rebel, a little earlier in our marriage when the girls were small. I decided I wasn't going to cook or clean unless he helped me with something around the house. My not cooking or cleaning didn't bother him one iota. And since he went somewhere practically every night anyway, he simply left earlier, claiming he was going to find *him* something to eat. Forget that I and his children had nothing; he was only looking out for himself. After a week of dishes piling up (somehow, he still managed to find ways and occasions to mess up a slew of dishes), I couldn't take it any longer. I cleaned up and went back to doing what I knew wouldn't get done if I didn't do it.

So when I came home from the flower shop, there, as usual, were his dishes waiting for me to load in the dishwasher. Zynique was starting to be more and more like her father: gone every night until it was time for her to come home. In fairness, she *was* working for Madame Perry and bringing in her own money. But she still resided under my roof and therefore, under my rules. I wasn't having any guys spending the night (accidental or not), and she had a set time to be home. I never knew for certain whether she actually adhered to the new post-high-school-graduate agreed-upon time, since most of the time, I was out like a light when 2:00 a.m. rolled around. The shop was much busier these days (thank the Lord!), so I was worn out and fell asleep as soon as my head hit the pillow.

Still, as I loaded Zeke's dirty dishes into the dishwasher and tried to think of something I could fix for myself to eat (since he'd eaten all I cooked and was left over from the night before), I couldn't help but lament (at least somewhat) that I'd turned down dinner with Ethan.

I grabbed a can of ravioli (Zynique's food of choice) out of the cabinet and opened it. As it heated in the microwave, I looked up toward the ceiling and laughed.

"God, now You know this is wrong, don't You? I know You see this kitchen and me here all by myself. I'm trying to do the right thing here, but it's not fair that it looks like I'm the one always on the wrong end of the fairness stick. But I want to thank You for grace. And I thank You for mercy right now. And I ask that You please forgive me for that small indiscretion from tonight. I really do need You right now. It's so hard to do right when you have someone like Ethan right there in front of you. Lord, You know what I'm dealing with. I'm trying my best to resist. But I'm going to tell You the truth, Lord, not to imply that You don't already know what's really going on inside of me. But Ethan is a challenge for me. He is.

"And it would help if You could speak to my husband . . . find a way to get through to him and tell him to at least meet me halfway. I know I've been praying this prayer for years now. And so far, nothing seems to have changed. In fact, it's starting to look and feel like things are getting worse. Because God, at least before, I had the girls with me. Now everybody's gone. Before, there was no one around to tempt me. Now there's Ethan. The sad thing about this, Lord, is that I don't want to ask You to take Ethan out of my life." I laughed. "I don't. I know I probably should. That's what I should be asking You to do right now. But I don't want to. I should be concentrating on me and my shortcomings instead of praying about Zeke and his. I should be asking You to make my heart not beat so hard when it comes to Ethan. But God, I'm being honest with You: right now, I like at least being able to talk to Ethan, even if it is only every now and then, and even if it's only as friends."

The microwave beeped—letting me know that my mouth-watering gourmet dinner was ready. Yum yum. Bon Appetit!

Chapter 25

Well reported of for good works; if she have brought up children, if she have lodged strangers, if she have washed the saints' feet, if she have relieved the afflicted, if she have diligently followed every good work.

—1 Timothy 5:10

It was the Monday before Thanksgiving. Zynique was still working for Madame Perry while putting her money away to be able to get her own place and, someday, her own dance studio. That's why Zynique hadn't been like a lot of her friends, most of whom had gone off to college. Zeke and I tried to convince her she should at least *look* at going to college while she worked. But her reasoning was that people generally went to college to obtain a career. What she wanted was to have her own studio, giving people an opportunity to experience the art of dance in the way that she had. She felt she was learning all she needed with Madame Perry while being paid.

Zynique had even convinced Madame Perry to start a class for senior citizens. It had turned out to be a marvelous idea, one that brought even more revenue to Madame Perry's studio and a lot of joy to a group that was excited about being able to stay in shape in this way. It was a win-win situation for everyone.

Zeke told Zynique it had been dumb of her to give Madame Perry that idea. He felt she should have saved it for her own studio. Zynique merely waved him off.

"Madame Perry is a wonderful person, Daddy. She's pouring everything she has into me. I'm glad I can do something in my own way to repay her."

"You *are* doing something," Zeke said, turning up the bottle of soda he was drinking. "You're working there, giving her the benefit of your knowledge and energy. Didn't you say she had cut back on her hours, essentially putting you in charge of her entire operation?"

"Yes," Zynique said, almost beaming at the mention of that.

"Well, frankly, I think the woman is a pretty smart cookie. She gets you to do most of her work while she sits back and gets to rake in the big bucks."

"Well, I think it's wonderful what Madame Perry is doing for Zynique," I said, adding my two cents. "Most folks don't want to share the knowledge of what they know with anyone else. Especially if they know you're doing or planning on doing what they're already doing. They view competition as a threat. Trust me, I know. That's why I've had such a hard time with my business. No one wants to help me. In fact, there are those who are trying to devise ways to pull me down."

"Crabs in the barrel," Zynique said.

I pulled back and looked at Zynique. "What do you know about crabs in a barrel?"

She beat the table with her hands as though it was a drum. "That's what Madame Perry calls it. She says our people especially are great about being crabs in a barrel."

"What does she mean 'our people'?" Zeke said, setting his empty bottle on the counter right there at the trashcan.

"Oh, Zeke, don't act like you don't know what she's talking about," I said, getting up and throwing his empty bottle in the trash as I gave him "the look" which didn't mean anything to him anymore. "You have a bunch of crabs in a barrel and as soon as it looks like one is just about to make its way out, the others reach up and pull it back down with them. That's what a lot of us do to each other. We're all stuck in a bucket that won't allow us to get anywhere. And when someone sees someone else about to escape, instead of the group helping that one out, which would make it easier for that one to reach back and pull others out, they all reach up and pull the one almost out back down with them."

"That's exactly what Madame Perry said," Zynique said. "I

think that's why she works so hard to help me. She says she might not have gotten out of the bucket, but if she can boost me up and over the top, maybe I can cover a lot more territory, more than she ever could."

"Well, personally, I believe Madame Perry just got her a good hustle going on." Zeke was now fixing himself a bowl of strawberry ice cream. "You watch, Zynique. When you get ready to spread your wings, she'll probably be the main one there with the clippers, ready to ground you."

"You don't know Madame Perry *at . . . all*," Zynique said.

Zynique's cell phone began to ring. It really didn't make sense to me that she'd gotten one. I knew everyone seemed to be getting one, but I didn't see something like cell phones achieveing a critical mass. *Why would anyone want to pay for a phone you carry around when you have a phone already at home?*

Zynique answered her cell phone. All of sudden, she started to shake her head, crying, and yelling, "No! No! Oh God, please no!"

"What's wrong?" I said. "Zynique? What's the matter?"

She waved me to be quiet until she was finished. When she hung up, she came over and fell into my arms. "It's Madame Perry," she said, finding it hard to get the words out.

"What about her?"

"She's at the hospital. That was her neighbor. He said she had my number posted to call in case of an emergency."

"Is she going to be all right?" I asked.

"I don't know. He didn't know. He just said she called him and the phone suddenly went dead. He ran over there and when he got there, she was lying on the floor. He called for an ambulance and they've taken her to the hospital. He said she was asking for me." Zynique placed her hand over her mouth as the tears continued to come.

"She was asking for you?" Zeke said.

"Mother, I have to go see her. I need to leave now. Will you drive me?" Zynique's hands were shaking.

"Of course I will," I said. "Let me run and get my purse." I turned to Zeke. "Do you want to go with us?"

"Nah. You two go on."

I was hoping he would go. It would have meant so much to Zynique if he had.

We got to the hospital and found where Madame Perry was. They had her hooked up to a breathing machine. When she saw Zynique, she tried to raise her hand but could only manage to point her index finger. Zynique rushed to her side and took her hand.

"You're going to be okay," Zynique said. "You just need to rest. They're going to get you all fixed up again. I know they are. And don't you even *think* about fighting the nurses and doctors. They're going to have you back on your feet and dancing again before you know it."

I looked at Madame Perry. Her eyes seemed to be pleading for me to come closer. I walked over and stood next to Zynique. Madame Perry began to move her eyes, as though she was trying to point them at the mask that covered her mouth.

"You want them to take that off?" Zynique asked.

Madame Perry nodded.

"I think she wants to take that thing off," Zynique said. "I think she wants to tell us something."

Madame Perry nodded again.

"Let me find a nurse," I said, then quickly left the room.

Just as I made it to the nurses' station, a patient's alarm must have gone off because a group of them jumped up and started running. It was then that I saw them rush into Madame Perry's room. I ran back there as well. Zynique was standing to the side now, crying. I went over to Zynique and gathered her in my arms. We stepped farther out of the way so we wouldn't hamper any of their efforts. A doctor and three nurses were frantically working on her. I didn't want Zynique to be there for this; I didn't want her to have to witness what was going on. But Zynique refused to leave.

Madame Perry died that night and her son, the only child she had, scheduled her funeral for the Saturday after Thanksgiving, which happened to be one day after Zynique's nineteenth birthday.

I was working full throttle, assembling sprays and floral arrangements for the funeral.

According to Zynique, Madame Perry had prearranged pretty much everything, so there really wasn't a lot for her son to have to do except execute what she'd put in place. And as only Madame Perry could do it, she'd left specific instructions that all of the flowers her family would be purchasing for her home-going celebration be bought from my place of business, The Painted Lady Flower Shop.

The dance studio was already closed for the week because of the Thanksgiving holiday. Madame Perry believed in family and that family should have time to spend and to be able to celebrate together.

Zynique was having difficulty pulling herself together after her beloved friend and mentor's death. I asked her to come and help me with the tons of orders I'd received. Honestly, I truly needed the additional help even though a month earlier I'd hired Mia (a lovely mother of two) to work for me part-time. Mia desperately needed the money, but she also wanted to be home when her two children got home from school. I needed a little help, but I didn't need anyone on a full-time basis. So this arrangement worked great for both of us.

Zynique needed something to occupy her mind. I felt she would appreciate being able to help put together the many flowers that had been ordered to pay tribute to Madame Perry.

Madame Perry was loved by so many. It was standing room only at both the wake and the funeral. At the funeral, Zynique wanted to say something during the time where people were allowed to speak for two minutes if anyone so desired. I didn't think it was a good idea, believing Zynique would break down as soon as she opened her mouth.

But she ended up surprising me. Zynique stood, took a deep breath, and began to tell people what an awesome person Madame Perry was and the many young women's and girls' lives she had changed just from them being at the dance studio and in her presence. She then proceeded to tell those in attendance something she hadn't even voiced to me.

"That night, right before she died, she called me to her

side," Zynique said. "My mom had just left out of the room to go find a nurse. Madame Perry wanted to say something, but she had a mask over her mouth that kept her from being able to speak where she could be heard. Well, anyway, as I said, my mom had gone to ask a nurse about taking it off for a minute to see what Madame Perry was trying to say. So Madame Perry and I were there alone." Zynique paused for a few seconds.

"That's okay, baby," an older woman yelled out from the audience. "Take your time. Take your time. We understand. We *all* understand."

Zynique smiled, and I could see her actually swallow before she began to speak again. I was praying hard for my child. She continued. "Madame Perry couldn't speak, but she used all she had within her to lift her hand and wave it in the air. Next, she placed her hand on her heart, then, with every fiber within her, she placed her hand on my heart." Zynique stopped again, looked up, and shook her head.

Zynique leveled her head, nodded a few times, then scanned the audience. "I knew what Madame Perry was saying without her having to utter one word. You see, I began working for Madame Perry a few hours a day after school when I turned seventeen. She really didn't need my help, not really; she just knew how much I wanted to do what she was doing someday. So she paid me to teach me what she knew. I didn't get it at seventeen; I got it when I began working for her full-time at age eighteen. Madame Perry was paying me hard-earned money to teach *me* what she knew. That's something to think about. So Madame Perry would drop little nuggets for me to put aside.

"One of the things she would always say about praising God was: 'If I couldn't say a word, I would just wave my hand.' Well, that's what she was telling me when she raised her hand the night she died. She was going to praise God somehow, anyhow. And the part where she placed her hand on her heart then placed it on mine? She was simply saying, 'I love you.' " Zynique paused, then quickly nodded. "So I'm telling each of you right now: Madame Perry loves you. And I'm thankful to God that He allowed someone like her to cross my path. Thank you."

Zynique sat down to thunderous applause even though it was

a funeral. I held her as she cried. As people stood and spoke of Madame Perry, I was reminded that this wasn't a funeral as much as it was a celebration of a wonderful spirit's life who had walked upon this earth. It made me want to do even more for God's Kingdom and His people.

At the gravesite, Claude, Madame Perry's son, made sure that Zynique got both a white and a red carnation from the standing spray he'd continually expressed to me was the most beautiful thing he'd ever seen when it came to flowers. It just so happened to be the one Zynique and I gave extra special attention and love to. It was the one from our family; the one with a small heart made up of vibrant red carnations inside of a larger white heart created with a combination of white carnations, Monte Casino, and white button pompons. A heart within a heart.

"Madame Perry will never really die," Zynique had said when we were discussing what we were going to make her from us. "Because I will always carry her heart and a part of her inside of my heart."

I thought it was beautiful that Claude wanted to be sure Zynique had something like that to keep.

"We'll put it in plastic and put it in the Bible," I said when we got home. "That will press it for you and you'll be able to keep it forever."

Zynique leaned over and hugged me; she wouldn't let go. "I love you, Mommy. I really do." She was really crying now.

Holding her tight like I had when she was a little girl (and glad that she let me be there for her during this time, instead of going off somewhere to herself as she'd been known to do), I said, "I know you do. And I love you, too, baby. I love you, too."

Chapter 26

The day started off slow, but by its end, all of that quickly changed.

Ethan called. That was a huge surprise. I hadn't talked with him since back in September when he'd called to tell me about his wife's breast cancer. It was pretty serious; they had to perform immediate surgery. She ended up having a double mastectomy. He'd been busy taking care of her for the past two and a half months.

"How's the family?" I asked.

"Doing well," Ethan said.

"And your wife?"

"She's coming along nicely. Chemo and radiation is no joke. She lost her hair and she got tired easily; in fact, she's still tired. But all in all, she's doing well. Thank you so much for asking."

"I'm glad she's doing well. I'll continue to pray for you and her both."

"Appreciate that," Ethan said. "Listen, I need to get out for a while. I've been essentially going from work to home to church and back, taking care of everything at home. That's pretty much been it. I was thinking about getting out and getting me some fresh air. I was wondering if you'd like to go to the park and walk today."

"Today?" I said with a spike in my voice. All I could think

about was that it was December and not the warmest day outside. Yes, people did walk during this time, but only the truly dedicated folks.

"Yes, today. I'd really like to see you. I was thinking we could bundle up and walk around the track while we talk. You know, sort of like old times."

"So you want to go walking today?" I scratched my head. "You do know we're off of daylight savings time so it gets dark a lot earlier now."

"Yeah, I know that. And if you can't or don't want to do it, it's fine. I really just wanted to talk to someone. You're wonderful at lifting my spirits."

"Oh, so you're just using me," I said, teasing him.

"No," he said in a serious tone. "I wouldn't dare do anything like that. I just wanted to see you."

"Hey. I was just kidding," I said.

"Well, I don't kid about something like that. Not when it comes to you. I know you probably don't entirely trust my motives as it is. The last thing I want is for you to think that I'm using you."

I looked at the clock on the wall. It was four thirty. The chance of anyone coming in now or before closing time at five was pretty slim. "Okay, we can go walking. Where?"

"Our usual place?" he said.

I giggled. "Oh, so now we have a usual meeting spot? You think you can call and just say 'our usual place' and I know precisely where you're talking about?"

"Yeah, it's pretty much like that. So can you leave right now?"

"Yeah. I can do that."

"Are you sure? I don't want to mess things up for you at the shop."

"It's fine. It's been slow today. I was thinking about leaving early anyway."

"Great. Then I'll see you in about fifteen minutes."

"I'll be there." And as soon as I hung up, I regretted saying I would. Now I'd have to find my walking shoes that I hadn't worn in over two months.

The phone rang again. I looked at the caller ID. It was

Zynique. I hurried to answer it. She hardly *ever* called me at the shop. Since Madame Perry's death, the dance studio had remained closed, orders from her son, until further notice.

"Hey, baby. What's up?"

"Mom, I just got a call from a lawyer's office."

"A lawyer's office. For what?"

"He said he was representing Madame Perry. He's been trying to reach me for days now. He wants to know if I can come over to his office."

"Did he say for what?"

"No. He just mentioned Madame Perry's name and asked if I could come to his office. It's not far from your shop. I told him I could come now."

"Now? Why would you tell him you would come today? Why didn't you schedule it for the daytime? Like tomorrow."

"Mother, you know how I am. I hate waiting. If you tell me something is a secret or a surprise, I want to know what it is as soon as possible. You *know* how I am. Besides, he said I could come today, so I want to go today."

"Well, you definitely don't need to go there by yourself."

"That's why I called you. I was wondering if you'd take off early and go with me."

"Today?"

"Yes, Mother. Today. We can meet up at the law firm."

"Where's your father? Is he home?"

"Yeah, he's here. Why?"

"Do you think you might like to ask him and see if he'll go with you?"

"You mean Daddy? We're talking about *my* daddy? You want me to see if *my* daddy, your husband, will go somewhere with *me?*"

"Okay, when you put it that way, I hear how it sounds. But you never know. This might be a turning point for him. He just might surprise us both."

"Hold on," Zynique said. I faintly heard her in the background asking her father if he would go with her to the lawyer's office. Zynique came back to the line. "He said no. He told me to ask you to go if I needed somebody to go with me. I told you. So will you go?"

I thought about Ethan. I'd just told him I would go walking with him. I couldn't exactly call him at home to let him know I wouldn't be able to make it. What if his wife answered the phone? If he had a cell phone, I could have called him on something like that. But I wasn't about to call his house.

"Mom, are you still there?"

"Yes, sweetheart, I'm here. Okay. Give me the address and I'll meet you at the lawyer's office."

Zynique rattled off the address. "Thanks, Mom. You're the best!"

"Excuse me? But what was that again?" I said. "I don't think I caught that."

Zynique laughed. "You're the best! I'll see you in a few."

When I hung up, I had to decide what to do, now that I'd essentially agreed to be in two places at the exact same time.

Chapter 27

That I may cause those that love me to inherit sub-stance; and I will fill their treasures.

—Proverbs 8:21

Zynique and I were only in the waiting area for five minutes before a tall, middle-aged, light-skinned black man came out of the office.

"Zynique, it's so good to meet you," he said. "Thank you for agreeing to come here on such short notice."

"It was not a problem," Zynique said. "I asked my mother to come with me."

"That's fine," he said, glancing at me as he nodded before extending his hand to shake mine. "It's nice to meet you as well."

I laughed to myself. He hadn't really *met* me since my daughter had apparently forgotten everything I'd taught her on the art of introducing people. I knew what it was: she was likely hung up on between him and me, whose name should be called first and that whole protocol. I started to do like I normally did and introduce myself, but I supposed "Zynique's mother" was enough for both him and my daughter.

His name was on his door, so I knew who he was: Justice Evans. He escorted us into his office. It was a nice-sized room, with lots of African memorabilia on the walls and other places. A lot of what I saw in his office was quite artistic. He gestured for us to have a seat in the chairs facing his mahogany desk.

Justice got straight to the point of why Zynique had been

summoned, which I not only loved, but appreciated. I hated when it took someone forever to get to the point.

Justice told Zynique that Madame Perry had hired him to handle her affairs after she was gone. To sum up everything in one neat package: Madame Perry left Zynique her house (worth more than my house) and her dance studio.

Zynique couldn't believe it. She kept looking at me like what she was hearing couldn't possibly be what he was saying. But it was true. All of the paperwork was there, and just like that: Zynique now owned a fully furnished house and a completely furnished dance studio, free and clear.

To be honest, I wasn't sure whether a just-turned-nineteen-year-old could handle so much at one time.

When we were on the elevator on our way to our respective cars not thirty minutes after we'd arrived, Zynique turned to me. "I don't believe this. I had no idea Madame Perry was planning on doing anything even *remotely* like this."

"It is something," I said. "I'm still processing what just took place in that office. With a stroke of a pen, you're now the proud owner of a fully paid-for house and a really nice dance studio."

"It's like you've always said. If we'll delight ourselves in the Lord, He'll give us the desires of our heart. I can't believe this happened though."

"Yeah, I do say that, don't I?"

"Well, God certainly blew me away with this one. I'm at a loss for words. I really don't know what to say."

"It's because of how you treated someone who was elderly," I said. "God is blessing you because of how you blessed someone who was up in age."

Zynique shook her head. "Madame Perry was the one who blessed me. Everything I know about dance and business, she taught me."

Ouch, that stung just a little bit. Zynique must have thought about what she'd said. "I mean everything businesswise that has to do with running a dance studio," she said.

"It's okay. I know what you mean. Madame Perry was really a great woman. And now this. . . ."

Our elevator reached the lobby. We stepped out. "Are you on your way home now?" I asked.

"No. I think I'm going over to Aiden's."

Aiden was Zynique's boyfriend. They'd been going together since she was a junior in high school. He seemed to be a nice enough guy. At least, he had his head screwed on the right way. He was both working and going to college. That said a lot about him right there to me.

"So you're not going home first?" I asked, making sure I understood her plans.

"No. You were there when the lawyer told me everything. So there's no reason for me to rush home and tell you." She smiled as though she'd made a joke.

"What about your father?"

She primped her mouth slightly. "What about him?"

"Don't you want to share your good news with him?"

"Mother, let's be real. You and I both know that Daddy's not at home right now."

"Well, he might be. He knew you were coming here. He just may have hung around to find out what was going on."

Zynique snickered, then leaned over and planted a kiss on my cheek. "Okay, Mother. You just keep on believing that. I'll see you later." She walked to her car.

I went home, and just as Zynique had predicted, the house was devoid of a living soul.

Chapter 28

Let no man say when he is tempted, I am tempted of God: for God cannot be tempted with evil, neither tempteth He any man.

—James 1:13

Once again, I began my routine of searching for either leftovers or something that didn't take long to cook. My life had changed dramatically since our children had grown up. I didn't cook as much as I had in the beginning. When the girls were growing up, I was one of those mothers who believed children should eat real food and not fast food every day of the week. In fact, fast food in our house was a treat. I soaked pinto beans and butter beans in hot water, waited on them to swell, then cooked them for two hours, careful not to overcook them. When I worked at Social Security, the slow cooker was my best friend, assisting me in our healthy eating endeavor.

After the two older daughters were gone, I stopped cooking as much. Maybe the right word isn't "as much" but more accurately "as often." After there were fewer bodies in the house, there was more food left over to put up. The problem with leftovers was: both Zeke and Zynique hated eating the same thing for more than two days straight—Zynique more so than Zeke, who would eat whatever he found if it meant he didn't have to fix anything.

When Zynique turned sixteen, she unofficially started working a few hours with Madame Perry, officially at seventeen. Two things that did for her: she was making her own money so she could buy more fast food; and she had an excuse not to be home and eat what I'd cooked.

So that meant I was cooking more for me and Zeke.

After I opened the flower shop, I found I had less time to fix meals, plus it was discouraging to cook when no one seemed enthused about what I'd fixed. So I cut back on cooking. Besides, Zeke was most times gone by the time I got in from the shop. I would fix something to eat, and he pretty much ate that for his dinner the next day so he could hit the streets that much faster.

My phone rang. I quickly glanced at the clock on the wall (the one that still had hands). It was a little after seven. I performed my normal routine of checking the caller ID first to see who was calling.

"Hello," I said, knowing that this was not going to be a pleasant conversation and surprised that I was getting this call here and at this hour.

"So you stood me up," Ethan said.

"No. That's not exactly what happened."

"Oh, it's *exactly* what happened. You didn't want to meet me, so you left me there wondering and waiting. I understand."

"You really shouldn't jump to conclusions before you hear all of the facts."

"Is it okay that I'm calling you at home right now?" Ethan asked.

"Yeah. Sure."

"So where's your husband?"

"Where he normally is at this time of night," I said with a little edge to my voice. "Your guess is as good as mine."

"Now *that* doesn't sound good," Ethan said. "So where is he normally at this time of night?"

"As I said: *your* guess . . . is as good as mine."

"You don't ever ask him?"

"No. Not really."

"I don't get that or see that with you," Ethan said.

"See what?"

"First off: I don't get him leaving you every night. However, I *really* don't see you just seeming to sit back and take it. It doesn't line up with my view of you."

"So how was your walk?" I said, quickly changing the subject. "Or did you wimp out when you figured out how cold it really was?"

He chuckled. "Cold does not bother me in the least. In fact, I laugh in the face of cold. And my walk was fine, after I finally decided to quit waiting on you and do it. I did wait for you a while before I figured out maybe, just maybe, you weren't coming. I had to cut my walk short though. It's not good being out there alone like that at night. They need to add some more lighting around that place."

"I don't think that particular park was created for night visits. If you want to walk during the night hours, you probably should go to the park near the college."

"So back to why I called," Ethan said.

"I thought you called to dump on me for leaving you without a walking partner."

"I did. But there's no reason to dwell on what's already in the past. Nothing I say now will get me back that time. So I'm looking forward. You say your husband is not at home?"

"That's what I said."

"What about your daughter? Zynique. Do you and she have plans for tonight?"

"She's the reason I left you to walk alone. I just saw her. And to answer your question: she has plans of her own and they don't include me."

"Poor baby," Ethan said in a jovial voice.

"Yeah, poor me."

"So I suppose that means you have no excuse not to meet me. I still would like to take you out to eat. And since you just stood me up—"

"I did not stand you up," I said. "My daughter called and needed me to meet her somewhere right after I hung up with you. And since I have no way of reaching you without possibly getting you in trouble with your wife, I couldn't call to let you know I wasn't going to be able to make it. Now if you had a cell phone, I could have called you on it. But I definitely wasn't going to call you at your house."

"Why not?" he asked.

"You're crazy. I'm not calling your house and take a chance on your wife answering the phone."

He laughed. "I get calls from women all of the time. I have to, in what I do. Had my wife answered, she would have just thought you were someone from church or something."

"Do you have caller ID on your phone?"

"Not yet. But I'm sure we're going to be getting it soon."

"Oh. Well, I guess if you don't have caller ID then she wouldn't be able to see a name."

"Precisely."

"Does she know about me?" I asked.

"You mean that you were the love of my life?" Ethan said with a smile in his voice.

I felt myself blush a tad. "I'm sure you didn't tell her that," I said.

"She knows a little about you. She knows your name and that I was crazy about you. Seriously. And she does bring your name up from time to time."

"Oh, I see what you've been doing now. You've been using me to mess with her."

"No, not really. But she does know that I possibly loved you at one time."

I wanted to hear more, but I felt this was really not a good topic to stay on. "Well, had I called and a name shown up on your caller ID, it would have been my husband's name. I just wouldn't want to call and get you in trouble if your wife hears a woman's voice. And I refuse to do like some folks who call my house and just hang up. The least a person can do is to say they dialed the wrong number."

"No one *dials* anymore," he said.

"Oh, so I see you're just full of jokey jokes tonight."

He laughed. "No, I'm just trying to keep the conversation honest and on point."

"Okay, so if the right word is not *dialed* anymore, then what is it?"

"Go to dinner with me and I'll tell you," he said. "Right now. Come on."

"You don't know the answer, do you? You don't know what we should be saying instead of *dialed*." I was trying my best to keep the conversation away from the topic of us meeting. But I *so* wanted to say yes to dinner with Ethan.

"It's *touch tone*. But the correct thing would just be to say *called*. I *called* the wrong number. Now, I was thinking we could meet for din—"

"So the correct phrase would be *touch toned* or *called the wrong number?*" I said with a chuckle. "That doesn't sound right at all."

"Okay, then I *punched in*," Ethan said. "What about say in thirty minutes? We could meet at your shop or wherever you'd like. Then we could get in my car and—"

"I'm sorry, but I *punched in* the wrong number?" I said. "Nope, that doesn't sound right either."

"All right, then *pressed*," Ethan said. "Now, what do you say? About dinner? With me . . . tonight. Let's go and—"

"Let's see now. I'm sorry, I *pressed* the wrong number . . . numbers. Now that might work. Although I still like *dialed*. Maybe *called* is the best word to replace the word *dialed*. I *called*—"

"Okay. If you don't want to go, then just say you don't. You don't have to keep trying to ignore me or change the subject while I earnestly ask you something." I heard the exasperation in his voice.

"I just don't think it's wise to even play with this. Ethan, you and I both know, no matter how many times we might say differently, that there's more going on between us than just friendship. We're playing with fire over a large, open bucket of gasoline."

"I need to talk. I promise: that's all I'm trying to do here. I need someone to talk to and you're normally the one person who makes me feel the most comfortable to be free and speak what's on my mind. But if you don't want to talk, then that's fine. I understand."

"I don't mind talking to you. I know that you need someone you can feel free to be yourself with—no mask, no pretentions, just an unadulterated you. And I'm glad you feel you can be that way with me. But you and I, out in public, is not a good idea, particularly not for you." I released a sigh. "You know how folks like to talk. Do you really want something like me and you together possibly getting out there? Really?"

"I eat with women who are not my wife, in public I might add, a lot," Ethan said.

"Yeah, but how many are you sleeping with or trying to sleep with?"

"What? Where did *that* come from?"

"I'm sorry." I really regretted how that must have sounded. "Who you sleep with or not is really none of my business. What you do, and with whom, is between you and God. I certainly had no right to say anything like that. I apologize."

"Then why did you say it?"

"Because . . . I don't know," I lied. The truth is I knew he wanted more than just to eat and talk when it came to me. So what made me think I was any more special than the other women he apparently met on the pretense of having dinner?

"Let me say this right here, right now. I have not cheated on my wife in over fifteen years."

"Then you're admitting that you *have* cheated on her?"

"Listen, this is not a conversation I'd prefer to have over the phone. Now, I'm going to go to your shop's parking lot. I'm leaving right now. I'll give you enough time to meet me there. If you don't show up, then I won't bother you anymore."

"Wait," I said, trying to stall for time as I thought a little more about this.

"I'm hanging up now. I'll be there in twenty minutes." He hung up.

Staring at the phone as the dial tone buzzed, I had to make a decision quickly. We weren't doing anything wrong. All he wanted to do was talk. And I could see him not wanting to have the type of conversation I was trying to have just now over the phone. Not with his wife and children around, possibly listening in. That would be bad; to get him in trouble because of what he might end up saying inadvertently on the phone.

I glanced at my watch. Eighteen minutes remaining. There was no real reason for me to always be left alone to sit in a big old empty house all by myself. I hurried and changed into a red pantsuit, then headed for the shop.

Chapter 29

But every man is tempted, when he is drawn away of his own lust, and enticed.

—James 1:14

When I pulled into the parking lot of my shop, Ethan's car was already there. He got out of his car, walked over to mine as soon as I was parked, and tried to open the passenger's side door. It was still locked. I unlocked it. He opened the door and quickly slid in.

"Thanks for coming," he said as he smiled. His eyes looked as though they were dancing. The inside lights in the car dimmed, then went out. "I appreciate this."

I turned on the overhead lights in the car. "Sure." I wasn't quite certain what was next after my arriving here.

"Would you like to get in my car and we ride together?"

"No. If we go anywhere, I'd prefer to drive."

"Okay. That will work for me," Ethan said. "Do you think my car will be okay if I leave it here?"

I hadn't heard of anyone breaking into vehicles around here, but then, most folks weren't here after dark. "I don't know. I think it might be better if you park it somewhere that's a bit busier than right here. I would hate for something to happen to your cute little gold Lexus."

"Okay, then I'll move it. Any suggestions? I mean, this is your side of town."

"I suppose it depends on where we're going. You said you wanted to get something to eat."

He smiled at me. Then began to tilt his head as though he were taking photos of me and his eyes were the camera lens. I could feel it more than see it, since there was just that one light on and it didn't light up the inside of the car all that brightly. "What do you have a taste for?" Ethan finally said, essentially breaking up some of the tension.

"Seafood," I said. "I love seafood. Golden fried shrimp is my favorite."

"I love seafood, too. So do you have a favorite seafood place?"

"I do. But it's a small little joint, not enough to really qualify as a restaurant. Which honestly, I'm still not all that comfortable doing with you. Going to a restaurant, that is." I sighed, frustrated with my clumsiness in expressing my words. "I'm not all that comfortable with going to a restaurant with you."

"Do they have takeout?"

"Yes."

"Then let's go get takeout at the place you're referring to. Then we can come back here and eat it in your shop. That's if you don't mind us smelling up the place with fish odor. But you have a table in there. It would be perfect," Ethan said.

I smiled. That was a very workable idea. We would be able to eat and talk without him getting into trouble, should the wrong person happen to see us together. "Well, if we're going to do that, I suppose you can leave your car here. We can ride over there and just pick up something to go." I nodded. "That will work."

"It works for me," he said. "Drive on, my lady."

I glanced over at him. "First you need to buckle up your seatbelt," I said.

"Yeah. I was just about to do that." He pulled the seatbelt and snapped it closed. I cranked up the car and drove to the seafood place.

It didn't take long to order and get back to the shop. Ethan and I made our way inside. I excused myself to wash my hands. When I came back, my mouth hung open.

"I hope you don't mind," Ethan said. "I'll pay the cost for whatever I used."

I couldn't say a word. He had a checkered blue and white plastic tablecloth on the table. And on the table were two lit candles in short crystal candleholders along with a small vase that contained two silk red roses. It was evident he'd opened one of the romance picnic gift packages I kept at the end of the counter. Blue plastic plates and matching utensils were also set. It looked so nice. And there were two plastic champagne glasses that I also included in that package.

"Wow, this is really nice," I was finally able to say.

He pulled out the chair for me. "I'm glad you like it."

I sat down. He was about to sit down across from me, then stopped. "Oh, I need to go to the bathroom," he said, then headed in the direction I'd just come from.

I nodded as I looked around while he was gone, taking in the beautiful setting and ambiance. It was so nice. All but one set of lights were off. It worked perfectly with the candles as neither of the lights wrestled anything away from the other.

Ethan came back and sat down. Once again, he said the grace. I smiled as I listened to his words that went well beyond thanking God merely "for the food we are about to receive for the nourishment of our bodies." He even thanked God for having a friend like me in his life. *Touching.* Caused me to put my hand over my heart.

"The fish and shrimp are absolutely wonderful," he said after digging in with both hands. His lips were greasy from the food. "You know all of the good places to eat, I see. Now, the place I had *planned* to take you is good." He shook his head. "But they can't touch this seafood right c'here." He pointed at an almost empty plate.

I laughed. "You are *so* silly. 'Right c'here,' huh?" I said, mocking the way he'd pronounced *here.*

"Woman, when you're throwing down like this, who has time to speak proper English? This c'here is some good eating; I don't know *what* you talking about!" He laughed a hearty, Santa Claus kind of laugh.

"I'm glad you like it. It is good though." I wiped the grease from my own lips.

"And the company I have the honor of dining with is *off the hook!*" He winked at me.

I tried not to grin . . . too much, anyway. "Glad I could be of service."

"Now, tell me: what would you have been doing had I not called and come up with this *brilliant* idea that is turning out to be a wonderful night between two good friends?"

I took a swallow of soda. "I would be at home, most likely, alone . . . feasibly reading a book, possibly scanning through a hundred cable channels, still to find there's really nothing good to watch on TV."

"Wow, forgive me if I begin to snore as you give the highlights of what *could* have been your night tonight."

"It might be boring, but I guarantee you that it's safe," I said.

"As opposed to?"

I bit my last shrimp. "As opposed to being here with you and all of your charm and great conversation. Which reminds me: we didn't finish what we were talking about earlier."

He smiled. "You mean about me having an affair over a decade-and-a-half ago? Or the fact that I haven't had an affair in fifteen years and it was only one night of weakness, which proves I've been relatively faithful to my wife?"

"You're not exactly being faithful right now."

"That's up for debate." Ethan wiped his mouth and hands with his napkin. He took a hard long draw from his soda's straw, causing it to make a noise when he'd emptied it. He shook the empty cup, rattling only remaining ice.

I picked up the champagne glass next to me and teetered it back and forth in the air. "You know, we didn't use our glasses," I said.

"Yeah, well, I started to pour my cola in mine. But hey, it worked out just the same. Next time, we'll use the glasses."

"So you're telling me that with all of the so-called dinners you've had with other women, you've not cheated on your wife with one of them? Not even come close?"

He had an expression that looked like he smelled something foul. "Nope. Not even close."

"Why are you here with me?"

"We're not cheating."

"It's close enough to it. This is as much of a date as I've ever seen."

He leaned back against his chair and smugly looked at me. "We are two friends merely—"

"Eating and talking," I said. "Yeah. I've heard that one before. Then what did your wife say when you told her we would be dining and talking together tonight?"

He chuckled. "You're not going to let this go, are you?"

I took another swallow of my soda. "Nope."

"Okay. I didn't tell my wife that I was meeting you, eating with you, and before you ask, she has no idea how much I value spending time with you."

I shook my head. "That's a bad sign right there. When you can't share with your spouse what you're doing, then it means you must be hiding something you shouldn't be doing."

"So I suppose that means you've told your husband all about us?" Ethan said with a warm grin.

"Us what? There is no *us*." I sat back against my chair. "Let's forget this discussion. Let's just finish up so we can get on back to our respective homes."

"I've missed you." Ethan leaned forward. "I've missed talking to you. I've missed laughing at your silly jokes with your silly self. I've missed . . . you."

I smiled, then twisted my mouth. "Wrong road. Time to detour. You need to find another road to ride on because this one is taking you completely in the wrong direction."

He leaned in some more. "Why exactly do you think I can't stay away from you? Why do you think after all these years I still feel joy every time I see your face? What would you call it, my beautiful little butterfly?"

"Soul ties," I said.

"Soul ties?" Ethan said. "Hmmm. An interesting phrase you've mentioned at least once before, I believe. So explain it better to me: what are soul ties?"

I stood up and began clearing off the table so we could leave. Ethan stood and took my hand, stopping me from picking up the empty plate I was reaching for. I looked down at his hand, then back up and into his eyes.

"What are soul ties?" he asked again. He took the back of his hand and gently touched my face.

I looked at him and all of a sudden all I wanted to do was cry. It was crazy. I wanted to cry for what we could have had. I wanted to cry for all the time we'd lost because of decisions we'd both made. I wanted to cry because there was nothing I would have loved more at that moment than to fall into his arms and let him hold me and love me forever. Forever soul ties, that's the way my perfect world would have looked. He and I, together as one. But instead, here we were inside of my flower shop, eating seafood from The Golden Market off of plastic plates with plastic forks, while drinking out of cups made from suspect material, at best.

He leaned down and softly kissed my lips. I didn't need this right now. For sure, I didn't need this. Not the way I was feeling about him. Not while we were alone in a place where no one could walk in and interrupt us before we made a mistake we might end up *positively* regretting later.

I pulled away, resisting the urge to taste my own lips now that he had tasted them. "Soul ties," I said, almost stumbling when I spoke, "is just what it sounds like. It's an unbreakable tie that binds two souls together. Nothing can separate that love. Not time, not distance, not family, not friends, not circumstances, neither height, nor depth, nor things present, nor things to come. Nothing seems able to break the bond." He took possession of me again. I tried to pull away. But truthfully, he had a hold on me in more ways than physically.

"Let's not walk away just yet," Ethan said. "Let me show you just how much I love you."

I laughed, which was just what I needed to make my escape from his embrace. "That was so old school. You want to show me how much you love me and let me guess: it includes the two of us having sex."

"Gee, why don't you just put it out there already," Ethan said with a laugh. "But yes, that's what we men do to show you women how much we really love you."

"And we 'women' take you 'men' wanting to have sex with us as your way of experiencing the best of both worlds without you caring about what *we* really want."

"And what is it that you women want? Why don't you school me?" He took my hand.

"Okay, class is in session. We want to be held. We want to be made to feel like you want us. Not want just our bodies, but us." I placed my hand over my heart. "We want to feel like it's not about what you can get from us, but what you can give."

"Oh, believe me, there's a whole lot I want to give you right now." He started swinging my hand. "You have *no* idea." He shook his head as he grinned.

I playfully hit at him. "Would you stop that? You're just being mannish now."

"Ooh, haven't heard that word since . . . middle school?"

"Ethan, we can't play this dangerously close to the line." I shook my head. "We can't. I can't."

"You still love me, don't you? Don't you?" Ethan said. "Come on. Say it. Tell me you love me."

"Ethan—"

He grabbed me around my waist and began to dance with me around the room. "Tell me you love me and I'll let you go."

"You need to stop this. I'm not playing with you. I'm telling you: this is a dangerous game we're playing."

"Tell me you love me and I'll let you go."

"If I say it, can we go home?"

"If that's what you want. I'd just like for you to tell the truth."

"Okay! I love you!" I said. "I love you. Now let me go." I pulled away.

He released me and became quiet. I looked at him as he stared at me in a way I had honestly never seen him ever do before. He then started to clean up the rest of the stuff off the table, even being kind enough not to throw the fishy-smelling things in my trash in the shop.

He walked to the door when everything was done, still not

having said a word. I was starting to become concerned. *Had I said something that cut him* too *deep? Had I hurt his feelings? What?*

I turned the shop's alarm on and locked the door. Ethan carried the trash as though he was going to put it in his car. I wanted to tell him bye, but I didn't know what was going on with him. Maybe it was best this way—just cut things off before we ended up doing something we would both regret.

I opened my car door as I watched Ethan. Having spotted the outdoor trash bin, he went and put the trash in there. He was on his way back to his car. But instead of stopping and getting in his car, he walked over to me as I'd continued to stand there watching him.

"You want to know the truth?" he said. "The truth is: I *love* you." He said it with such sincerity. "I honestly and truly never *stopped* loving you." He kissed me on my cheek, turned around, and left me standing there without looking back. He got in his car and sat there. I got in mine. He waited until I pulled off, then followed me as I drove away, staying close, but far enough, behind me. When I came upon my exit to my house, I turned on my blinkers. Ethan turned on his. I was starting to get a little nervous, thinking he might possibly be following me home. I exited; he kept going straight. I breathed a sigh of relief.

I arrived home around ten o'clock. As usual, no one was there—leaving me alone *yet* again to contemplate and to try and make sense of what had ended up being quite an eventful day.

Quite eventful.

Chapter 30

Confess your faults one to another, and pray one for another, that ye may be healed. The effectual fervent prayer of a righteous man availeth much.

—James 5:16

I wanted to talk to someone about what was going on with me, specifically between me and Ethan. But that was easier said than done. One: I didn't want to give any of my friends an occasion to judge me. And two: my two best friends were too much like refrigerators gone bad—they couldn't keep nothing!

Several of my friends have told me something like this. But I've never really had anything quite like this to happen with me before. Sure, men have hit on me. I've even had stints of being impressed with a few guys who have caused me to jokingly say aloud (along with both Shelia and Kelly), "Now I could get with *that!*"

Shelia and Kelly knew I was merely kidding (even if I knew that they absolutely weren't). Anyone who *really* knew me knew I'd *never* act on anything like that. So those times with me running my mouth were essentially harmless.

But this situation with Ethan was totally different.

This had me moving toward doing something I knew I shouldn't, with a man who was *not* my husband. It didn't matter that I'd known Ethan long before I ever met Zeke. It didn't matter that I'd loved Ethan back when I wasn't even sure I knew what love was.

And now, he was telling me that he'd never stopped loving me. He had professed his love for me. And there was no one I could discuss this with. No one. It was so frustrating. In all honesty, I should have been able to talk to my pastor about this. But he would have *loved* having something like this to hold over my head. Pastor Hutchings had tried many times himself to kiss me. There was no way I would confess to him that another man had not only tried, but succeeded, where he'd failed. That would have merely communicated to him that he just needed to be more persistent . . . possibly try harder.

Nope. My pastor was definitely out, as was his wife who suffered from her own case of diarrhea of the mouth. I didn't feel I needed to talk to a psychiatrist since there was nothing fundamentally mentally unstable about cheating. Well, maybe unstable isn't the best choice of words. Let's just say people have been cheating since the days of the Old Testament.

I categorically couldn't tell my mother. She'd likely pull out her bottle of oil and start anointing me and anything else within my immediate vicinity. My three sisters saw me as the responsible one of the family. Definitely couldn't tell any of them.

And my brother?

Well . . . let's just say he would have affectionately slapped me on my back, congratulated me, and said, "Welcome to the club! It's about [insert a curse word here] time." As quiet as it's been kept, I know for a fact that two of my three sisters and my only brother *all* have cheated on their spouses at one time or another. They'll deny it, but I know the truth.

My sisters had good reasons. One sister was married to a stone fool (fool is used biblically here: he used to say there was no God) who didn't deserve a wife. He treated her so badly. Another sister's husband was sleeping with pretty much anything that wore a skirt, breathed, and would let him. She cheated on him to let him know that he wasn't the only one who could garner attention in their house. Her husband straightened up for a few months before he went right back to his old ways. That sister eventually got tired and left him, only to return six months later. My baby sister has never married. She has commitment issues. Sharon has a good man (a *really* good man) she's been with for some ten years, but she refuses to settle down. "It's just not in my nature to commit myself forever . . . to tie myself forever to one person . . . one soul," she told me. "Nope. That's not me."

Then there's Baby Brother, a straight-up dog (my sincere apologies to dogs). That's pretty much all I need to say about him. My mother used to tell him he was like a dog chasing a car. "Should the dog catch it, he doesn't have a clue what to do with it," Mother said. Still, Baby Brother loves the chase. And those women slow enough or who stopped long enough for him to catch them? Sure, he'd stay with them for a few months before he was right back out there, running and barking at the next good-looking, two-legged "vehicle" passing his way.

So as much as I would have loved to talk about . . . confess all that had taken place between me and Ethan over this past year and four months, I didn't have anyone I honestly felt comfortable enough to tell. I couldn't tell a soul he'd bought me flowers. I couldn't tell how he and I had kissed on more than one occasion. I couldn't tell how he made me feel like I was the most beautiful thing he'd ever laid eyes upon, even though I was much, much older than when he and I first met. I couldn't tell how he'd magically created the most romantic night I'd had (ever, honestly) practically out of nothing when he set that table with candles and flowers and we laughed and ate some of the best seafood on this side of Heaven. I couldn't tell anyone he'd just told me that he loved me.

There was no one I could tell what was causing me to smile for what seemed like no reason whatsoever. How butterflies were setting up residence in my stomach, fluttering around whenever I saw Ethan or heard his voice.

There was no one I could talk to or tell any of this . . . except *for* Ethan. And from everything I'd gotten from him, it was the same with him. At this point, the only real confidantes either of us seemed to have . . . were each other.

Chapter 31

That ye be not slothful, but followers of them who through faith and patience inherit the promises.
—Hebrews 6:12

The next morning I got up earlier than normal and went to the shop. I wanted to change some things around to make the place more appealing (at least that's what I told myself when I got up that early). The truth was: I didn't want to be bothered with Zeke. The more I thought about things, the more I was starting to resent the way Zeke treated me. Why did he have to leave me by myself almost every single night? Why didn't he and I go anywhere fun together? Why didn't we go on trips together like other families or merely now as a loving couple?

I've never even been on a cruise. As inexpensive as they are these days to take three-, four-, or even seven-day cruises to places like the Bahamas, I've never gone. All of my friends have. Even my mother has been on a cruise, my Medicare-card-carrying seventy-one-year-old mother. The last time she went was two years ago, she and five of her gray-haired slash wig-wearing friends: the fearsome six, I call them. She'd invited me (more out of sympathy, I believe, than that she really wanted me to hang with them). But in full disclosure: I didn't want my first experience on a cruise to be with a bunch of elderly women who probably got giddy and excited over the mention of shuffleboard.

The fact is: both time and life were passing me by. And all I really had to show for my participation was picture calendars I saved each year and a houseful of *stuff* that, when I'm dead and gone, will most likely end up in an estate sale, the trash, or, mercifully, donated to folks who come by in trucks and pick up items for charity.

Yes, I'd had children and they *were* and still *are* the loves of my life. But children are supposed to leave you and go on to live their own lives, hopefully with the love of their lives. You can't hold on to your children forever (although maybe someone should tell my mother that . . . namely when it comes to my baby brother).

When I arrived at the shop, I couldn't help but smile a little as I replayed the events with Ethan from the night before. I wasn't sure exactly where things were going with us. He'd made it clear that he wasn't planning on divorcing his wife any time soon (after that initial breakdown I was able to help him through). He wanted to be there until at least his youngest child graduated high school. So as for anything seriously developing between the two of us, even if it did happen, we were looking at about nine years down the road.

The phone rang. It was my home number. I hurriedly answered it, wondering who was calling.

"You need to get home right now!" Zeke yelled before I could get my "hello" out good.

"What's wrong? What's going on?" I asked.

"You just need to get here as quickly as you can."

"Are you okay? Tell me what's going on."

"It's your youngest child."

My heart skipped a beat then seemed to stop. "What's wrong? Is Zynique all right?" I hadn't even thought about checking on Zynique before I left. I was in too big of a hurry to get out of the house before Zeke woke up. But her car was there. I thought for a moment. Yes, I'd seen her car parked in its usual spot.

"Physically, she's fine. But I think she's lost her mind!" Zeke said. My heart began its normal beating again.

"Zeke, calm down and tell me what's going on." I didn't see

a reason for me to come home just because he and Zynique were at it again.

Zeke can be a little over the top when he wants to be, mainly because he never has to deal with anything at the house. The home and the children were always *my* responsibility. When any of the children were fighting? "You need to handle those children of yours." They ask him a question. "Where's your mother? Go ask your mother." They need money for something. "Go get it from your mother." They need a little love and attention from their father. "Where's your mother? Go get a hug from her; she's the hugger of the family." When it's time for someone to discipline any one of them? "Go tell your mother what you did. Go on now! Go tell your mother."

So when Zynique and Zeke were at it for whatever reason this morning, the first thing he instinctively did was bring it to me.

"All I can tell you is that you need to find your way back to this house and handle this child of yours. I don't have time for this!" Zeke said it so loud I had to pull the receiver away from my ear.

"So when do you think you're *ever* going to have *time for this?*" I said.

"Listen, you need to quit all this talking and make your way back home. Because if this child says one more smart word to me, I'm not going to be responsible if I go off on her."

"Okay, Zeke. I'll be there in about fifteen minutes."

"Don't be saying that and it be an hour before you drive up. I have stuff to do."

"As do I," I said.

"Well, this is my day off and I don't plan on spending it with some child snipping back at me. And on top of that: you left without making me breakfast. I don't know what's wrong with both of y'all. It must be PMS or something. Y'all are both acting crazy."

"Zeke, I think you need to dial it back a notch. Because just like you're not in the mood, I'm not in the mood. Now, I'll be home as soon as I can." I hung up and shook my head. My redecorating ideas would have to wait.

When I stepped inside of the house, Zynique was in the den saying something to her father while she was crying.

"Hey! Hey!" I said. "What's going on here?"

"I should have known he would call you," Zynique said. "He can't ever handle anything by himself."

"All right now. I done told you," Zeke said. "You'd better watch your mouth."

"And if I don't, what are you going to do?" She stared at her father, shutting down her crying voice completely. "What are you going to do? What, Dad?"

Zeke looked at me. "You see what I told you. The girl done lost her mind. You'd better help her get a handle on herself."

"And if Mother doesn't, then what are *you* going to do?" Zynique asked. "Huh?"

Zeke looked at me as though he was saying I needed to hurry up and take control of this. I merely matched his look, thinking of the many times I had handled things like this when he should have. *Was there any wonder the girls thought I was the mean one of us two?* He always let me do all the dirty work. Well, not this time. This was his fight. I was going to stand back and let him handle it today.

Zeke turned his full attention toward me. "Are you going to just stand there and let this child disrespect me like this?"

I was determined that all I was going to do was be a fair and just referee. If one of them truly went out of bounds, I would call them on it. So far, I hadn't seen that. Zynique was talking to her father about something. He didn't want to deal with it, so he thought he was going to put it off on me. Normally, I would have taken it, but not this time. Not today.

"Woman, are you listening to me?" Zeke said, raising his voice at me.

"Yes, Daddy; she can hear you. But maybe she's telling you to stand up for yourself for a change. Maybe Mother is tired of fighting alone all the time. Have you ever thought about her and what she feels? Do you ever consider her feelings when you're doing things?"

He turned to Zynique. "Yes, ma'am, I do consider your

mother's feelings," he said before turning back to me. "Don't I, baby?"

I didn't say a word.

"Daddy, why don't you leave Mother out of this? You were the one who came and woke me up out of *my* sleep talking about get up and fix you some breakfast."

"And you were the one who got smart and asked me what was wrong with my two hands."

"That's right. I'm not Mom. I'm not your maid. My job is not to cook for you or clean up after you," Zynique said with her hand on her hip.

"And that's why you're not going to end up with a man. You're going to have to live here with us because ain't no man out there going to want some lazy woman who refuses to do her womanly job."

I almost burst into a laugh when he said that. *Is that what he thinks when it comes to me? That I'd better do that to keep a man?* It would be funny if it wasn't so sad.

"Daddy, let me straighten you out before you go out in public and say some of this male chauvinist junk to somebody else who just might tell you off in a way you've obviously not been told off before."

"I've been told off plenty times before." Zeke then looked at me. "So you're actually going to just stand there and let your daughter talk to me this way?"

I tried not to smile, but it was so hard.

"Both of y'all done lost your minds! You"—he looked at Zynique—"are over here talking to me as though you don't remember that commandment that tells you to honor your mother *and* your father. And you"—he turned to me—"acting like you don't hear this child running off at the mouth, acting like she hasn't gotten any home training when it comes to how to talk to grown folks."

"Well, if I had been waiting on you to do any home training, this is what you would have gotten, if not worse, considering you were never *home* to do any training." I said that so calm, I almost scared myself.

"Okay," he said to me as he nodded, then turned to Zynique. "You know what? You keep on, and I promise you that you're going to be looking for a place to stay. If your mother doesn't handle this, I'm gonna show you how tough I really can be. I'll send your little tail packing. Let you see how it feels to be out there on the streets with nowhere to live. I bet you'll be glad to get up and fix me some breakfast from here on out." He nodded as he smirked.

"Zeke—" I said.

"Hush up, *wo*man!" He snapped at me. "There's no need in you trying to step in now. You wanted to stand there like a cat was holding your tongue. Well, you keep standing there with your mouth closed while I handle my business."

I tried again. "But, Zeke—"

"I told you to hush up!" Zeke said to me. "I don't know why you women can't be obedient the way you're supposed to be. Submit. Have you ever heard of that word while you were in church? 'Wives, submit yourselves to your own husbands, as unto the Lord.' Yeah, that's in that Bible you be toting around all the time."

Zynique started clapping and singing. "Yay! Daddy knows a scripture! Daddy knows a scripture!"

I gave Zynique my look that told her "Don't go overboard." She knew that look; all of my children knew it. It's the look that doesn't require you to open your mouth, but the one receiving the look, knows *precisely* what's being said.

Zynique turned back to her father. "Do you know what the rest of that scripture says?"

"You mean where it explains to the wives that the husband is the head of the wife?" Zeke said.

"Not that one, Daddy. I'm talking about the one farther down that tells the husbands to 'love your wives, even as Christ also loved the church, and gave himself for it.' That one."

I was impressed. My baby knew her scriptures. *Go on, Zynique!*

"And FYI: the word *submit* there, Daddy, merely means to re- spect. But I was told you earn respect. And to get respect, you had to give respect. You don't respect Mother. You treat her like she's gum under your shoe."

"That's not true," Zeke said. "That's not true." He shook his head and glanced my way.

"Okay, when is the last time you took Mother out?"

"What?"

"Oh, I'll wait; I have time," Zynique said. "When was the last time you took Mother anywhere? To a nice restaurant, out to a movie, to a concert, a play, for a walk in the park? Okay, a nice restaurant may be too much to ask of you. So how about Mc-Donalds, Burger King, Arby's, Rally's? When was the last time you opened up a can of soup for her when she was sick? Helped her bring in the groceries? Oh, that's right. You can't help with groceries because you're too busy not being here when she comes home with them. Mother buys the groceries, loads the groceries, brings the groceries home, unloads the groceries, puts the groceries away, and cooks the groceries. And what is your part in this whole grocery process?"

Zeke looked as though he was really taking in what she was saying and seriously trying to come up with a rebuttal.

"I'll tell you what your part looks to be from my viewpoint," Zynique said, continuing without missing a beat. "You eat what she cooks and complains if it's not to your liking. And you think I'm going to be like Mom, here? Waiting on some man hand and foot the way Mom does? When she can't even get a thank-you out of you?"

Ouch, now that stung a little.

"Oh, and Daddy, had you allowed Mother to speak when she was trying to tell you something a few minutes ago, I'm pretty sure she was about to tell you that it really won't hurt me if you put me out. Right now, today, if you like."

"Is that right?" Zeke said.

"She's right," I said, deciding it was time to bring this little exercise to an end.

"And why is that?" Zeke said, turning to me with a smug look. "Because you think this is your house and I can't put her out?"

"No," I said. "Because, my dear husband, your daughter has her own house now."

He started laughing, reaching a level of sheer exaggeration. "Zynique?" he said, pointing at her. "You're talking about that daughter right there? So Zynique has her own house. Oh, wait a minute. Let me guess." He laughed. "It's already paid for and everything. Right?"

I smiled while Zynique smirked. "Yeah, that's pretty much it."

His laughter began to temper. "So what did you do? Buy her a house? I mean you seem to give your children, especially Zynique, everything else they want."

"Nope, I didn't buy her a house."

"Had you gone with me last night you would know what happened," Zynique said, folding her arms.

"All right, Miss Smarty Mouth. What happened?"

"Madame Perry left me her house," Zynique said, then grinned.

"She left you her house?" Zeke said. "What do you mean she left you her house?"

"Just what I said. She left her house to me. She also left the dance studio in my care," Zynique said.

Zeke looked at me. I nodded.

"What about her son? Didn't she have a son?" Zeke said. "I'm sure that's not going to go over well with him. If I were you, Missy, I wouldn't start counting my chickens before they hatch."

"You are always so . . . corny," Zynique said.

"Clichéd," I clarified.

"I'm just trying to tell Little Miss Uppity here that she might want to watch her mouth with me until the deed has been transferred into her name," Zeke said. " 'Cause I know how folks can be when it comes to relatives and inheritances, anything associated with someone getting something that someone else thinks they should have gotten or are entitled to. So Zynique, you might want to wait and see if that child of hers doesn't contest the will or something before you start rising up at your mother and me."

I frowned, wondering how he was all of a sudden including me in this.

"Okay, Daddy. Whatever." Zynique waved him away.

"All right now. Don't say I didn't warn you. Just keep on . . . you hear?"

Zynique huffed, then left the room.

"Do you believe that?" Zeke said to me.

"Believe that you called me from my place of business for something like this?" I said.

"So you knew about this already," Zeke said. "And just when were you planning on letting me in on this piece of breaking news?"

"Who, me?" I patted my chest. "I planned on telling you last night after I came back from Zynique and me meeting with the lawyer. Let me see now, why didn't I happen to do that?" I snapped my fingers. "That's right! You weren't here when I got home." I started walking toward the front door.

"Hey," Zeke said. "Where do you think you're going?"

I stopped and turned around. "Back to work," I said.

"Back to work? Well, who's going to fix me my breakfast?"

I walked back over to him, lifted his hands, and began to examine them.

"What are you doing?" he asked, glancing between my face and his hands with a slight look of concern.

"Oh, just checking your hands. They appear to be working fine to me, too," I said.

He snatched his hands out of mine. I again walked away. Just as I opened the door to go outside to my car, I heard him yell after me, "And I have *too* brought in groceries! A few times! I have, too!"

Chapter 32

Not that I speak in respect of want: for I have learned, in whatsoever state I am, therewith to be content.

—Philippians 4:11

Christmas was only a week away, and I didn't even have my Christmas tree up and decorated. Everything had gone smoothly with the transferring of the deeds on the house to Zynique. And since it was fully furnished, she'd already moved in. I wasn't sure how I felt about her being in a house by herself. But she was grown now, technically speaking. And as she and I had discussed even before she ended up blessed with that house, it was time for her to be getting out on her own.

In the past, I was always excited about Christmastime. Especially when the girls were young and looking forward to what would be under the tree. We had our own ritual coming up to the big day. We would turn on Christmas music, put up the tree—each year having purchased one new ornament to put on the tree. Each child had her own special ornament that marked the day she was born. We would drink hot chocolate and have the best time. *Memories . . . precious memories.*

Of course, Zeke had never participated in the decorating of the tree. The most I could ever get him to do was to bring the boxes of decorations upstairs from the storage room. So it was no surprise that he didn't feel funny about this year.

Zanetta wasn't going to be there this year. She had decided to make the Air Force her career and was stationed too far away to come home for a few days and get back in time even if she had wanted to. Zion called, right as Zynique was moving her things into her new home, to inform me of *her* good news.

"You say what?" I said, stunned.

"Married, Mom," Zion said. "I got married!"

"Wait a minute. Are you saying that you're getting married, so I need to start planning a wedding? Is that what you're saying?"

She laughed. "No. I'm saying I'm already married, so you won't have to worry about either the planning *or* the expense, not when it comes to me, anyway."

"Who was worried about an expense? I was looking forward to it." I had to sit down. I was utterly disappointed. "So you're telling me that you got married?"

"Yes, Mother. And he's a wonderful man!" I could hear the love oozing from her voice.

"So . . . is he Haitian?"

"He's not, but his father is. He's in our group. And guess what else, Mom?"

I was afraid to even try to guess. "What?" I said putting a swift end to the guessing game before it got started.

"I'm a mother!"

"You're a what? A mother?! Oh, baby. You were pregnant." I couldn't help but be disappointed and it showed. "Why didn't you tell me? Did you have the baby over there? Is that why you got married? You know you didn't have to get married just because you were pregnant—"

"Mom! Mom! Slow down. I didn't get married because I was pregnant." She laughed. "You get so wound up and nobody can shut you down. Malik has a son."

"So is Malik the name of my new son-in-law? A son-in-law you didn't think you should bring home for us to at least meet before you tied your souls forever together?"

"You're too much," Zion said with a chuckle. "Why don't you tell me what you *really* think?"

"I thought that's what I was doing."

"Mother, I'm only joking," Zion said.

I released a sigh of relief. "I have to give it to you. For a minute there you had me going. I thought you'd married some river-rat your daddy and I had never met and that you were now a mother. Whew! Thank God you were only joking."

"No. The part about me being married and a mother is all true. I was joking about you telling me what you really think. I can tell you're not that excited about this. Of course, I also expected that from you. Listen, I can't talk long. I just wanted to let you know that I'm married to a wonderful man named Malik Merisier, I'm Zion Merisier now, and I'm the mother of an amazing three-year-old son named Jonah."

"All right. Then, I suppose congratulations are in order," I said, trying my best to sound happy for her. There was no purpose in ruining this conversation trying to get her to see what a huge mistake I believed she may have made. Besides, the spirit of Christmas was upon us, a time of glad tidings and good cheer. "Congratulations!"

"Thank you," Zion said. "Is Dad around?"

"No, honey. He's not here."

"Okay. Well, tell him that I called and that I'm sorry I missed him."

"Will do," I said. "So when do we get to meet our new son-in-law and his three-year-old?"

"*Our* three-year-old," Zion said, correcting me. "There is no 'my and his' with us; only 'ours.' "

"Okay . . . *your* three-year-old. When are you coming home?"

"We'll likely be back in the states sometime in March."

"Are you coming home to stay?" I crossed my fingers and said a quick prayer.

"Maybe," Zion said.

That was good news. Maybe I could grow to like this Malik after all. If he was bringing my child back this way, he couldn't be all bad, right? Prior to this call, I had almost become convinced Zion was never coming back. Now, we were at a "maybe."

"Mom, I'm going to get off the phone now. These calling cards don't give as many minutes when you use them for international calls."

"Well, thanks for calling. It was good hearing your voice."

"Oh!" Zion said. "Have you put up the Christmas tree yet? What am I saying? Of course, you have," Zion said. I could hear the smile in her voice. "You always put the tree up right after Thanksgiving."

"Well, this Thanksgiving was a bit hectic. Madame Perry died."

"Madame Perry died? When? What happened?"

"The Monday before Thanksgiving. You know she was up in age. Her heart just gave out. The funeral was the Saturday after Thanksgiving. I was really busy that week with flower orders for the funeral and everything. It was something."

"How is Zynique taking it? She loved her some Madame Perry, even more than the rest of us. The last time Zynique and I talked, she was working for her. Is Zynique doing all right?"

"It was hard, but she made it through. She even spoke at the funeral."

"Zynique spoke? You mean little don't-ever-want-to-speak-in-public Zynique spoke at her funeral? We're talking about my baby sister Zynique?"

"Yes, your little sister Zynique. It was very touching, too."

"So is she there now or out with that guy she's been dating?"

"Actually, I don't know where she is," I said. "She has her own place now."

"Zynique moved into an apartment? Is she sharing it with Iesha or Darlene?"

"It's not an apartment; Zynique has a house. And she's not sharing it with either Iesha *or* Darlene. It's all hers; she owns it."

"A house? Zynique is living in a house?"

"Yes."

"Her *own* house?"

"Yes."

"And she's not renting it?" Zion said.

"No. She owns it outright. No mortgage at all. Free and clear. Owns it."

"Listen, Mom," Zion said hurriedly. "The voice just said I only have a minute left. Tell Zynique to write me and tell me what's going on with her. I'll see you all soon, I hope! I love you. Tell Dad I love him, too."

"Love you, too, baby," I said.

"Oh, and Mom? Merry Christ—"

We were disconnected.

And that's about how I felt with all of my children right now—disconnected. Everyone was going about . . . living their own lives the way they chose. Zanetta would not likely be settling down anytime soon. I was a little worried about her, especially since we were at war now. I thought Zanetta might be in a prime position to be flying in a combat area. She and others assured me that there's a 1994 combat exclusion policy banning women from ground combat units. Zanetta mentioned it when she was fussing about the unfairness of it. Other people brought it up to make me feel better about her doing this at all.

Zanetta stated women have, for years, served in ground combat situations. "They just don't get credit for it," Zanetta said, which she contended hinders women from getting promotions . . . senior flag ranks, the three and four stars primarily.

Zeke was the first person to mention anything about Bin Laden even before the news said the attack was most likely orchestrated by him. I'd never heard of a Bin Laden before. But Zeke watched that type of stuff on television, so he was familiar with Bin Laden and what he'd done in the past. When it was official that Bin Laden was the one that had orchestrated the 9/11 attacks, Zeke couldn't stop talking about it, telling every bit of information he thought that he knew about him. I just wanted Zanetta to get out of the military and do something else.

But Zanetta has always been headstrong. She's going to do what she wants, no matter how nervous it makes me.

"Mother," Zanetta said. "God has not given us the spirit of fear. Isn't that one of the scriptures you like to quote to reassure us that we should never be afraid?"

"Yes, I know. And I'm not saying that I'm in fear. I would just prefer you not put yourself in harm's way of any kind, if you can at all avoid it. You're a woman, who, of all things, managed to make it to a position where you're allowed to fly planes, likely now over hostile territory. What if you get shot down and taken prisoner? Do you have any idea how—?"

"Don't, Mom. Don't speak that negative on me. 'For God hath not given us the spirit of fear, but of power, and of love,

and of a sound mind.' That's what Second Timothy, one-seven
says."

"I know, I know. And you're right." I let out a sigh. " 'Life and
death is in the power of the tongue.' So I'll not speak or think
anything negative on this again. I believe God has charged angels to watch over you. So I'm going to be content in knowing
that a thousand may fall at your side and ten thousand at your
right hand—"

" 'But it shall not come nigh me,' " Zanetta said, finishing
Psalm 91:7 she and I began quoting religiously the first day I
learned she'd signed up for the Air Force.

"Okay. I'm good," I said, reassuring myself more than her.
"I'm content."

And that's what I was doing right now. Learning to be content in whatever state I found myself. Our girls had all flown
the nest. And I was by myself now, with the exception of the few
times Zeke and I passed each other coming and going.

This Christmas would be the first time that I would not have
a Christmas tree up in our house. Not because I was too busy;
but because no one, except me, was there to care. I was good
though. The shop was busy and it had a festive look. All in all, I
was content. I was content. Or so I thought.

Chapter 33

And let us consider one another to provoke unto love and to good works.

—Hebrews 10:24

Zion came home in March just as she'd said back in December she might do. I met Malik, who turned out to be a really nice guy. He was dark skinned, which didn't bother me in the least. I only mention his hue because Zion had always appeared sort of color-struck when it came to the guys she liked. Every one of them, since she was in middle school, was light skinned with curly hair. Malik was dark and completely bald. And since he was only twenty-five, his baldness came from deliberate effort.

I wasn't sure how I would act with the three-year-old, but he was such a little charmer. He gave me a hug and followed me around asking me all kinds of questions. I instantly fell in love with Jonah.

"Guess what?" Zion said with a giddiness that clued me in that whatever the "what" was, it was going to be a doozy.

"What?"

"I'm pregnant!"

My eyes widened with delight. "You are?"

"Yes! The baby is due on the twenty-third of October. Malik and I are over the moon about this!"

I reached out and pulled her to me. "My baby is going to have a baby!"

She pulled away after a few seconds. "That's why Malik

wanted us to come back to the states. He wants us to settle down and take care of our own, at least for now. He's such a wonderful man. He doesn't want me to work outside the home either."

"Really? So how do you feel about that? Not working, I mean."

"Oh, I'll be working. I'll be doing the greatest, most difficult but equally rewarding job there is to do—the work of a stay-at-home mother. I told Malik that if we added up what we'd be paying for someone to keep our children and paid that to me, I'd be pulling in some major cash. Forget adding in the cost of a maid to take care of our house." She grinned. "We're looking for a place now."

"Wow. So how is that going? Do you need me to call that realtor I know? She did a great job for my friend Shelia. They just bought a new house last year," I said. I left out the part about her husband buying the house because she'd busted him with another woman and it was his way of trying to change the subject.

"We're not going to live in this state," Zion said.

"You're not?" Now I was getting a bit upset. Malik had scored major points with me for getting my child to move back to the states. He was about to lose those points, now that it looked like he was still taking my child away.

"Malik was offered a job in Cambridge, Massachusetts, at MIT. It's a great opportunity for him and for us."

The university with the brilliant folks? Well, I couldn't argue with that!

Chapter 34

But call to remembrance the former days, in which,
after ye were illuminated, ye endured a great fight of
afflictions.

—Hebrews 10:32

Ethan called me four times from the time I became a
mother-in-law and an instant grandmother, to the week I
had been blessed to witness the birth of my first biological
grandchild—a baby boy Zion and Malik named Jeremiah.

Here I was, each time Ethan called, with reports of joyful
happenings in my life, while Ethan was (over that same time
frame) reporting on two medical problems that had occurred
with his wife, as well as updates of her subsequent recoveries.

"Miss me?" Ethan said at the end of November.

"Now why would you ask me something like that?" I said.

"Just checking. Not that it's been intentional, but I've been
neglecting you."

"Listen, Ethan, you said it yourself: we're just friends. So
there's really nothing between us for you to neglect."

"I never said that. I never said there's nothing between us."

"Well, okay: I'll say it. There's nothing between us. You have
your life—"

"And you have yours," Ethan said. "You're mad at me, aren't
you?"

"Mad?" I chuckled. "I'm not mad."

"Yes, you are."

"No," I said, more strongly and deliberately. "I'm not. Trust
me: I have plenty to keep me busy. Plenty."

"So what are you saying? That you don't have time for me?"

"What I'm saying is: I don't have time to worry about stuff like this."

"Wow, I guess I'd better get on my job a little better," he said. "What job?"

"My job of making sure I don't lose you again."

I laughed. "Well, good luck with *that*. I think you're what they would call a day late and a dollar short."

"And you need to come up with more original material if you plan on shooting me down," Ethan said. "But I'm not going to lose you again. We're tied together forever. That means if you go down, then I'm going down with you and vice versa."

"Cute line. Although I don't know how well that little line will apply to our situation."

"Did you even hear a word I said the last time I saw you?" Ethan said.

"What are you talking about? Are you talking about last year? When we went and got seafood and ended up eating it in my shop? That last time?"

"Okay, so you *do* remember the last time. Frankly, I can't get the thought out of my mind. It was really nice. I'd love to do something like that again. In fact, I was planning on doing something like that again. It's just things started happening in my family and I had to take care of them."

"I understand. You don't have to explain anything to me."

"But I do. I don't ever want you to feel the way I made you feel all those years ago. I messed up with you once; I don't plan on doing that ever again. Not ever. Whatever I have to do to ensure that you stay in my life, that's what I plan on doing."

"Ethan"—I said his name with a soft sigh—"do you know how crazy what you just said sounds? Look: I don't matter. You have a wife; you have a family. And regardless of what you feel for me . . . toward me . . . your first obligation is and, as it should, will always be to them."

"I know. And I'm not saying that I'm not doing my job at home. I just don't want you to feel as though you don't matter or that you're not important to me," Ethan said. "Because you're important to me, very important."

"Can we just change the subject?" I said.

"Can I see you?"

"You know, I don't think that's a good idea," I said.

"Because you're upset with me," he said matter-of-factly.

"No. I told you: I'm not upset with you."

"Then meet me. Or better yet; let me pick us up something to eat one day this week and bring it by the shop. We can do like we did last year."

"So what is this? Every year you're going to come by my flower shop, feed me, and we'll be straight until the next year?" I was really only teasing, but when the words came out of my mouth, it sure didn't sound that way, not even to me.

"You really *are* upset with me." Ethan's voice sounded resigned.

"Look, I don't think you and I should talk anymore."

"Because you're upset with me."

"No. But if we're able to go this long without talking to or seeing each other . . ." There it was again. Maybe I *was* upset with him about all of this and I was denying it, even to myself. But here he was *yet again* treating me as though my feelings really didn't matter and I was supposed to dutifully sit around waiting on him. "Look, I have to go. I'll talk to you later." I promptly hung up, not giving him a chance to say another word.

Chapter 35

Ye have not yet resisted unto blood, striving against sin.

—Hebrews 12:4

The thing about telling someone you care about to leave you alone (whether it's family, friends, or otherwise) and they do what you ask, is that it really can mess with your head. You tell them as though that's what you truly want them to do, and on some level you believe you really do. But when they oblige that request and stop calling or coming around, your mind starts an intense internal dialogue.

"Maybe they didn't care about you like they said. See, I told you that you were only being used. Why was it so easy for them to just walk away? Huh? Huh? Have you thought about that? Are you thinking about that? If they really and truly cared, they would, could never have walked away. You'd think they would be as miserable about not having you in their lives as you are about not having them, but that doesn't appear to be the case now does it? If they really loved you they wouldn't have walked away, at least not without putting up a bigger fight. It merely proves that you weren't as special and as important to them as you thought."

The Painted Lady Flower Shop was going strong now. I could hardly believe it had been a little over five years since I first opened my doors. I now had a full-time deliverer and both a full- and a part-time worker taking and putting together orders. Since our country had gone to war, business had really picked up. People were buying tons of flowers either before a soldier deployed or upon their return. Balloons were popular even though you could buy them at almost any grocery store these days. I was thankful for my customers. Then there were the weddings and babies being born (not always in that order) that boosted sales. June was booming.

The phone rang. I answered it while continuing to arrange the vase of flowers I was putting together.

"Hi. Yes. I'm looking for the owner," a deep masculine, slightly familiar voice said.

"This is she," I said.

"Yes, ma'am. I was wondering if you might be able to help me," he said with an overexaggerated, Southern drawl.

"I'll certainly do my best," I said.

"Well, you see . . ." And that was when I recognized the voice on the other end, fake-sounding Southern drawl and all. "I was wondering if I might be able to have a personal, private consultation with you." It was Ethan.

I took the cordless phone and hurried into my office, closing the door to keep anyone from overhearing.

"How are you?" I said, lowering my voice just in case.

"Better, now that I've finally gotten to hear your voice. You're a hard woman to catch up with these days," he said.

"Who, me? I don't think so. You must have me confused with someone else."

"No confusion here. I'm talking about you, little butterfly, with your little flittering self."

"Like you've really tried to catch up with me," I said, then just as quickly hated that, after all this time, I was falling for him—going there *yet* again with him.

"I *have* called you there. You weren't in and I didn't leave a message. I even called your house, twice in fact. There was no answer."

I didn't remember seeing where he'd called my house, although there had been a couple of numbers on my home caller ID I didn't recognize. I looked at the name and number coming through now. It wasn't familiar. The name said D. Roberts. *Of course. Denise Roberts, his wife's name.*

"So you have a new number, I see?" I said.

"I'm pleased to say that, in addition to my home number, I now have a cell phone."

"Wow. Must be nice."

"It comes in handy, especially when I travel."

"It says D. Roberts."

"It does? Oh, I didn't know since I don't call myself." He let out a short laugh. "My wife got the phones. I guess she must have put them all in her name or something," he said. "Now you'll need to look out for my calls on this number. They've cracked down on folks using the phones at work, so I don't make personal calls from my work number much anymore, if at all."

I almost said he probably wouldn't be calling me much from his cell phone either. But I was able to monitor my words better and I kept that thought in my head.

"Okay, so how about that private consultation I just asked about?" Ethan said.

"What do you need?"

"I need to see you and tell you that in person."

"Is this business related?"

He started chuckling. "That's according to whose business we're talking about."

"Okay, is this about ordering flowers?" I asked, making it clear I was speaking of *my* business.

"Nope. It's not about ordering any flowers. But if that's the only way I can see you, then fine; I'll be glad to talk about flowers with you."

"Listen, Ethan. You've had a lot going on. I've had a lot. Of course, it's been nothing like you though. We've both had things going on. And honestly—"

"I won't take no for an answer," he said, calm and even. "I need to see you. Alone. So tell me when and where."

I didn't want to stay on the phone arguing; I could never be certain who might be listening. "Okay," I said.

"Okay?" He said it as though he was taken off guard or something. "Okay, then," he said with gusto. I could hear the smile in his voice. "When and where?"

I tried to think of a safe, neutral place. "Our usual," I said. It had been more than a year since I'd last seen him. I wasn't sure how I'd react. Maybe I was finally over him. Maybe I would see him and say hello without butterflies taking flight in my stomach.

"Today?" Ethan said, bringing my attention back to our conversation.

"Yeah, that will work."

"What time?"

"How about six?" I said.

"I need to pick up Jacquetta from gymnastic practice at six. Can we make it either later or earlier?"

"Why did you ask me what time if you have something you have to do already?" I said. "I know: you were hoping I would say no, weren't you?"

He laughed. "You are so funny. I was praying you would say yes. But I admit that I was shocked you didn't make me suffer longer than you did. So I can meet you at two or six-thirty. What's good for you?"

If I chose two o'clock, that meant I wouldn't have to be with him as long. It would give me an out to leave if things got heated. "Two o'clock works for me," I said.

"Then two o'clock it is," he said. "Well, my break is almost over. So I'll see you today at two at the big park."

"Okay," I said.

"Bye," he said.

"Bye," I said but I didn't hang up. I waited on him to hang up first.

"Bye," he said again with a definite grin in his voice.

"Bye," I said, this time singing it. I held the phone a few more seconds. "Well, hang up," I finally said to him.

"Bye," he said one final time, making me that much more eager for two o'clock to hurry up and come.

Chapter 36

*For that which I do I allow not: for what I would,
that do I not; but what I hate, that do I.*
                                        —Romans 7:15

The clouds began to move in a little after Ethan and I hung up the phone. I thought the rain might hold off until later in the evening. Instead, it started raining just as I pulled my car into the park. Ethan was already there in his car waiting. I backed my car in alongside his. As soon as I parked, he jumped out of his car and stood in the pouring rain waiting for me to unlock the passenger-side door. I unlocked it with the master button on my side, and he quickly got in.

"Man, that rain is coming down now," he said, rain rolling down from where it had landed on his head prior to him getting into my car. He wiped the rain off his face and top of his head with his hand.

"I can see that," I said. The rain was pounding the windshield and the roof of my car. I had never just sat in the car and listened to rain hitting it before. It had a real calming beat and effect to it.

"I suppose walking is out today," Ethan said, smiling at me as he stared.

"Suppose so," I said, thinking there was no way I was going to get my hair wet. Not today.

"Oh, come on. Why don't we do it?" Ethan said.

"Do what?"

"Walk in the rain. Wouldn't that be fun?"

"It might be fun," I said, slowly exhaling as I spoke, "if we were little kids. It might be fun if I didn't have to worry about my hair getting drenched."

"Your hair looks beautiful," he said, admiring my hairstyle. He touched one of my curls. "Come on. Let's do it."

I jerked back. "Do what?"

He laughed. "Well, that, too," he said, raising his eyebrows repeatedly as he grinned. I knew what he was talking about. He'd told me how much he wanted me. "I'm absolutely gamed, willing, ready, and able. But I was really still talking about walking in the rain." He began to sing, "Walking in the rain with the one I love."

I playfully hit him, mostly to get his hand out of my hair. Touching my hair as he was singing to me with the rain pounding down on the roof like that was more than I could stand.

He leaned in and kissed me. Just like that. No warning or anything. And I'm not going to lie: I *absolutely* wanted this man, I wanted this man, I *wanted* this man! I was trying to pray, but all I could think to say in my mind was *Lord, help me. Lord,* please *help me.* That man knows he knows how to kiss! *Have mercy!*

Before I knew anything, his hand was touching my thigh. I was wearing a longer-than-normal dress, one that reached down to my ankle, in fact. But somehow, his hand was in a place it had no business being.

I pulled back. "Ethan, we need to stop," I said.

"I want you so badly," he said, his eyes dancing around my face as he spoke.

"That's what you say now. I keep telling you: I know you. If you mess up and do this, you're going to regret it. Then I'll have to hear you beating up on yourself about what you did. You may even turn on me—accuse me of tempting you. I'm not going to let you do this. I'm not going to let *us* go there."

"Please," he said. "I love you so much. I just want to be with you." He kissed me again.

I didn't want to, God knows I didn't, but I found the strength to push him away. One of us had to be strong. "Ethan, you know what could happen if we give in to this."

"Yeah, I know: fireworks," he said. "Ecstasy like I've never experienced before in my life."

That wasn't exactly what I was going for. I had to be strong. "Think of your family," I said. "Do you really want to do something that might mess things up at home? What about God? Do you really want Him seeing you fail?"

"Right now, I don't want to think about anybody except you and me." He touched my face with the back of his hand. "We've denied ourselves for so long. Don't we deserve some happiness? Don't you and I deserve to experience true love and to express our love? Don't we?"

"Honestly? No, we don't. You and I aren't married to each other, Ethan."

"See, there you go again. You're just trying to punish me for us not being together. I told you: I messed up. But I also don't bear all the blame. If you had just waited on me—"

"Look, I don't want to rehash this again. You want to say it was my fault; I still believe it was yours. I loved you so much. You knew how much I loved you. But it wasn't fair for you to think I shouldn't have anybody while you had two, who knows, maybe even three or four girls at the same time."

He fell back against the seat and leaned his head back. "There you go. There you go again." I could hear his frustration. "If you don't want to be with me then just say that. Bringing up all this old history doesn't address where we are right now." He closed his eyes.

He looked so peaceful there with his eyes closed. I wanted to reach out and caress his face. But I stayed strong and stayed with the discussion. "I'm sorry, but I think that it does. It kills me that you and I could have been together . . . legally. If you had just chosen me . . ."

I hated the way that last part came out. It was so weak and pathetic. He hadn't chosen me; he had chosen her. And at least I thought enough of myself not to wait around on him to decide whether or not I was worthy of him to choose me. So I moved on. And in the end, he'd married that same girl he was with when I first met him. He must have loved her a lot. So why was he here with me? Why was he now making me feel all dirty inside? And what if I said yes to us right now? Are we supposed to do this in the car like two teenagers on a date with no other place to go?

"What are you thinking about?" Ethan asked, interrupting my convincing thoughts. He was looking directly at me.

I smiled a quick smile. "Just trying to make the right decision. I know you think you want to do this, but Ethan—"

"You know what? Don't worry about it, all right? You don't want to. And you know I'm not the type to force anybody to do something they don't want to do. If you don't want me, I'm a big boy; I can handle it."

"It's not that I don't want you, Ethan," I said. "I do. And you know that I do so don't even try any of that reverse psychology junk on me. You also know that I don't play games. I detest when grown folks play games. I've been honest with you; all I want is for you to always be honest with me."

"And I honestly would love to be with you right here, right now," he said with a chuckle that broke up the tension a bit.

I laughed, too. "So what were you planning? For us to get into the backseat?"

He looked back there and did a quick smile. "You know there *is* enough room."

I shook my head. "You are crazy."

"Seriously, though: I really wouldn't mind us getting a room at a hotel. But that's a bit difficult for me to do, giving who I am."

"True."

"And besides, we wouldn't have much time today. I have a ton of things to do, one of which is picking up my daughter at six."

"See there. So it looks like this is all working out for the best."

He lowered his head slightly and looked up at me. "Would you go?"

"Go where?"

"To a hotel with me? If I were to get us a room, would you be with me then?"

I smiled and gazed into his eyes. He was serious. "You and I both know what we should do. We both know what's right."

"That wasn't what I asked you," Ethan said, taking my hand and caressing it. "If I got a room, would you be with me, if only for one night?" He smiled. I knew he was thinking about the song Luther Vandross sang with those exact words: *If only for one night.*

His cell phone starting playing a tune; he continued to hold my hand. "You'd better get that," I said. "It might be important."

He let go of my hand, looked at the incoming number, and answered the phone. It was his wife. I could hear her voice. "Where you at?" she said.

"What do you need?" Ethan said.

"You weren't at home when I called there so I was wondering where you were," she said.

"I'm on my way home," he said, then glanced over at me. I bowed my head and said a prayer of thanks to the Lord. I thanked Him for stopping what almost happened here. I thanked Him for reminding me with this phone call exactly where I stood on the totem pole of Ethan's life.

Ethan clicked off from his wife and turned back to me.

"You need to go," I said with a stern yet calm voice.

"But you didn't answer my question."

"Your wife is waiting on you. You need to go home to your wife."

He leaned over to kiss me; I turned away. He took my hand and kissed it. "I love you, little butterfly. I really do."

I turned and looked at him. "I know," I said. "I know." I took my hand from his. "Now go." I forced a smile so he wouldn't have to worry about me at this point.

He nodded, opened the door, and hurried back to his car. Once again, he was man enough to wait on me to pull off first. He then followed behind me until it was time for us to have to part ways.

Chapter 37

*I find then a law, that, when I would do good, evil is
present with me.*

—Romans 7:21

After that, Ethan made sure he called me on a more regular basis. It was always easier (and safer) for him to call me, instead of me calling him. We argued about that from time to time. If I hadn't heard from him in a couple of weeks when he called, I would make some smart remark about it. He would then come back with how I never called him.

"I'm trying to protect you," I said. "I would never do anything to hurt you."

"I know," he said. "But you make me wonder if you love me as much as I love you. It looks like I'm the one running after you. Maybe you don't care about me as much as I care about you."

"I don't care what it looks like. I'm the one who's waiting around, just in case you call," I said, admitting a real truth. "Sure, I could call you. But what if I call and you're with your wife? What do you say when she asks you who was that on the phone? Or worse: what if I call and she happens to answer your cell phone?"

"That's true. But it would be nice to know that you care about me as much as I care about you. That's all I'm saying. Do you have any idea how hard it is for a man to let a woman know he's vulnerable?" Ethan said.

"That's the problem with you men. If you'd quit trying to strategize on how to win and just be honest and forthright, women would have an easier time with you," I said.

"If you women wouldn't take what we give that's vulnerable about us—like how much we really love, just like and as hard as y'all do; it's just we don't happen to show it in the same way that y'all do—then use it against us, more men might open up. But as soon as you women learn we really care about you, you start dogging us out."

"We do not." I almost laughed. He *was* slightly telling the truth. Some women did do that and I knew *that* for a fact.

"Yes . . . you . . . do. Look at you even. You know I'm head-over-heels, crazy about you. So what do you do? You dress all pretty and sexy—"

"I do not," I said, then I started giggling like a thirteen-year-old girl.

"Ah, you know you do. You be wearing those cute little outfits, knowing that you're killing a brother who can't have you because you've already let him know he's not going to be able to get with that. That's torture and you know it. It's like seeing somebody starving and eating a meal right smack-dab in front of them without even letting them taste it. You can look at it. You can have a whiff of it. But you won't be getting any of it."

"You need to stop!" I said with laughter peppered throughout my words.

He was laughing, too. "Then you have *the nerve* to act like I'm not showing you enough love, so you're going to punish me."

"Ethan, stop saying stuff like that. You know none of that's true." I tried to be serious after having laughed.

"Well, I'm going to show you just how much I care. I'm going to still call you, even though you're not doing one thing to indicate you care about me."

"I love you, you hear?" I was stone-cold serious.

"I hear you. But talk is cheap. Anybody can say the words. Ask any man trying to get in some woman's pants. He'll say those words like they're nothing."

"So are you confessing your strategy to me? Telling me you love me because your ultimate goal is to get me into bed?"

"Woman, please!" he said, quickly and forcefully dismissing my statement. "I tell you that because it's true and you and I promised not to play games with each other. I'm going to love you forever. That's what I've concluded. Because if I could walk away from you, believe me I would do it. But for some reason, I can't. I can't walk away. Not for good, no matter how hard or how many times I try. And I *have* tried."

"Same here," I said, being honest.

"Which one? Love me forever or walk away?"

"What you said," I said, getting back into a teasing mode again.

"What did I say? Because you act like you don't know what I say," Ethan said.

I released a breath. "I'm going to love you forever," I said, repeating what he'd said. "Because if I could walk away from you, believe me, I would have done it when you walked in the shop that day. In fact, I would have run away."

"Oh, so you would have done it? Is that why you act like you do sometimes? You're trying to make *me* go away for good?"

"You're the one who keeps bouncing around like a rubber ball. One day you want to see me; the next day you're saying we need to walk away from this situation. One period you want to talk every single day; the next period I hardly ever hear from you. You can go for weeks without calling me. There was even that time it was months. Then you'll just show up out of the blue and want to act like nothing's happened. We go on as though it hasn't been that long since we last talked. It's confusing, at least for me."

"But you're still hanging in there with me," Ethan said.

I smiled. He always spoke truth to the situation, even if it might turn out to be something that—in the end—hurt my feelings. "Yes. I'm still hanging in there with you."

He had to get off the phone, so we hung up. I stared at the phone, and all I could think was: *What on earth am I doing? Really? Will somebody please tell me . . .* what *am* I *doing?!*

Chapter 38

And every man went unto his own house.

—John 7:53

A lot happened in both my and Ethan's worlds over the next four years. Some folks were telling me what was going on with me and Zeke was the devil being the devil and being on his job. My pastor even taught on that subject for several weeks during Bible study. Pastor Hutchings said the devil was messing with good folks, Christian folks because we were a threat to him and his work. "If the devil ain't messing with you, you must not be doing enough for the Kingdom of God," he'd said.

Of course, Pastor Hutchings was preaching on this because he knew folks were hot to get rid of him. And the folks who were after him weren't the devil, either. They were church members, fed up with all the mess and antics that seemed to always follow him. The latest hot mess was him making up conferences he claimed he was attending, getting extra funds from the church, when in actuality, he was covering for his latest affair with his newly hired, high-maintenance secretary, half his fifty-eight-year-old age.

It is true: some problems can be attributed to the devil. But I believe people give much too much credit to the devil. Sometimes it's things we do that get us in situations. Sometimes things just happen. The Bible says that it rains on the just and the unjust. Many times the good and the bad that happen in our lives are merely part of the ebb and flow of life. In this life, we're going to have our share of troubles. What I found that takes many folks out and makes it hard is when things come one after the other and you don't seem to get a chance to catch your breath.

Zeke happened to be home when I got there, and it just happened to be a day through the week. Zeke hadn't been home like this since the girls were in school when he would at least be there for a little while before taking off. Now that all of our girls were grown and out of the house, he didn't bother being home when I got there (unless there was nothing left over to eat or he wanted me to cook him something special). The only other time was when he's sick, which hadn't happened often.

"Hi, baby," he said, greeting me as soon as I stepped inside the kitchen.

"Hi," I said.

"Can I get something for you?" He looked at me. "Is there anything in the car you need me to get out for you? Packages . . . groceries . . ."

"No," I said, looking around wondering whether I had interrupted something he was trying to hide. "I'm good. So what are you doing home?"

"I live here," he said almost as though he was insulted.

"Is that right?" I walked to the den and sat down; he followed me. "I would never know that."

"I bought some Chinese food for dinner. Would you like me to fix you some?"

I really became suspicious then. I stood up.

Zeke stood up. "Where are you going? I'll bring a plate in here to you."

"Actually, I was going upstairs to change."

"Upstairs," he said, then glanced toward the staircase.

"You look fine the way you are," he said.

"Is there some reason you don't want me going to my room?" I asked, staring him in his face now.

"No. I just wanted us to talk. You know, we haven't done a lot of that lately. Talk, that is."

"And whose fault is that?" I asked.

"It's mine. It's all my fault."

Okay, now I was *really* suspicious. "Is someone in our bedroom?" I asked him point blank as I shoved my hand on my hip.

He jerked back and frowned. "Someone in our bedroom?" He chuckled. "Woman, please! I'm not crazy now. You know I wouldn't have another woman in our bedroom."

"Okay, what about a man?" I said.

"Oh, you're really tripping now," he said.

"Then why are you trying to keep me down here? And why would you happen to have bought dinner? What's going on, Zeke?"

He grabbed my arm. "Nothing is going on. I bought dinner for us. I wanted us to sit and talk. You know, the way we used to."

"You mean the way we used to before we got married? Because we sure haven't done much talking since then."

Zeke nodded. "You're right. You're right. And you know what: I'm going to do better. Now come on back and sit down." He pulled me back over to the couch and gently led me to sit down. "You sit right here and I'm going to go get our food."

I nodded. And as soon as he left the room, I got up and went upstairs. I looked in the bedroom. Everything appeared normal; nothing was out of place or in there that shouldn't be. I checked our closet and then the bathroom. Both were fine as well.

Since I was upstairs, I decided to change into one of the caftans Zanetta had sent me from one of her overseas excursions. Zanetta was scheduled to come home to visit us in two months during her leave time. I couldn't wait to see her; it had been a year since her last deployment.

"Satisfied?" Zeke said when I came back down to the den.

"Oh, yes," I said. "I love this purple one. Zanetta knows how much I love purple—"

"I'm not talking about that muumuu thing you have on. I'm

talking about the fact that there was no one in the house." Zeke then put some pepper steak and rice into his mouth and began to chew.

"I didn't go looking for anyone," I lied. "I went to change and I did that. I told you, Zeke: I'm not going to be chasing behind you to see if you're fooling around on me. I'm not."

"But you still looked when you went upstairs." He shoved another forkful of food into his mouth and looked up at me as he chewed.

I sat down. "Yes, I did look. But it's because it's my house. And you won't be bringing anyone in here, defiling my bed with anyone—man or woman."

He frowned, stopped chewing, and swallowed hard. "You really think I would be with a man? You really believe something like that about me?"

"Zeke, I'm going to tell you: I hope you wouldn't, but I don't put anything past anybody these days."

"Well, trust me on this: you don't have to worry about me and another dude. I'm strictly a ladies' man." He must have thought about how that sounded because he quickly added, "And you're the only lady for me."

"Humph," I said. "That you're a ladies' man, I might believe completely. Me being the only lady . . . I'm not so sure."

He patted the place next to him. "Come over here and eat. The food is getting cold."

I got up and went and sat down next to him, saying grace after I fixed me something to eat. Lifting up a forkful of steak, a piece of pepper, and a bit of onion, I suddenly stopped and stared at it.

Zeke started laughing. "It's okay," he said, then took my wrist and guided the food resting on my fork to his mouth. He put it in his mouth and began to chew. "It's not poison. You're really tripping now."

"I was going to eat it," I said, spearing another helping. "It's just, I'm wondering what's going on with you."

"Can't a man treat his wife to dinner? You're always saying I never do that. Well, I'm doing it right now."

I nodded and speared another pepper and steak. "This is good."

"Yeah, I absolutely love their food." He then must have thought about what had just slipped out of his mouth. "I go there when there's nothing here at home to eat. That's how I know about them."

"Yeah, I bet," I said, not falling for it and wanting him to know I wasn't falling for it.

We chatted for about fifteen minutes. It was really nice talking to Zeke like that. We talked about Zanetta coming home and how at the rate she was going (minus that one time she seemed to have found someone and mentioned the word "marriage") she would likely never settle down and have a family.

Zion was making plans to come home along with Malik and their two children around the time Zanetta would be here. Zion was the type that never wanted anyone to know when she was having financial challenges, but I sensed that might be the case. At first Zion said she was most likely coming by herself. Then she started saying she might bring the children. Then Malik might be coming with them after all. If Zion was having financial difficulties, she would be trying to figure out how all of them could get here, in spite of the challenge.

Zynique and Aiden had gotten serious to the point where they were talking marriage. She was running that dance studio like a pro who'd been doing it all of her life. I guess in a way, maybe she had. Madame Perry had poured everything she had and knew into Zynique. Now Zynique was plowing full speed ahead.

Madame Perry's son might have gotten all of her fishes (which I hear was a pretty nice chunk of change), but Zynique ended up with the pond. Meaning: the son was given the fish (money) and Zynqiue ended up with the pond (where a lot of those fishes came from). Madame Perry's son didn't contest any of her final desires. That just might have been because she'd put something in place that if he did, he'd lose what she'd willed to him.

Zeke and I touched on a little of that. I was relaxed now and enjoying myself.

"Listen," Zeke said, setting his plate on the coffee table. "Now that we're talking about family and all, my sister called today."

My antennae immediately went up: the first red flag.

"Which sister?" I asked.

"My baby sister . . . Yvonne."

That was the second red flag.

"What does she want? Or should I say, how much does she want?"

He smiled and nodded. "I know; usually she calls when she needs to borrow some money. But believe it or not; she doesn't want to borrow money this time."

"Okay. So what *does* she want then?"

"You know what's been going on with my mother," Zeke said.

His mother lived in Jacksonville, Florida. She'd packed up all of her belongings and moved there some fifteen years ago after Yvonne begged her to come and help out with her four children when they were young. Two years ago, Zeke's mother was diagnosed with Alzheimer's. Now here was Yvonne calling Zeke.

"Yes, I know," I said.

"Well, Yvonne wants us to let Mama come and live with us," Zeke said, turning squarely to me now.

"She wants your mother to come here and live with us?"

"Yes."

"And what about your other three sisters?"

"What about them?" Zeke said with a frown as though he wasn't following me or better yet: didn't like where I was headed with my questions.

"Why didn't Yvonne call any of the other three sisters?"

"I don't know. I didn't ask her," Zeke said.

"Well, maybe you need to call Yvonne back and ask her."

"Why?"

"Because, Zeke: Your mother has four daughters."

"And my mother also has one son—me. And if she needs somewhere to live, then why *not* call me?"

"You want to know why not call you?" I stood up and looked down at him. "Do you really want to know why not you? You're asking *me* why not *you?*"

He stood up. I know it was because he didn't like me towering over him. That's how Zeke is: he always wants to feel like he's dominant and the one in control. "Yeah, I'm asking *you* why not *me?*"

"Okay, if you want to go there; we can go there."

"See, right there," Zeke said as he pointed down at me. "That right there is why I can't stand talking to you."

"Why, because you thought you were going to butter me up and then lay at my feet what's going on with your family?" I said.

"My mother needs somewhere to stay. We have this house here with plenty of room for her. There's nobody here but me and you. You're supposed to be such a great Christian. Oh yeah, you can see about other folks' mothers. You can help feed the homeless. But when it comes to my mother, you want to start some drama," Zeke said, scratching his head.

"Zeke, this is nothing against your mother personally. But let's be real and fair now. Your mother hardly ever did anything for our children. She never kept them overnight. She wouldn't pick them up when I needed help. In fact, she's hardly ever stepped foot in our house the whole time we've been married. And now your little sister is concluding that she doesn't want to be bothered—"

"Yvonne never said she didn't want to be bothered."

I nodded my head nippily several times. "She wants us to take your mother in now, is that right?"

"Yes."

"Well, then she's saying she doesn't want to be bothered," I said. "Your mother gave up everything to be there for your sister so your sister wouldn't have to be inconvenienced. Your sister has practically had a live-in babysitter and maid with your mother being down there. Zeke, don't front me: you know I'm telling the truth."

"Yeah . . . well . . . so," Zeke said. "What's that got to do with where we are now? My mother needs somewhere to stay. She needs someone to take care of her. We have a place here. You and I can take my mother in and take care of her."

"And therein lies my biggest problem with all of this," I said, folding my arms. "This 'you and I' will quickly become just me. I'll be the one taking care of your mother while you'll still be out in the streets like always."

"I said I'll help and I will."

"Zeke, you *say* a lot of things. But when it's time to *do*, you're MIA. I have enough on my plate right now. I can't be doing this all by myself."

"I told you: I'll help you."

I shook my head. "Nope. I'm not going to do it. You're not going to put this on me. You're not. Your mother has taken care of them; you would think one of them . . . somebody . . . would step up and return the favor now that she needs them."

"Oh, so you're going to punish my mother because she didn't do anything for you and our children? Is this what this is all about?"

"No, Zeke! No!" I stepped up to him. "It is *you* not getting it. You don't get it!" I shook my head. "I have allowed you to do me the way you have in the past. Well, it stops here and now." I pointed my finger at the floor.

"Just because it's my mama. Fine! Fine! I will call my other sisters and see if one of them will take her in since you don't want her here."

"It's not that I don't want her here, Zeke. You always try to make me out to be the bad guy. It's just I know I'll be here doing all of this on my own, just like always. And you'll be at a casino, the horse and dog track . . . somewhere gambling, hanging out with your buddies, or whatever you do that I don't have a clue about."

He went and snatched up the phone's receiver. "I'll call Carolyn and ask her if Mama can stay with her." I stood there as he glared at me. "What's Carolyn's number?" he finally said after a few seconds.

I couldn't do anything but laugh. He didn't even know his own sister's number. Yet I'm the one who's always wrong.

Chapter 39

Jesus went unto the mount of Olives.

—John 8:1

Ｎone of the other sisters would agree to take their mother in. Sure, they each had what they considered a valid reason for not being able to. Carolyn was dealing with health issues of her own (although she wouldn't tell any of us what those issues were). Jestina was having major marital problems and believed her mother's presence would most certainly push her marriage over the cliff and into the awaiting ravine. The only sister (as far as I was concerned) who had a valid reason for not taking in their mother was Charlene, the third sister, who was essentially homeless but now blessed to be in a halfway house. She'd gotten her life together after throwing most of it away on decades of first alcohol, then crack. Charlene really wanted to do this for her mother; she just wasn't in a position, homewise, to do so.

So me with my always-looking-for-a-solution self, suggested that Charlene move in with their mother in Jacksonville and take care of her there. Frankly, I thought it was a win-win all the way around. Charlene would now have a place to call home, their mother would be able to stay in her own house, and none of the sisters would have to disrupt their lives.

That idea was shot down quicker than an inbound missile trying to make its way into the United States from a hostile country. The other sisters didn't trust Charlene. They all said they were proud of the progress she'd made in rehab, but they believed the temptation of being around all of their mother's "stuff" would be too much for Charlene to overcome.

"She'll just backslide if we put this much temptation at her hand. Then we'll end up with even more problems than just taking care of Mama," Carolyn said while she, Zeke, Jestina, and I were all on a conference call.

I countered by pointing out that Yvonne could still take care of their mother's business and financial affairs just as she was doing much of it now and to just allow Charlene to move in to take care of her. They weren't going for any of it. Of course, I would later learn that Carolyn and Jestina were already trying to take away the power Yvonne had over their mother's affairs because they didn't trust or like what Yvonne was doing either.

In the end, Zeke's mother ended up at our house. I was able to get them to hold off until after Zanetta came home for her visit along with Zion and her entire family. I was glad about that because after Zeke's mother arrived, I was wide open, working from sunup to sunup. There really was no true break for me.

I still ran the flower shop. In the beginning, I had to take Zeke's mother in with me. But that quickly became a problem as the disease worsened rapidly. She didn't like living at our house. She kept saying that she wanted to go home, but home wasn't our house. I suspect home wasn't even her house in Jacksonville. Before she arrived, I'd gone to classes on dealing with Alzheimer's from a caregiver's point of view. It had been helpful in preparing me for what to expect. They expressed to us that as caregivers, we needed to watch our subjects like a hawk. They were good at wandering away, we were informed, most times trying to go home—home usually being a place that no longer exists in real life, but rather in time and in their minds.

I stopped Zeke as he was on his way out the door, not fifteen minutes after I stepped foot inside the house from the shop and ten minutes after the sitter left for the day. "Zeke, I thought you said you were going to help me."

"I was here for a minute," he said. "Now, I've got to get out of here."

"But you were here with the sitter who was here doing all of the work. The sitter just left. You know she leaves as soon as I get here. I need your help when I'm here, Zeke." I was almost pleading now.

"Listen," he said, looking deeply into my eyes. "I can't take seeing my mother like this. It's hard for me to be around her this way. That's not my mother in there." He pointed toward the bedroom we'd created for her on the main level out of our sunroom. "That woman in there actually cusses. My mother never cussed. Never. That woman calls me names. My mother always thought I was 'the stuff.' "

"She doesn't know what she's doing or saying," I said.

"Still, I can't be around her. I can't stay here with her like this."

"This is just what I told you would happen. You're leaving this all on me."

"Look, I'm sorry. I know I promised I'd help you if we did this. But you're a strong woman. You can handle Mama. As a matter of fact, Mama likes you. Me? She acts like she doesn't even know who I am."

"It's not her, Zeke. It's the disease. Your mother can't help it."

"I know that. I get that. But I can't stay here and watch it." He leaned down and kissed me on the cheek, then headed out the door.

"Hey, you," Zeke's mother said to me when she came into the den where I was left standing. "I'm hungry. When is somebody going to fix me something to eat?"

"Hi, Mama Olivia," I said.

"I don't know why you insists on calling me somebody's mama. I told you I don't have any kids. And I prefer being called Olive. Olivia is an old person's name. I don't know why anyone would name somebody an old name like that."

"Okay, Olive."

"So who's going to fix me something to eat? That sorry little yellow man that was here ain't good for nothing. I don't even know why you bother letting him in your house. I would put his sorry tail out so *quick* it would make his head spin. The door would hit him before he cleared it good."

"That's Zeke, Olive. Zeke is your son."

"Humph! That ain't no son of mine. I wouldn't have a child as no good and as sorry as that one. Whenever I do have a son, you'd better believe I'm going to teach him how to treat a woman. He won't be nothing like that one that was here earlier." She sat down. "So when are you going to take me home? I don't like being here. I want to go home." She started to cry.

I carefully sat down next to her and hugged her. "You can't go home. You have to stay here with me. I'm going to take care of you, okay?"

"Don't nobody want me," she said, crying even more now. "Don't nobody want me! That's why I'm here." She tilted her head. "Why don't nobody want me?"

"I want you," I said, hugging her some more. "And I'm going to go fix you something to eat, all right?"

She nodded. "You're a good person," she said. "You're a really good person. You have a good heart. I know God is going to bless you, too. But you really need to get rid of that no-good man you have hanging around here. Can't you see? He doesn't care about you. We women know these things. That man doesn't think about anybody but himself. He's selfish and self-centered, do you hear me? He don't care *nothing* about you."

"I hear you, Olive. But don't you worry about me, all right?" I stood up. "Would you like me to turn on the television for you while I fix you something to eat?"

She nodded.

"Okay. Now, I need you to be good while I'm in the kitchen. Don't try going out of the front door. All right?"

"I can't get out no way," she said. "Y'all have me locked up in this place. I don't know what I did to make you lock me in here like this." She looked at me with a primped mouth now.

"We have the doors locked for your safety. You keep trying to leave," I said.

"That's because I want to go home." She looked into my eyes, softer now. "You ever been someplace that was real nice, but no matter how nice the place was, it just wasn't home?"

I smiled and nodded. "Yeah, I know how that feels. It's just you can't leave me. I need you to stay here with me." I swallowed hard. "I need you, okay?"

"You're a nice lady; a good person. They don't want me and that's why I can't go home. Nobody wants me. Okay. I'll stay here. You don't have to worry about me trying to leave. If they don't want me, then they don't want me. It's their loss, right?"

"Right." I hugged her again, then went into the kitchen to fix a few of the things I knew she'd eat since she refused to eat a lot of things I cooked for her. My ultimate goal was always to get her to eat. Otherwise, she'd end up in the hospital with a feeding tube. And I didn't want that.

I didn't want that at all.

Chapter 40

And early in the morning he came again into the
temple, and all the people came unto him; and he
sat down, and taught them.

—John 8:2

E than called me at the shop.
   "Can you get away for a few minutes?" he said.
   "What's up?"
   "I need to talk. I'm about to go stone out of my mind. Can
you meet me?"
   I thought about what I had to do at the shop. It was a good
time. "Sure."
   "The usual spot?"
   "That will work," I said. I told my workers I would be back
shortly and headed for the park.
   Ethan wasn't there when I arrived. I waited fifteen minutes
before I started thinking he might have called the shop to tell
me things had changed and I was already gone. This was when
I started seriously thinking again that I needed a cell phone, especially now that Olivia was living with us. If anyone needed to
reach me during times when I was out of pocket like this,
they'd be out of luck. I decided to check into the various cell
phone companies and get a phone before another week went
by. Zeke needed a phone as well, since I never knew when I
might need to find him.
   Ethan pulled into the space next to me. He smiled through
his window, then hurriedly got out of his car, jumping into
mine.

"Hi there," he said with a huge grin on his face.

"Hi."

"Thank you *so much* for coming."

"It's fine. It's not a problem."

"I'm just about to lose it," he said. "It seems like it's just been one thing right after another."

"Is it your wife? Is she sick again?"

"No, it's my mother this time." He started wiping at his eyes. "I'm sorry. I'm sorry. But my mother is just such a special woman and now—"

I touched his hand. He grabbed my hand and squeezed it. "My mother is diabetic. She was visiting out of town with one of my sisters last week. While there, she got sick. They rushed her to the hospital. Her blood is not circulating in her leg the way it should. They say there's a clot. We finally got her back home to a hospital here." He squeezed my hand again. "They want to amputate her right leg." He wiped his eyes some more.

"Ah, Ethan, I'm sorry."

He lowered his head. "I know. I know, folks have done it and it's okay." He raised his head back up. "But my mother is eighty."

"So what does your mother say about all of this?"

"She's okay with it. She says if it'll save her life, she can lose a leg. My mother is a trouper. Her children are the ones seemingly falling apart about it."

"Well, if she's okay with it, then half of the battle is won."

He squeezed my hand again. "I know. I just needed to see you today. I needed to look in your face." He looked at me, smiled, then lifted my hand to his mouth and placed a kiss on it.

"It looks like everybody is dealing with something," I said, looking for something to take my mind away from the kiss on my hand. "Zeke's mother is staying with us." Ethan and I hadn't spoken much since Zeke's mother had come.

He put my hand back down but continued to hold it. "Yeah, you told me the last time we talked."

"She's getting worse. I'm telling you: Alzheimer's is no joke."

"I'm sure. My mother is dealing with a little bit of dementia. I know this memory stuff can be something else."

"So is your mother set to have the surgery?" I asked.

"Yeah. She's having it tomorrow. I just needed to see you . . . to talk to you . . . face to face, before tomorrow."

"You know that I'm here for you. I know it's hard when things are going on."

"You're always here for me. And I thank you for that. Just being able to talk to someone makes it so much better to deal with." He let out a deep sigh. "But what about you? How are things going with you and your mother-in-law?"

"I'm pretty much doing everything after the day sitter leaves."

"Your husband's not helping you?"

"Nope. He leaves as soon as I walk in the door. It's just like it was before his mother came. Only now, I'm taking care of his mother while he's out doing who knows what."

"Why don't you make him stop?"

"And just how am I supposed to do that?" I tilted my head slightly to the side.

"Tell him he's not going anywhere. That he's going to stay there with you?"

"You tried that with your wife," I said. "How did that work out for you?"

"Touché," he said. "But my situation is different from yours. I can't physically make my wife stay home if she doesn't want to. You can't make grown folks do what they don't want to do."

"That's my point exactly. I could whine about him being gone all the time, and let's say he decides to stay home because of my whining. He'll just make me miserable because he doesn't want to be there. I want him to *want* to be there with me." I looked at Ethan and wrinkled my nose a little. "Does that make sense?"

"It makes perfect sense to me. And I can tell you: if you were my wife, I wouldn't want to be away from you any more than I had to be. You would get tired of looking in my face and probably be begging me to go somewhere and leave you alone."

I laughed. "Sure," I said, letting him know that I was skeptical of his statement.

"I'm serious. I would love to be with you. I hate right now that I only get to see you on occasion. If you were my wife . . ."

"Okay, Ethan." I put my hand up to let him know I didn't want to go there.

"So your husband is not helping with his mother?" he said, politely getting back more to our original conversation.

"Nope," I said. "He comes home from work, takes a shower, puts on his fancy clothes, eats something. Right about that time, I come home. And he exits, stage right."

"And this is *his* mother?"

"Yep."

"But you're doing all the work while he's still out there living it up?"

"Oh, but you don't understand," I said. "He can't bear to see his mother this way. He can't stay there with her like she is now. That's not the mother he grew up knowing," I said, mocking Zeke.

"Wow. That is so sad. It's his mother and you're left doing all of the work." Ethan angled his body more toward me. "Let's go get on the swing."

I grinned as I pulled my head back. "What?"

"Let's go get on the swing over there." He nodded toward the playground. It was early morning on a school day. No one was at the park except for the two of us.

I nodded. "Okay." We got out of the car and walked to the swings. I sat in one while he stood there. "You're not going to swing?"

He went and stood behind me. "I'm going to push you," he said and began to gently push me.

"You're going to have to push a whole lot harder than that," I said, pumping my legs to help get me going.

He pushed me some more, stepping back as I began to go higher. Not one minute into my swing, I felt the swing when it hit him. I turned around as I was still swinging. "Oh, no!" I said before being able to stop. I jumped off, stepped around to him, and watched him holding his chin. "Did I hurt you?" I asked, trying to see what damage had been done. "Let me see."

He grinned as he held his chin. "It's not too bad. And it wasn't your fault. I should have been paying better attention to what I was doing instead of watching your behind."

I playfully hit at him. "You need to quit."

He laughed. "I'm serious. I guess God just smacked me for looking at your rear end. God was saying, 'Stop that, boy.' Pow! Right in the chin."

"You are so crazy," I said.

"Okay." He rubbed his chin some more. "Get back on the swing so I can push you again."

"I don't know. I feel bad that you got hurt."

"Will you sit down already," Ethan said in an authoritative voice. I obliged. He began to push me again, this time stepping back far enough not to get whacked.

When we finished, Ethan and I prayed together. We both had a lot on our plates. And now, more than ever, we needed the Lord along with His peace that surpasses all understanding.

Chapter 41

And of some have compassion, making a difference.
—Jude 22

Following the last time we saw each other at the park, Ethan and I talked by way of the telephone at least once a week, encouraging the other. I soon acquired a cell phone, which I later learned was a huge mistake. Now everybody felt it their duty to hunt me down and find me whenever I wasn't at home or at the flower shop. I was exceeding my allotted minutes and, after two months of doing that, I was forced to upgrade to a more expensive plan with more allocated minutes.

Then there was Zeke. It was only after I got us each a phone and I presented him with his that I learned the grand news: he already had a cell phone.

"When did you get one?" I asked with obvious confusion on my face.

"About a year ago," he said as though it wasn't a big deal.

"A year ago? So who is paying the bill?"

"I pay it," he said as though that was a stupid question for me to even ask.

Well, it was a huge shock to me. "You pay a bill? You mean that you *physically* pay a bill? Then why won't you *physically* pay any of these other bills that come streaming into this house, including the new ones associated with your mother? Bills, by the way, that take money out of *our* pockets because your sisters think they're entitled to your mother's check and the money from the selling of her house."

I didn't even want to get started again on the subject of his sisters and how they were keeping his mother's Social Security checks and hadn't shared any of the proceeds received from the sale of her house with either Zeke, or Charlene for that matter, even though Zeke and I were bearing the total responsibility of taking care of their mother. I was going to fight them on the Social Security check. (I'd worked for the Social Security Administration so I was more than knowledgeable about things like this.) Zeke didn't want me doing that, at least not at this time. But back to him physically paying a cell phone bill and why he couldn't physically pay any other bills in this house.

"Because I give you the money for the bills and you pay them," he said.

"I get that. But then why not give me your cell phone bill and the money for it and let me pay it like you *let* me pay all of the other bills?"

"Why do you always have to make a big deal about everything?" he said with an air of frustration.

"I'm not. I just didn't know you had a cell phone, that's all. And I'm left to wonder why you felt you should keep something like having a cell phone a secret. I mean, lots of folks have cell phones. Zynique has had one for years now."

Zeke tried to act like he was busy straightening the magazines on the coffee table. "It wasn't a secret. Not *really.*"

"It was a secret to me. I'm also curious why you felt you needed a cell phone. Your job doesn't require you to have one. You didn't think it important to give me the number, so it couldn't have been for my benefit." I paused a second. "Who all has the number to even call you?"

He looked up at me and stared like an animal seconds away from being hit by a speeding car. "You mean in our family?"

"In our family or otherwise."

He quickly looked back down. "Nobody."

I can always tell when he's lying.

"Okay," I said, standing now with my hand on my hip. "So

you're telling *me* that you have a cell phone and no one knows your number? A phone you've had for what? About a year now?"

"A year . . . a year and a half. But yeah, I'm telling you I have a cell phone and, pretty much, no one has the number, unless they got it off their caller ID when I called."

"So you just have the phone for . . . what reason now?" I said, my neck jutting out slightly.

"Why do I have to go through the third degree with you about everything?" He sighed. "I have a phone. It's available in case of an emergency. I use it to call out if I need to. You know phone booths are becoming obsolete. What if I break down? I need a phone so I can call somebody."

"And what about me?" I said. "What about the fact that your mother has been here all this time and you've never let me know I could get in touch with you in case I had an emergency, in case *I* needed you. You know, during those times when you leave because you 'can't take it,' and I'm here all by myself with *your* mother."

"I hardly turn the phone on anyway, so it wouldn't have helped you to have the number. I told you: I got it for emergencies."

"And what about if I was to break down? I guess I was just out of luck, huh? It doesn't seem like you cared about *me* breaking down or me being out there without a way to contact anyone if I needed help," I said.

"You could have gotten a phone anytime you wanted, so don't try and guilt-trip me on that one." Zeke stood up.

"Go get your phone bill and let me see it," I said.

"Do what?"

"Go get your cell phone bill and let me see it."

He chuckled. "Now you're *really* tripping. I don't have my bills; I throw them away after I pay them."

I rubbed my forehead. He was starting to give me a headache. I turned and began walking away.

"Where are you going?" he said. "I told you I throw the bills away."

I turned back around. "Zeke, honestly I really don't care

about your cell phone bill. If you want to keep secrets, go ahead and keep them. I've told you and I meant it: I'm not running behind you. I'm just not going to do it."

"Then where are you going?"

"To check on your mother," I said. "She's been sleeping a lot lately. I'm going to make sure she's all right." I turned back and went to his mother's room.

Olivia was resting fine, but her excessive sleeping was a sign that her health was swiftly and vastly deteriorating.

That was back in June. On December fourteenth, Olivia died. There was insurance money that should have been used for her funeral and burial. But true to form, Carolyn (the daughter named on Olivia's insurance policy) didn't let anyone know that. It was left to me to figure out how to take care of the funeral and burial costs. Olivia's funeral became the first order of business our newly installed, thirty-three-year-old pastor, Terrell Godbee, performed. He did a *marvelous* job.

After everything was over, Zeke learned about the insurance money when he blew up at Carolyn about us having to pay for everything, while they dictated their funeral desires but not one contributed a dime. It was only then that Carolyn decided to reimburse us *half* the money we had incurred, using *some* of the insurance money.

The next year, on April fifteenth, Ethan called. I was surprised when he called me at my home.

"My mother passed away today," Ethan said, his voice cracking as he spoke.

"Oh, Ethan, I'm sorry."

"We knew it was coming," he said. "After the leg amputation, she was doing quite well. Mama always had such a beautiful attitude when it came to life and living life to its fullest. She was doing what she needed to do to get better. Then she contracted pneumonia; fluid built up in her lungs. The doctor was talking about some other things going on inside of her. They wanted to do more surgery. Mama told me she didn't want them cutting on her anymore. She said she was tired; that she was ready to go home. A few days ago, I went to see her and we were alone. She told me she could see the door, but she didn't know how to open it. She asked me to help her open the door." I could tell he was crying now. It was breaking my heart.

"Oh, Ethan, I am *so* sorry." I tried to keep from crying, but I couldn't hold back my own tears. "That's powerful."

"I told her to go on through the door if she wanted to. So today, she went through the door. She went home and now she's with the Lord."

"I don't know what to say," I said. "That is really something. Are you okay?"

"Oh yeah; I'm okay. I just wanted to tell you. When she died, all I wanted to do was talk to you. You were the first person on my mind."

"Well, I'm glad you called. I'll be praying for you and your family."

"Thank you," he said.

"Is it okay if I send a card of condolence to the family? I don't want to do anything that would make you feel uncomfortable."

"Sure. That's fine. You can send a card." He then gave me his home address.

"I hope you know that you made a difference in your mother's life. I want you to know that you did," I said.

"Yeah. I know." His voice cracked. "And I hope you know how much of a difference you made in your mother-in-law's life," he said.

I nodded even though he couldn't see me. "Thanks for that," I said. "You know, you're the only one who has said that to me."

When I hung up, I cried.

Chapter 42

*For I would that ye knew what great conflict I have
for you, and for them at Laodicea, and for as many
as have not seen my face in the flesh.*

—Colossians 2:1

It had been ten years since Ethan first called my flower shop
that fateful day in August that had reconnected us to each
other again. Surprisingly, he called the shop on the exact same
date he'd phoned ten years earlier.

"Happy Anniversary," he said.

I was shocked that he'd remembered and even more
shocked that he was calling to say happy anniversary. Zeke
barely ever remembered our wedding anniversary, my birthday,
or his children's birthdays, and here this man was remember-
ing the first day he'd called my shop some ten years ago.

"Thank you," I said with a grin that I'm sure he detected
through the phone.

I *so* needed this right now. I'd been feeling a bit bummed out
and, quite frankly, unloved. This past weekend I'd been hon-
ored at a small business convention in Orlando, Florida, for my
company and I'd asked Zeke to come with me. Zeke never
wants to go anywhere with me. But I thought because I was
being recognized for my dedication and hard work that he'd
surely go to this. Well, I was *surely* wrong. He refused to go no
matter how many times or ways I asked. I even told him he and
I could have a mini vacation while we were in Orlando. "We can
go see Mickey Mouse, Shamu, Universal Studios theme park,"
I'd said. Zeke didn't care about a vacation (at least not with

me) either. So once again, while everyone else had someone, I was alone, trying to pretend that I was okay with being all by myself.

"Are you busy tonight?" Ethan said, quickly snapping me back to the present.

"No," I said. "Why?"

"I'd like to take you to dinner or something. You know: to celebrate."

I smiled, but this time, more nervously. As though he could see me, I shook my head. "I don't think that's a good idea." Ethan knew how I felt about me and him going anywhere in public to places like dinner or a movie. I'd expressed the same position each time he'd presented that type of an invitation to me.

"Well, this time I'm not taking no for an answer. So unless you already have something planned that you can't get out of, then you and I are doing something special tonight to celebrate our tenth year anniversary of being reignited friends."

"Ethan—"

"Please let me do this," he said in a soft tone. "Look, if you're not comfortable being out with me around here, then we can go someplace where no one knows either of us. I just want to see you. If you like, we can even have dinner at the shop again. I don't care what we do or where we go; I just want to be with you."

"Ethan, I hear you, I do. But I'm going to be honest: I don't think it's good for you and I to do something like this, not giving the way we feel about each other."

"And how do we feel about each other?"

"You know," I said, ensuring that I wasn't talking too loud.

"No, I don't know. Why don't you tell me? Tell me. How do we feel about each other?"

"We're more than just friends. You know it and I know it. And if we keep playing with fire the way we do, somebody's eventually going to get burned."

"Stop speaking negative things. Isn't that what you're known for always saying? You know there is power in the words that you speak."

"I know. And I'm really not trying to speak negative things. But I *am* being real here. You and I both know what happens every time we see each other."

"I know what goes on with me. I can't speak for you," Ethan said. "You get my heart pumping. My hands get all warm. You cause me to smile no matter how bad of a day I may have had, or am having. You make me feel like I'm truly somebody."

I laughed. "Oh, you don't need me to make you feel like you're somebody. There are plenty of folks in your life that do that for you quite well, quite well."

"And still . . . no one does it like you do. You're not a kiss-up. You tell me what you really think. I can trust you and what you say. I can't do that with everybody. There's only one: you. And I want to celebrate my being blessed with you in my life . . . you being a part of my life. I'm not sure what we'd call what we are. I just know that I'm glad my world includes you again." He sighed loudly enough for me to hear him. "So tonight, we're going out and doing something special. That's not up for de-bate. What we *can* debate is what we do and where. That, I'll leave up to you."

I was thinking that, in truth, he and I had really never gone to dinner before, not even when we were youngsters. But I also never wanted to do anything that could hurt him, no matter what I really wanted. "How about you surprise me," I said.

"So you're leaving this all up to me?" There was skepticism in his voice.

"Yep, I'm leaving it all up to you."

"And you won't open your mouth about whatever I decide? Not one word."

"Whatever you decide, I'll go along with it." Although he couldn't see me, I contorted and crinkled up my face.

"Great," he said. "Where can we meet so I can pick you up?"

This part always gave me pause. Whenever we were going to ride together in the same vehicle to a destination, that thought always made me nervous. There were just too many variables that could go wrong. At least when we were in our separate ve-hicles, no one would be able to say (with assurance anyway) that we were together.

Ethan cleared his throat to get my attention.

"I heard you," I said.

"You're not changing your mind on me already, are you?" he said.

"No. I was just wondering whether it's a good idea for us to ride together. Maybe you can just tell me where you want to go, and I can meet you there. That way, let's say if we bump into someone either of us knows, it could always look like you and I also merely ran into each other."

"You're still afraid, aren't you?"

"Not for me," I said. "I just don't want to mess anything up for you."

"I told you already that I eat out with folks, and that includes women, all the time. No one is going to think anything if they happen to see you and me out together. I'm telling you."

"Still, I don't want to put you in that situation. Maybe it's because I know we're not innocent in what we're doing. Dinner between me and you is not just two friends out eating or someone needing advice or counseling."

"What are you talking about? You counsel me and give me advice all the time. In fact: if it hadn't been for you that time when I was ready to walk away from everything, and I do mean *everything*, who knows where I would be today."

"You would have come to your senses," I said. "You'd be exactly where you are now."

"I don't know about that. You truly don't know how far gone I was before you came back into my life. My marriage was pretty much all over but the shouting. In reality: you're the one who can be credited with saving it."

I laughed.

"Don't laugh. I'm serious. You saved my marriage and my family nucleus. So tonight, you and I are going to celebrate. And tonight . . . it's all about you."

"Still, I'd feel better about meeting you wherever you're planning. I'll drive my car there and you can drive yours. We'll still have a great time. Trust me."

"Okay. I'll text you the information."

"You're going to text me?" I said. "Hold up. When did you learn to text?"

"I'm still working on it. It takes me a while, but I get it done." He chuckled.

"All right. I'll be looking for your text."

Five minutes later, Ethan's text came through. The address was unfamiliar, so I was going to have to use my GPS to find it. But for all practical purposes: Ethan and I were scheduled to go to dinner at seven o'clock. *He'd finally talked me into it!*

Chapter 43

*That their hearts might be comforted, being knit to-
gether in love, and unto all riches of the full assurance of understanding, to the acknowledgement of
the mystery of God, and of the Father, and of Christ.*
—Colossians 2:2

Even before I pulled into the parking lot to the address
Ethan had texted, I could see what a *major* problem this
could end up being.

I'd gone online to check out the restaurant. Somehow I'd
failed to notice that this upscale, exclusive dining place was located in the heart of a grand hotel. The butterflies in my stomach awakened and immediately began fluttering.

It's going to be fine. It's going to be okay, I continued to say in my
head as I parked my car in a spot well away from the main entrance. I wasn't quite sure how to do this. By this I mean: do I
go inside and wait for Ethan to meet me? What if he's already
inside waiting on me while I'm sitting here trying to get it together and someone sees him and starts thinking he's booked a
room at the hotel or something? *Scandalous.*

Ethan and I hadn't discussed this part. I pulled out my cell
phone and thought about calling him to find out what I was
supposed to do, now that I'd arrived. I laughed at how silly I
was being. It was dinner. That's it—dinner. The selected restaurant just happened to be inside of a hotel. I just needed to get
out and go to the restaurant like we'd planned.

Still . . . walking inside the lobby of the hotel (with its beautifully artistic marbled floor, magnificent three-tiered chandelier

hanging down from two-and-a-half stories up, mammoth squared columns, and a floral arrangement as wide as I am tall) made me feel self-conscious. I couldn't help but feel that any-one who was there heard me coming as my four-inch-high heels tapped, echoing throughout with each step I took. I tried walk-ing more softly.

Hurriedly, I glanced around to see where the restaurant was located. The last thing I wanted, at this point, was to have to go to the front desk and ask. The place was so huge.

"Need some help?" a man's voice whispered, his peppermint breath practically blowing coolness into my ear. I smelled his perfectly applied cologne before I ever turned around. *Heav-enly*, was my first thought.

I turned, about to ask which way to the restaurant, when I stopped and began to smile. "Hi," I said almost like a teenage girl who'd happened upon her favorite pop singer.

"Hi," Ethan said back as he smiled down at me.

I slowly released the breath I'd taken in. At least now I didn't feel so awkward. "This place is huge," I said, glancing around, mostly so I wouldn't just be staring at him, which honestly I could definitely have done all night.

"I've seen larger," he said. "Shall we?" He held out his arm to escort me.

I wasn't sure me grabbing onto his arm in a public venue like this was a good idea. "Ethan," I said with a final tone to it.

"If you'd rather not," he said, reluctantly lowering his arm.

We strolled into the restaurant that was equally as beautiful and luxurious as the lobby we'd just stepped out of. It wasn't crowded by any means. Ethan and I sat at a table in an area off to ourselves, raised up from the main floor.

"What does it mean when you look at the menu and there are no prices?" I asked as I looked over the menu.

"It means that you shouldn't worry about what you order and just get whatever you want." Ethan grinned, then cocked his head ever so slightly.

I didn't want to seem rude, but I didn't want him spending

an arm and a leg eating what we could get at most other restaurants for far less.

"Please don't ruin this night for me," Ethan said, touching my hand. "Do you know how long I've been saving up for this night?"

I frowned. "Saving up?"

"Yeah. You see: I've really never taken you out, even though we've known each other for some thirty-eight years now. This may be my only time I get you to go with me to dinner, so I'm putting all I've saved up over the years into this one night."

"Hmmm," I said, smiling as he gazed into my eyes with a sparkling glimmer.

"So order whatever your heart desires and don't worry about the cost. Believe me: this is nothing to what it would have cost, had I gone to a psychiatrist and worked out my issues, instead of having done it with you. I'm actually getting off cheap. And my company tonight—both beautiful and smart. It doesn't get any better than this."

I tried not to blush. Joking is one way I generally mask my uneasiness. But he was making me feel so special; I held back my urge to make a joke.

We ordered, talked, ate, and laughed. And when it was time for dessert, Ethan told the waiter, "I have dessert covered already. If you'll just bring my check, I will appreciate it." He then looked at me.

"So you have dessert covered, huh?" I said in a teasing, almost flirty voice.

"Yes," he said, leaning in. His look took on a serious tone. "You said I could plan this night, right?"

"Yeah. Kind of."

"Well, I ordered dessert from Bake Me A Wish! Something chocolate."

"Oooh," I said, leaning in as well, making it much too close for comfort.

"Yeah. *Heavenly* chocolate. Not devilish . . . Heavenly."

"So, what are you planning on doing? Bring it in here and we eat it here?"

"No."

"Eat it in the car?" I said, pulling back my body a little more.

"No."

"What then?"

"I've reserved us a room."

I sat back totally against my chair. "Ethan—"

"It's just dessert," he said. "We don't have to do anything more than have dessert in there."

I began shaking my head slowly. "That doesn't make any sense. You mean to tell me that you rented a room just for dessert?"

"Yes."

"Please tell me you didn't rent a room in this place." I looked around.

"I did."

"Ethan, this place is expensive. Why would you do something like that? You just threw your money away. You're paying for a night in a luxury hotel just to eat dessert?"

"Believe me: dessert with you will be worth every penny, and then some."

I cupped my hands around the back and sides of my neck. The butterflies in my stomach were really flapping their wings now.

The waiter returned with the check. Ethan paid it with cash. "The rest is your tip," he said to the waiter.

"Thank you, sir," the waiter said with a huge grin.

Ethan stood, came over, and held my hand as I nervously stood up.

He already had the key to the room, so there was nothing for us to do except head for the elevator. I looked around as though, any minute, someone would call either my or Ethan's name, and bust us for sure.

Ethan placed his hand on my back. "It's going to be all right. We'll eat our dessert, and when you're ready, all you have to do is say the word, and we'll leave."

I didn't say anything the whole ride up or down the long corridor. In my head, I felt I should turn around before we reached the room and take myself on home. My heart said differently. We reached the door, he put the plastic keycard in, a green light lit, he opened the door, and we stepped in. The torte, a champagne bottle (of white grape juice), two champagne glasses, and one unlit candle were waiting on the table.

Chapter 44

And this I say, lest any man should beguile you with enticing words.

—Colossians 2:4

I can't tell you why it went down the way that it did; it just did. It was midnight and raining hard. Being the gentleman that he is, Ethan didn't want me having to go to my car in all of that rain.

"I'll go check out, get my car, pick you up at the front entrance of the lobby, and take you to your car," he said, as we stood at the doorway. "Give me about ten minutes."

I nodded. He then kissed me lightly on my lips, smiling as he held the box of remaining cake I was taking home with me. I bit down on my bottom lip to keep from grinning too much.

Thoughtful and caring, Ethan was now topping off the perfectly wonderful night this had already been by offering to keep me dry from the downpour taking place outside. A night that, were I still keeping a diary as I'd religiously done in my teenage years, I would definitely have recorded the triple-D-plus, play-by-play minutes—dinner, dessert, and deliciously divine.

After I felt Ethan had gotten things squared away and that it was okay for me to go downstairs, I stepped into the hallway and headed for the elevator. The elevator stopped and the doors opened. I was just about to step in when I heard, "Hold the elevator, please!"

I turned to see who was getting on with me, ever mindful always of other people and of my surroundings, and I couldn't be-lieve my eyes.

"Well, well. Looky who we have here," the man said, looking me up and down as though I was his first meal after a three-day fast. "If it's not Little Miss Church Lady, Third Row." He was re-ferring to where I normally sat in church.

"Deacon Willie Price," I said, not believing that of all people for me to run into, and here of all places, it would be him. The man had a love-hate relationship when it came to me. He wanted to get with me, but, because I wasn't interested, he wanted nothing more than to make my life miserable. Plus, he was none too happy when I voted against him and his gang to get rid of our former pastor and hire a new one.

"So what are you doing here"—he made a show of looking at his watch—"and at this time of night?" he said with that dirty-old-man grin he was known for.

I didn't have an answer. I mean: my mind went totally blank!

"Is your husband here with you?" he asked.

"Funny meeting you here as well, Deacon," I said, recovering slightly and deciding to turn the tables back on him. "Is your lovely wife here with you?"

"As a matter of fact, she's not. I was here meeting up with a client." He had a smug look.

"How wonderful," I said with a lift to my voice as though I was really happy for him. "Productive, I hope. Your meeting, I mean."

He nodded. "Quite productive. And you're here again for what reason did you say?"

I nodded, then smiled. "Oh. I didn't say. Mainly because I don't see where *my* business is any of *your* business," I said. He was accustomed to my curtness.

He grinned. "True that. But a woman being out at this time of the night, at a place like this, no less, can cause a more curi-ous—I'd dare say devious—person's brain to think of all kinds of reasons you might be here. Especially when it comes to a good little church lady such as yourself, who, I suspect, is normally at home this time of the night. Of course, I'm sure your hus-band—Zeke, isn't it?—is probably downstairs waiting on you, since you appear to be leaving. You *are* leaving, aren't you?"

I didn't respond, glad that we'd finally reached the lobby floor. I stepped out of the elevator and quickly headed for the exit. Deacon Price was right on my heels. I stopped and turned to him.

"Oh, I'm just walking you out," he said to a question I hadn't asked. "Wouldn't want anything to happen to one of our fellow church members, now would we? I wouldn't be able to live with myself if something were to happen to *you*. That new pastor of ours, the one y'all voted in, would most definitely be upset if he learned that I hadn't been my sister's keeper here, when I had the opportunity. Isn't that one of the many things he's trying to change about us since he's come in and taken over? Trying to get us to repent and clean up our old ways?"

"Thank you, Deacon Price, but I'll be just fine. I really don't need you to walk me out."

"Oh, but I was on my way out anyway. It's really no trouble . . . no trouble at all. I need to get home to the Missus the same as I'm sure you need to be getting home to your old man."

He was definitely either fishing or baiting me now. He wanted me to slip and say something to confirm, one way or the other, what was really going on here. My best strategy was to say nothing or as little as possible.

Just as I was about to go through the first set of doors, it suddenly dawned on me that Ethan would be waiting for me when I walked out. He didn't have any way of knowing that I knew this man. And knowing Ethan the way I did, as soon as I cleared the outside door, he would be out of his car and running to open the passenger door for me. I couldn't take a chance that Deacon Price might see him or his car.

I stopped completely.

"What's the matter?" Deacon Price said, also coming to a sudden halt.

"Nothing."

"Well, aren't you going outside? I told you that I'll walk with you."

I smiled. "I just remembered: I think I may have forgotten something."

"Oh. Well, then, I'll just wait for you here while you go back and get it," he said with a smirk. "I have time."

"You really don't have to wait on me, Deacon."

"I know I don't, but I *want* to."

"Well, I don't want you to," I said, forcing a smile to temper the words. He continued to stand there with that ridiculous smirk on his face. I turned and headed back toward the elevator. My phone started vibrating in my purse. I answered it.

"Hey, what's going on?" Ethan said. "I'm out here. I saw you coming to the door, but then you turned around. Is something wrong?"

"Yeah. I just ran into a man from my church," I said in a whisper, afraid the large area would carry like an echo.

"Seriously?"

"Yeah. Seriously. He was asking me what I was doing here; he wanted to walk me to my car. I didn't know what to do. I knew you were outside waiting," I said. "You need to go on and leave."

"I want to be sure that you're all right."

"I'll be fine. You go on," I said.

"Are you sure?"

"I'm sure. I don't trust this guy at all. He's a sneaky little devil. He's been looking for something to use against me forever. I wouldn't want him doing anything to get at me and end up bringing you into it with me," I said.

"How about I just hang back while you go to your car? I don't want to leave you with somebody like him. I don't trust him."

"He's not going to do anything to me," I said. "I'll be okay. You go on."

"Still, I don't want to leave you here by yourself. You go on to your car; and just know that I'll be close by, watching until I know that you're safely inside your car."

"I'm telling you: I'm going to be—"

"Please don't argue with me," Ethan said. "Go to your car, and I'll be here looking out for you. All right?"

"All right." I clicked off my phone, took in a deep breath, slowly released it, found my car keys, then started again toward the lobby door.

"Well, that was fast," Deacon Price said, stepping up beside me.

I didn't say anything else to him; I just kept walking with my face straight ahead. The automatic doors opened as we approached them; I strolled through quickly.

"You sure are walking fast," he said, speeding up to catch up with me. "If you'll just slow down a tad, we can use my jacket to keep your hair from getting wet in all of this rain." He had taken off his suit coat and now held it over us.

I started walking even faster, jogging a little.

"Hey, I told you slow down!" He jogged to keep up with me.

The rain was *really* coming down. I ran full out to my car, high heels and all, happy I hadn't parked on the other side of the entrance as I'd thought about doing, so I didn't have as far to go now. I worked swiftly to put the key in the lock, wishing now I had a car with one of those keyless remotes. Deacon Price walked up on me before I could get the door opened. I didn't like how close he stood behind me. When I finally opened the door, I jumped in, hair dripping wet. He stood there, his body preventing me from closing my door.

"Thanks, I'm here now," I said, my hand on the handle, the inside of the car getting wet.

"Okay. You know, I was thinking maybe you and I could go to dinner sometime. We can even come here, although I'm not sure I can afford this restaurant. Other folks generally pay whenever I *do* eat here. But for *you* now . . ."

I shook my head. "I don't think so." I made a show of pulling at the handle.

"Well, I'll tell you what: we can talk about it later. Okay?"

"There's nothing to talk about. I'm not interested."

"Oh, okay. Like I said, we'll talk later. Maybe I'll be able to change your mind."

"I doubt it," I said, with my hand on the armrest making a show of my effort to close my door.

"Well, I suppose I'll see you at church on Sunday," he said.

"Okay." I sang the word. "Bye now." I pulled the door, slightly tapping him as it was taking him too long to move. He stepped out of the way. I shut the door and immediately locked it, started my car, and drove away.

Chapter 45

And the scribes and Pharisees brought unto him a woman taken in adultery; and when they had set her in the midst . . .

—John 8:3

I stepped into church not thinking anything major would be happening on this particular Sunday. Well, I was definitely in for the surprise of my church life.

For some reason, Barbara Price, Deacon Willie Price's wife, kept staring in my direction from the choir stand. I didn't have a clue what that was about, unless her husband had told her he'd run into me at the hotel, which I *highly* doubted since I'm sure he didn't want her to know he'd been there. Barbara could get her dander up about things, but for the most part, she and I had managed not to have any major problems with each other. Then Pastor Godbee stood and asked if anyone present was in need of prayer and Barbara raised her hand as she stood and started walking toward the pastor, which didn't make sense to me since the customary thing to do if you wanted prayer was just to come to the front and quietly stand.

"Pastor Godbee, before you do any of this, I have something I need to get off my chest and my heart." Barbara held a large, gold-colored envelope in her hand.

Pastor Godbee wasn't anything like Pastor Hutchings, who routinely allowed such disruptions in the service without question. "I'm sorry, Sister Price," Pastor Godbee said, "but now is not the appropriate time for—"

"Well, we need to make it the appropriate time," Barbara said as she strutted in her one-size-too-small blue dress toward the pulpit. "Because we have a huge problem here that needs to be addressed. We have members in our congregation who need to come forward and ask for forgiveness for their sins."

"Sister Price, this is highly out of order. Generally, I open that up after the sermon."

"Forget about order," Barbara said. "These folks are sinning, to be more specific, committing adultery. And I for one am not going to sit idly by and allow it *or* them to continue as though it's not happening. Not while I'm a member here. And considering my family was one of the ones that started this church one hundred and nine years ago, I don't plan on *not* being a member here. Ever."

By this time, gasps were flowing throughout the congregation.

"Sister Price, you and I can discuss this after we dismiss. I'll be glad to talk with you then. But I refuse to allow you to disrupt our regular service in this way."

"You're not going to have to *allow* me. I'd like to see you try and *stop* me. Because this is coming out right here right now *today*. Evelyn Payne has been after my husband for months now, and it's time we stop acting like we don't know that it's happening."

People were twisting and turning to locate Evelyn who was directly behind me, now standing with her hand over her heart.

"Yeah, that's right," Barbara said to Evelyn. "I know about you and Willie. I been knowing about the two of you; I just didn't have proof. Well, guess what? I got proof now." She waved the gold envelope in the air. "So what you got to say about that now, Ms. Evelyn? Huh? Yes, that's right! I got pictures of you from Friday night. I know what you did on Friday. And before you try to deny it, know that pictures don't lie! So you might as well come on and confess and ask for forgiveness."

Evelyn placed her hand over her mouth and ran out of the sanctuary. I turned back around to the front, ashamed of what had just happened. Pastor Godbee was busy trying to get Barbara to sit down and stop her clowning.

But it was more than apparent that Barbara wasn't close to being finished, nor was she going to be quieted *easily* or, apparently, anytime soon.

In fact, she was merely getting warmed up.

Chapter 46

They say unto him, Master, this woman was taken in
adultery, in the very act.

—John 8:4

"Oh, but I'm not finished, Pastor Godbee," Barbara said. "I'm just getting started. You keep talking and preaching about us living holy. Ever since you arrived here, you've been talking about how we're called to be holy. You say you're not going to let us continue our wrongdoings and thinking this mess we been doing don't stink in God's nostrils. Well, unless folks start confessing their sins and start to doing it now, I don't know how you're planning on any of these folks getting better." She had one hand on her hip and was wiggling her head like a bobble doll now.

"Just like alcoholics, gamblers, and any other addicts' anonymous," Barbara continued, "folks who are sinning need to stand, say their names, and confess what they are. All of these phony folks walking around here trying to act like they're such good, upstanding Christians. Teaching Sunday school; working with our youth," she said, directing her full attention to me now. "Trying to tell folks, young and old, what 'thus saith the Lord' when they're doing all kinds of manner of sins themselves."

I frowned, wondering where she was going with this and why she was concentrating her attention in my direction.

"That's right! I'm talking about you, Mrs. Thang!" She pointed at me. "Yeah, you, Mrs. Holy Steamroller. Talking on

Sundays about how good God is while you're sneaking around, meeting other folks' husbands at expensive hotels and stuff on a Friday." She pulled out the eight-by-ten glossy photos and tried to hand them to Pastor Godbee. "Take a look at these, Pastor!" Barbara flapped the photos in his face. "Look and see if you don't find some familiar faces in these photographs," she said.

"Sister Price, we're not going to make a mockery of these services or God's house."

Barbara waved the photos in the air. "Yes, that's right. You got caught!" She said, now walking toward me. "And I got proof of what you were doing on Friday night. That's right . . . it's right here in living color." Her husband stood up and blocked her. "Oh, I guess Willie here has something he wants to confess," she said to him.

"Baby, I'm sorry. I'm sorry. But you of all people know how busy the devil is."

"Oh no, darling. We're not going to blame the devil for this. So don't even try and protect her. She knew what she was doing," Barbara said. By now, several of the deacons were trying to get hold of Barbara and take her out of the sanctuary. "Get your hands off of me!" she said, snatching her arms out of their grip just as quickly as they'd grabbed her. "I'm telling you: you touch me again and I'm going to call the authorities on you!"

Pastor Godbee shook his head to relay to the deacons not to put their hands on her.

Barbara came stomping over and stood in front of me. "I can't believe you would do something like this. Not you. Evelyn committing adultery? Sure. I know for a fact that she's been after my husband for years now. And he's so weak"—she glanced back at Willie—"all she has to do is wave her deceased husband's insurance money at him and, he's such a dog, he's as good as there. But you?" She shook her head. "You want to tell the congregation what you were doing at a hotel like this on this past Friday night? Yes, ma'am, that's right: you've been caught!" She waved the white backs of the glossy photos in my face. "You were caught in the act . . . the *very* act of adultery."

I didn't know what to say. Not knowing what the photos showed, I certainly wasn't going to say anything that might implicate Ethan in any of this. Not at this point for sure. But Barbara had pictures. The proof was there in her hand. I wanted to see what she held, the pictures she was waving around like they were nothing. One bright factor in all of this was that after all of my complaining and fussing about Zeke hardly ever going to church, at least he, and none of our children, were present to witness any of this.

Chapter 47

Now Moses in the law commanded us, that such should be stoned: but what sayest thou?
—John 8:5

"Yes, she committed adultery," Barbara said, pointing at me. "And I have brought her to you. And not only do I have pictures, but I have a witness. Willie, was she at the hotel as late as the midnight hour or not?" ·

Willie shook his head, then reluctantly nodded in the affirmative.

"So you can testify that she was physically there?" she said to Willie. "These photos aren't likely doctored or Photoshopped? And speak so folks can hear you!"

"She was there," he mumbled, looking at me as he said it.

Barbara turned back to Pastor Godbee. "So what are you going to do about this, Pastor? What are you going to do about this here *righteous* member of yours?"

"First, we're going to have order. Then we will do things *decent* and in order," Pastor Godbee said.

"This *is* decent and in order," Barbara said. She flung the photos my way. They landed near me but, thankfully, either face down or covered up by another.

I sat there, wanting to but refusing to move toward them to gather them up.

"She was caught in her sin," Barbara said, alternating her look between me and Pastor Godbee. "My husband and I both caught her and have brought her before you and this assembly of *supposedly* baptized believers. In the past, at least before you came, anyway, and started changing how we do things around here, we would make our young women who had babies out of wedlock come to the front and ask forgiveness for their caught sins. Like I said, that was before you came and put a stop to us forcing them to do that."

Pastor Godbee looked at me, looked at the photos face down on the floor (close enough that I could have stood up, taken two steps, and retrieved them), then back at Barbara who was standing there glaring at him as she waited on him to say something now. It was obvious that this was not so much about *me* as it was about her contempt for our newly installed, thirty-three-year-old pastor.

Barbara and Willie Price both had been upset about Pastor Hutchings' dismissal. But Pastor Hutchings had become too much. He was sleeping with a new woman like clockwork every six months. He was coming up with new ways to get money out of the church funds and the members who believed the sun rose and set on him—Willie and Barbara being two of the ring-leaders. The Prices had enjoyed prominent positions and recognition within the congregation when Pastor Hutchings was the congregation's leader.

But after 85 percent of the congregation said enough with Pastor Hutchings' shenanigans and requested that he either resign or be fired and it was done, Barbara and Willie (along with about twenty other members) went on a holy crusade against the newly selected pastor, Terrell Godbee. I guess they wanted to make things so miserable for him that he would leave before he settled in good. Pastor Godbee was much younger than Pastor Hutchings and this was the first church he'd been appointed to as a pastor. Maybe his detractors thought his age and inexperience would override the anointing practically no one could deny was on his life.

In any case, it became clear (at least to me), that what was happening today wasn't *really* about me and the man I've loved since the very first day I laid eyes on him when I was thirteen—well, closer to fourteen—years old. The man I couldn't refute that my soul was somehow tied to. A man

I loved and probably would love forever, even though I was married . . . committed to, and yes (even though Zeke didn't treat me the best) loved. It's hard to explain how someone can love the one you're married to while equally loving someone else. But in my own way, I did love them both.

My mother once told me, "Love is not mechanical. You can't turn it off and on like a faucet. There is no lever, switch, button, or plug to disconnect. I wish there was. It would make so many lives, especially women's, much easier. But when love is hurting you . . . breaking you . . . making you become someone that you're not, you have to learn—in spite of that love—to walk away. If loving someone tears you down instead of making your life better, then learn to love *that one* from afar."

I never figured out why she knew so much about the topic. But as you get older, you find that life is enhanced by experiences. I suspect my mother was speaking from a place of experience. She obviously knew something about love and losing, and love and settling. I don't know; she never told me. Maybe I should ask her now. Mom just hates telling things that might tarnish our image of her even a little bit.

Thinking of my own daughters, I can only hope that if they ever need to know something like this, they'll feel comfortable enough to ask me. And that I won't feel compelled to appear so perfect to them, that I'll actually tell them the truth.

The *whole* truth, nothing but the truth, so help me God.

Chapter 48

This they said, tempting him, that they might have to accuse him. But Jesus stooped down, and with his finger wrote on the ground, as though he heard them not.

—John 8:6

Pastor Godbee didn't say another word to Barbara. He walked back to the pulpit in his long black robe with the double red stripes down each side that I loved seeing him in, and opened his Bible.

I can't speak to what anyone else might have been thinking, but I was wondering if this might have been too much for our young pastor. I don't know if they teach them how to get an irate member to sit down and stop disrupting the service (short of physically removing them) in seminary. I'd seen someone only once before being forcibly removed from a sanctuary (not our church). It's never a good look when a few men appear to be dragging or carrying someone, a woman particularly, out of a church house. And knowing Barbara, she'd surely be kicking and screaming, claiming that she was being assaulted, if any of them tried to carry her out.

Then the police would be called, and how would that all play out? According to how slow the news cycle was for that day (or maybe even because of the potential sensationalism), it might make the evening news. Forget about the number of folks with cell phones who would have assuredly recorded the actual event, as it was happening, and would have it up on YouTube as soon as it was over.

Pastor Godbee nodded a few times at a still-standing, fifty-

eight-year-old, defiant Barbara Price, who was breathing hard
now.

"In the gospel according to Saint John, we find so many
great scriptures. There's the first chapter where it declares, 'In
the beginning was the Word, and the Word was with God, and
the Word was God.' We learn that John came to bear witness to
the Light, 'that all men through him might believe.' That John
'was not that Light, but was sent to bear witness of the Light.
That was the true Light, which lighteth every man that cometh
into the world.' We see that Jesus 'came unto his own, and his
own received him not. But as many as received him, to them
gave he power to become the sons of God, even to them that
believe on his name.' In John 3:16, we find, 'For God so loved
the world, that he gave his only begotten Son, that whosoever
believeth in him should not perish, but have everlasting life.'

"In John 4:24 we learn from the spoken words of Jesus that,
'God is a Spirit: and they that worship him must worship him in
spirit and in truth.' If I may, I'd like to talk to you today from
the subject: *Forever Soul Ties.*" Pastor Godbee smiled, nodding as
though he were saying *Amen* to himself. Barbara reluctantly sat
down.

"I'm not going to be long today. My mentor in the Lord has
a saying, 'If you come strong, you don't have to be long.' So I'm
going to say what I need to say, and then I'm going to leave it
alone. One generation here, back in the day, might have said it
this way: 'I'm going to hit it and quit it.' "

A few folks chuckled, although the tension in the building
was so thick you could tell people were being careful about
even breathing too hard.

"For the benefit of those who may not have heard the termi-
nology before, let me say something about soul ties. Soul ties
can be a good thing or it can be a dangerous thing. It can happen before you even realize it's happened. It can begin as simple as two folks helping each other out. It can take root with
two folks starting out as mere friends. It then grows as they sow
into each other's lives by telling the other what they're dealing
with. You see, everyone wants to feel as though they matter. And

when you find someone empathetic to what you're going through, that can be a wonderful thing. With the right person and in the right context, soul ties can be a blessing. The problem is: many times two people are talking while the other one is listening when it should be their spouse they're cultivating this stronger bond with.

"But Pastor, what do you do when your spouse won't talk to you? What do you do when you've tried talking, but the other person doesn't want to hear it or they don't have time for you? What do you do then, Pastor Godbee." Pastor Godbee nodded as he smirked slightly.

"I'm so glad you asked," he said in a teasing manner. "I know it's hard, but you need to know what you're dealing with. Yes, I could tell you to keep trying to talk to the one you're married to, but I know that doesn't always work. I'm saying that you need to be aware of illegal soul ties. Don't put blinders on talking about you're just friends. Folks love to say that. 'Oh, we're just friends.' Now you know *good and well* friends don't have any business kissing each other in the mouth! Yes, I said it. I'm not going to sugarcoat this today. This is too important to dress it up!"

There were lots of sounds from oohs, aahs, gasps, and laughs being made now.

"Don't ooh and aah me," Pastor Godbee said. "I'm going to say it, because if I don't, then I can be accused of spiritual malpractice. That's right, *mal-*practice. God knows all about this stuff, so it's not like God is shocked by what I'm saying to you right now. You don't believe me, then get your Bible and read it sometimes instead of using it for decoration on your living room coffee table or toting it around to fool or impress other folks."

A few people chuckled, some touching somebody sitting next to them.

"In the wrong situation, soul ties can be dangerous because, once a bond is deep enough to touch the soul it becomes more than just physical. Lust is basically surface. With lust, you're moved by your senses. Sight—you see something or someone;

it looks good to you and you want it. Smell—someone's cologne catches your attention or you recall 'things' whenever you encounter the scent again.

"Truthfully, lust is easier to walk away from because surface things can change. By that I mean: that fine specimen who caught your attention, causing you to almost drool . . . oh, you know the one I'm talking about. Well, she or he can gain weight and all of a sudden you're not 'feeling' the way you used to. That pretty face that once made you stop in your tracks. Well, it can start sagging, you know: it's not the face you 'fell in love with.' Feelings change. 'The way you made me feel when we first met back when I thought you were perfect? Now you're starting to get on my last nerve and I wish you'd go on some-where and leave me alone.' That voice that used to whisper sweet nothings in your ear? Now you can't stand to hear them even breathe. 'And you'd better not touch me; all I have to say is don't touch me!'

"Yes, things on a surface level can change," Pastor Godbee said. "But when it's a soul level, it's not about surface stuff. Soul ties are so deep, you can't even describe it. You can't tell any-body what it looks like. You can't attach a smell to it. You want to explain what it feels like, but it doesn't feel like anything you've ever felt before. You'd like to recreate the sound but how do you make the sound that a soul emanates? And when it comes to describing the taste? Oh my goodness!" Pastor God-bee grabbed the top of his head and stomped around a few times.

"Oh my goodness! All you want to say is, 'Oh, taste and see that the Lord is good!' " He stood still and smiled. "That was what David said in one of the Psalms, Psalm 34:8 to be exact. 'O taste and see that the Lord is good.' Soul ties are a different type of bond than any you'll ever experience. It's a tie that looks beyond your faults. It's a love that doesn't make sense to others observing it from afar. It's a bind that you'll go to great lengths to protect if you have to. You don't want to hurt the person you're tied with, no matter what *you* personally might lose in the process."

Pastor Godbee stepped back down. "Forever soul ties. For-

ever . . . soul . . . ties. You know, forever is a long time. Forever
meaning nothing can separate us. Neither height nor depth,
nor things present, nor things to come. I'm talking forever soul
ties. The scripture asks what shall separate us from the love of
God. It goes on to say that *nothing* shall separate us. For while
we were *yet* sinners, God loved us. God loved us so much that
He gave His only begotten Son. God loved us so much that
even before the world was formed, He made a way for us to get
back to Him. Jesus loved us so much that He gave His life for
us. And now we have a High Priest in Heaven, sitting at the
right hand of Father God, making intercessions for us. That's
forever soul ties.

"We mess up, and Jesus is right there, pleading on our behalf. Showing God His blood that He shed and that now blots
out our transgressions. Does that mean we should purposely
mess up, purposely sin? God forbid. No. Because every time we
sin, it's like driving a nail into Jesus' body all over again. I don't
want to do that to the One who hung on the cross in my place.
But we do miss it sometimes. We do. I know some of you think
you're perfect. And I know we should strive to *be* perfect. But
the fact is: we miss it sometimes. Sometimes we mess . . . up. If
this wasn't the case, there would have been no need for Jesus to
have died on the cross. You just need to be careful of the ties
you make down here on earth. Watch and pray. And when you
find things heating up in your life outside of God's perfect will,
then you need to get out quickly. Don't diddle, don't daddle,
just flee." Pastor Godbee stood in the aisle now.

"Do you know how to cook a frog?" He flashed a quick smile.
"Some of you may have heard this before. But for the benefit of
those who haven't and to remind those of you who have, I'm
going to tell you how here today. The way to cook a frog is to
put the frog in the water while the water is tepid. A frog will sit
there when it's not uncomfortable or causing pain. You then
turn on the heat. The frog will get used to heat, not realizing
what's happening until it's too late. Well, I come to tell you:
that's how some of you end up in your messes. The devil puts
you in a pot of tepidness. You sit there being all content, glad
for the swimming pool, if you will."

People laughed.

"Then the devil turns on the heat. It's getting hot, but you think you've now moved to the whirlpool stage. Thinking how nice it is to spend time in your very own Jacuzzi. Then it quickly becomes like a sauna. And before you know anything, you're cooked and you didn't even see it coming. By the time you realize what is truly happening, it's too late, and someone is now having you for dinner."

"Oooh," a few folks said. "Now, that was good, Pastor!"

Pastor Godbee chuckled, then walked back to the pulpit and picked up his Bible. "Let me ask you: what pot have you found yourself in? Have you cheated on your tax returns? Claimed dependents you 'borrowed' to lower the amount you owed? Oh, that's right: the IRS sort of put the brakes on some of you on that one. Have you ever upped the amount that you donated to charity and to the church?" He nodded. "You know you didn't give that much to the *church house*. Oh, I hear you saying there's nothing wrong with doing any of this because it's your money and you should be able to keep more of it. But did you know that's called stealing? It is. It's stealing.

"Let me ask you: are you talking about folks on the phone under the guise of 'praying for them'? Sitting around fanning flies and telling lies." He grinned. "Okay, let me get current with you. Let me get 'jiggy with it.' Are you downloading music illegally? Downloading movies illegally? Making bootleg copies of music and movies and selling them, with your faded-ink-label self? Oh wait! Are you the one *buying* the bootleg copies? I think they call that being an accessory to the crime. Buying boosted and stolen purses. Now you *know* don't no Gucci purse sell for that amount, especially when you're buying it off the street or from the back of a car from a guy who has to up and move his operations at the first sign of the police."

Folks laughed.

"Are you taking pen and paper, other things from off your job for your children's school supplies? Anybody sneaking and watching porn on the computer? Oh, and this isn't addressed just to the men. Women are doing this, too, so don't front." Pastor Godbee nodded as he wriggled his nose a few times. "Some of you women are *something* else!" He shook his head. "Wait a minute: how about this? Have any of you classy ladies ever bought a nice outfit, kept the tag on it, then took it back and got a full refund after the event you wore it to was over? Men, are any of you *not* taking care of your own children? I'm talking about financially and being physically present. Well, the Bible calls a man who won't take care of his own worse than an infidel. Are you claiming you don't know why you're not losing weight when you know during the midnight hour you're sitting there with a tub of chunky monkey double fudge ice cream? Oh, I'm almost finished," Pastor Godbee said with a grin.

"I see some of you squirming. Are you borrowing money and not paying it back? Is there anyone here tipping out on your spouse but you think you're okay because you've kept it hidden well? You think you're in the clear because no one knows. Well, allow me to drop this 411 on you. God knows. Yes, He does! Oh, yes, He does. God knows all of these things, with your *holy* self." He looked in his Bible.

"Let me wrap this up," Pastor Godbee said. "I'm going to bring this to a close now," he said. "Some of you have questioned me as to why I put a stop to the little exercise y'all used to do by forcing pregnant young women to come forward after their babies were born." He placed the ribbon between the pages and closed his Bible.

"The reason I stopped doing that is because the sin is in the fornication and *not* in having the baby. See, some of you missed that. The baby is not the sin. The sin was the *act* of *fornication*. And with her getting pregnant, I'm still left to ask: where's the daddy of the baby? She didn't get that baby all by herself. There's no more immaculate conceptions, not after Mary the mother of Jesus. So where is the guy? Why is he not being made to come forward? Then there are those who are fornicating and no visible evidence is produced because no one got pregnant due to the use of birth control pills and other birth control methods, and those who *were* pregnant, but opted instead to have an abortion. The sin is still there. But because a baby didn't materialize, you believe there's no reason to repent for the sin? God forbid! That was the wrong message this congregation was, and some congregations are still, sending."

I heard someone a few rows behind me, under her breath, say, "Humph. That's exactly why some folks don't like you. Coming up in here changing things."

Pastor Godbee looked her way as though he'd also heard her. He continued on. "The young ladies who were fornicating and not getting 'caught' weren't being made to come forward. The young men fornicating weren't being made to come forward. In fact, many of you merely said, 'Boys are just being boys' as though that gives our young men a pass to not keep themselves holy. Then there are you 'older folks' who are doing '*your* thang.' You know: shucking and jiving; dipping and hiding. Fornicating . . . committing adultery, you name it. But none of *you* were bum-rushing the altar, asking for forgiveness. Stealing. Killing folks with your mouth. Having other gods before the one, true God. Bearing false witness against your neighbor. Disrespecting your mother and father as though the expiration date for that comes when you get grown." Pastor Godbee nodded, then opened his Bible back up.

"I'm closing. I'm closing. In the gospel of John, chapter eight verse seven, it says, 'So when they continued asking him, he lifted up himself, and said unto them, He that is without sin among you, let him first cast a stone at her.' " Pastor Godbee looked around, then set the Bible on the lectern.

"I'm going to do something differently today," Pastor Godbee said. "I can hear some of you saying, 'What else is new?' I'm going to open the doors of the church. But instead of you coming up here the way we customarily do it, I'm going to ask Deacon Jones to make sure that the door to the fellowship hall is unlocked. And I'm going to allow you to first examine yourself. And if there's something you've done wrong that you haven't repented for . . . you haven't asked God to forgive you for, or maybe you *have* asked, but the fact is: you know there's something in your life that you're guilty of. Whether it's a sin of omission or *commission*, I want you to go out that way"—he pointed at the main doors of the sanctuary—"and I want you to make your way to the fellowship hall. The doors of the church are open." Pastor Godbee nodded.

"But if your hands are clean enough and you find that you're able to cast a stone at my sister here"—he pointed at me—"who has been brought before me—justly or not—and no punishment is warranted or can be administered to you for your sins, then you stay in here, and we'll let the 'stoning,' metaphorically speaking, of course, begin. Weigh your own sins. Again: the doors of the church are open."

Pastor Godbee walked over and quietly asked the church secretary for her notepad and a pen. Walking back to the center of the sanctuary, with the notepad in hand, he stooped down, and without saying another word, simply began to write.

Chapter 49

And they which heard it, being convicted by their own conscience, went out one by one, beginning at the eldest, even unto the last: and Jesus was left alone, and the woman standing in the midst.
—John 8:9

P astor Godbee stayed at the front and continued writing, on occasion looking in a certain direction at someone in the congregation. One by one, people got up and quietly exited, starting with some of the oldest members of the church. I sat there, knowing that at this point (for whatever reason), I was the centerpiece of what was transpiring here today. Deacon Price stood up to leave and tried to get Barbara to stand. She yanked her arm back from him and frowned, no doubt about to go off on him.

"Woman, don't make me have to out you," Deacon Price said louder than I've ever heard him speak to her. "Because if I have to, I *will* do it," he said. "Sure as my name is Willie James Price. Now you know what you don't want these folks here to know about you. Don't make me go there."

Barbara glared at him, made a loud huffing sound, went and snatched her purse from where she'd left it, and stormed out the door.

When the last person had exited the sanctuary and there was no one left except me and Pastor Godbee, he stood up and walked over to me. Stooping down, he quietly gathered up the photos. Not knowing what was on them I couldn't help but hold my breath. Only, Pastor Godbee didn't look at any of them. He handed them to me face down. I lifted up my head and looked at him as he looked at me.

"Where are your accusers?" Pastor Godbee asked as he made a show of looking around. "Has anyone condemned you?"

I looked around more thoroughly. The place was completely empty. "No one."

"John eight, verse ten says, 'When Jesus had lifted up himself, and saw none but the woman, he said unto her, Woman where are those thine accusers? hath no man condemned thee?' My sister in the Lord, I don't know what's on those photos." He nodded his head toward my hand. "I don't know what you may or may not have done. But I do know that we all have sinned and come short of the glory of God. I do know that much. I do know that after we give our lives to Christ, we are no longer classified as sinners but former sinners now saved by grace. Do we sin after we're saved? Of course we do. But glory to God, He no longer calls us a sinner. So don't you ever say or think to yourself again that you're a sinner. Because you're not. So don't speak those words against yourself. Okay?"

I smiled and nodded, tears streaming down my face now.

He touched my shoulder, then patted it twice. "I'm going to the fellowship hall to see how the intercessory prayer warriors are doing. Hopefully people went to the hall and not out of those doors and to their cars. But if you will, I'd like to meet with you briefly in my office after everyone has cleared out."

I nodded, wiped my eyes with my hand, looked at him, then forced a smile.

After Pastor Godbee left to go to the fellowship hall, I took a deep breath and slowly turned over the photos I now held in my hands. Before I had time to think about it or stop it, a loud gasp escaped from my mouth. I quickly clamped my hand over my mouth, almost disbelieving what my eyes beheld.

Chapter 50

She said, No man, Lord. And Jesus said unto her,
Neither do I condemn thee: go, and sin no more.
                                                    —John 8:11

Pastor Godbee called me, Barbara, and Willie Price into his office together. Barbara was still acting all huffy. It was more than obvious she didn't want to be in there. Personally, I would have preferred not being there with either of them as well.

"I called Sister Evelyn Payne to ask her to come back and be here with us," Pastor Godbee said. "But she informed me that she has no time for these 'childish shenanigans,' her words exactly. Sister Evelyn indicated to me that she was both hurt and embarrassed by what transpired today during service."

"She needs to be more than embarrassed," Barbara said. "Did you look at those photos, Pastor Godbee?"

"No, ma'am, I did not."

"Where are they?" Barbara asked, making a show of looking around.

"I let our sister here have them," he said, indicating me.

"Give those photos to Pastor Godbee," Barbara said. "I want him to see that what I did was not out of order."

"Sister Price, I really don't need to see—"

"Oh yeah, you need to see them," Barbara said, cutting Pastor Godbee off. "I didn't go to all of this trouble for people to accuse me of being a tale-bearer or as bearing false witness against anybody. I have proof, and I want you to see what I'm talking about." Barbara turned to me. "Give Pastor Godbee the photos, unless you've already torn them up or something, which if you have, know that I have more copies."

"Please go on and just give the photos to Pastor Godbee," Deacon Price said. "I'm telling you: this woman is not going to rest until she's been shut down and up."

I opened my pocketbook, slowly pulled out the photos I'd placed back in the gold envelope they'd originally been in, and handed the envelope to Pastor Godbee. It was apparent he didn't want to look at them. But to move things along, I suppose, he took them out of the envelope and began to flip through them. He then handed the photos over to Deacon Price for him to see.

Deacon Price went through them, then frowned as he quickly looked over at me. There was a photo of Evelyn Payne going into the hotel, one of me going in, as well as one of Deacon Price . . . all separately, and alone. The other photos were when Deacon Price and I stood at the lobby door and he'd taken off his suit jacket and was trying to cover me, and one when he stood over me at my car. That was it.

Deacon Price sighed as he shook his head. "This is what you were making all that ruckus about?" he said to his wife with disgust. "These?" He flapped the photos.

"Give me those!" Barbara snatched the photos out of her husband's hand. "Let me make sure Little Miss Perfect here didn't get rid of any pictures." She proceeded to go through them. "Well, they're all here. The proof is right here, Pastor!" Barbara said, shaking the pictures she now held in her hand at Pastor Godbee.

Deacon Price grunted and shook his head. "Those photos my wife was waving around in service today show nothing more than me being a gentleman, trying to keep my sister here, *in the Lord* I might add, from getting drenched. This doesn't prove we—or anyone else—were committing adultery. She and I bumped into each other, and I was merely trying to make sure she was safely escorted to her car. That's it. And Barbara," he said, turning to his wife, "you ought to be *ashamed* of yourself. If anybody should, you're the one who needs to be asking for forgiveness around here. Falsely accusing folks like that." He shook his head. "A shame and a disgrace."

"No," Barbara said. "No! You're *not* going to turn things around on me. You've been tipping out on me. I hired someone to follow you. I got photos here. Okay, maybe I didn't get the ones of you and her or you and Evelyn, if Evelyn's the one you were with Friday night, in a hotel room together—"

"You didn't get any photos of us being in a hotel room together because we weren't in any room together. I told you I was going to meet a potential client," Deacon Price said. "There's a restaurant in there. People have to go inside of that hotel to get to that restaurant."

"But you never said it was in a hotel," Barbara said. "Okay, so maybe you weren't doing anything with this one here"—she threw a hard glance my way—"but what about Evelyn? I bet you and Evelyn were together and not at no restaurant, either. Yeah, you two are smart. Of course you wouldn't be caught with Evelyn like you were caught in the picture with *her*. But you can't convince me it was a coincidence that Evelyn was there at a hotel on the same day that you were there."

"So in other words, you're admitting that you falsely accused your sister in Christ"—Pastor Godbee nodded at me—"in front of all these people today? Is that what you're confessing, Sister Price?"

Barbara forced a smile. "I didn't know all of it. But I felt if I had a problem, I needed to get it out in the open. Okay, so I was partly wrong." She turned fully toward me. "I'm sorry. I apologize for any embarrassment I might have caused you."

I was crying a little, thinking about all she'd taken me through today. And all I was getting from her for my troubles was an "I'm sorry." Still, I nodded my okay.

"But that doesn't mean Willie here is in the clear, or that little husband stealer Evelyn Payne is either."

Pastor Godbee raised his hand. "That's enough, Sister Price."

"But—"

"I said that's enough."

Barbara jumped to her feet, slapped the photos down on the

desk in front of where I sat, and said, "Come on, Willie! Let's get out of here. I'll be doggone if I'm going to sit here and let some wet-behind-the-ears preacher try and tell me when I can speak or not. Oh, and Pastor, you can consider this as our official notice that we'll no longer be members here." She started for the door, then stopped. "Come on, Willie!"

Deacon Price got up slowly. "Pastor, she doesn't speak for me. I'll see you at Bible study Wednesday night. And sister, I *profusely* apologize for what you've had to go through today. If there's any way I can make things right, please let me know."

"Willie!" Barbara said, tears now streaming down her face.

Willie nodded and left, closing the door gently behind him.

Chapter 51

For God is not unrighteous to forget your work and labor of love, which ye have showed toward his name, in that ye have ministered to the saints, and do minister.

—Hebrews 6:10

Pastor Godbee shook his head as the Prices left. "Wow," Pastor Godbee said, falling hard back against his teal leather chair. "Praise God for Jesus." He sat up straight, then leaned forward. "I'm so sorry you had to go through that. But you certainly handled yourself with grace." He shook his head once more.

I didn't say anything, still stunned by everything that had transpired on this day.

There was a loud knock on the door. Pastor Godbee stood to his feet. "That must be my mentor and pastor friend I called before you all came in. He said he was going to come over as soon as he got away from his church. I'm sure that's him now. Do you mind if he comes in while you're here?" Pastor Godbee said.

I shook my head. "No. It's fine with me."

Pastor Godbee placed his hand on my shoulder as he walked past me. "I know it's been a trying day. But I love this man. Maybe he can say something that will bless you and help you to heal, following what you've been through today."

"Pastor Godbee, you've truly been wonderful. But I don't mind meeting him."

"I thank you for that, Sister. Not many of us pastors have outbursts like what took place today, at least not during a church service. I'm going to ask my pastor friend to pray with us. He's a powerful man of God." Pastor Godbee hurried and opened the door. "I thought it was you," Pastor Godbee said. "Come on in, Pastor."

"I got here as fast as I could."

I turned and looked, unable to believe my own eyes. I stood to my feet.

"Pastor Ethan Roberts, I'd like you to meet—"

Ethan was already standing in front of me. "We've already met," Ethan said.

"Oh, you two know each other?"

"Yes," Ethan said. I could tell he was fighting hard to keep from smiling. I was as well.

"Small world, huh?" Pastor Godbee said. "But of course, I would think my sister here would know you since you are a gifted pastor and preacher in the city. Who probably *hasn't* heard of you, at least around these parts?"

I didn't say anything. I was stunned into almost absolute silence.

"She owns a floral shop," Ethan said. "The Painted Lady Flower Shop, I believe. Beautiful workmanship. I've patronized her shop on more than a few occasions." Ethan smiled.

"That's right," Pastor Godbee said. "I keep forgetting that my sister here is an awesome businesswoman in her own right. She's a great worker for the Lord, too; been *extremely* helpful since I arrived here. But today was a trying day for us all."

"So tell me what happened?" Ethan said to Pastor Godbee. "That's if you don't mind me asking."

"Oh, I certainly don't mind. I couldn't tell you much when I called you earlier," Pastor Godbee said, indicating for us to have a seat. We sat in the chairs next to each other. Pastor Godbee walked around his desk and sat down, then proceeded to tell Ethan everything as it had happened down to the photos that were being waved around inside of the sanctuary.

"So your member, the one that almost knocked me down when I was on my way in here, brought photos she'd had taken of this sister right here at a hotel on this past Friday?" Ethan glanced my way before allowing his eyes to engage my eyes.

"Yes," Pastor Godbee said.

Looking back to Pastor Godbee, Ethan asked, "Did anyone *see* these alleged photos?"

"Oh yes," Pastor Godbee said, standing up and picking up the photos that were face down on the desk where Barbara Price had left them.

I immediately sensed Ethan tense up. I shook my head quickly to put his mind to rest.

Pastor Godbee held the photos as he spoke. "They were photos of people going into the hotel and a few with our sister here coming out." He held up and turned around the photos of me and Willie Price, standing next to each other, toward us. "These are the photos that mostly had the man's wife up in arms. Apparently her husband was trying to be a gentleman by walking her to her car and using his coat to shield her from the pouring rain when she was leaving a restaurant that just happens to be located inside of the luxurious hotel."

"I'm familiar with that restaurant. I've eaten there many times myself," Ethan said.

Pastor Godbee nodded. "Of course, his wife jumped all over this and broadcasted to the entire church that she'd caught the two or three of them, I really don't even know at this point anymore where she was going with all of this, in an affair."

"Wow," Ethan said, looking through all of the photos now. He looked back up at Pastor Godbee. "Talk about drama in the church house. Now that's church drama there." He shook his head in disgust.

"Yeah." Pastor Godbee shook his head as he smiled a bit. "But God stepped in, directed me on what to do, and set things right."

"Well, I must say: in my twenty-something years of pastoring, I've never personally encountered anything quite like what you experienced today," Ethan said. "Honestly though, it doesn't appear you needed me after all."

"Oh, it's always good when you have someone who has your back," Pastor Godbee said. "I had all of those involved in here before you arrived. As you see, the deacon and his wife left already. Truthfully, I had no idea how things were going to turn out. I'm glad you came though. I just might have needed you to help me lay hands on some folks. But everything worked out, thank the Lord."

Ethan smiled and nodded a few times. "God is good . . ."

"All the time," Pastor Godbee said. "And all the time . . ."

"God is good," Ethan said.

"Well, I thank you for coming, Pastor Roberts. You just don't know what this means to me. To be able to call you my mentor *and* a friend, then to have you show up like you did today, ready to do spiritual battle, knowing all that you have to deal with and do yourself," Pastor Godbee said. "That's huge . . . it's major. I just thank God for putting someone like you in my life. You've been a true blessing. You really have."

"No problem. I'm just glad things worked out the way that they did. But you know what Romans 8:28 says," Ethan said.

"The way folks wear that scripture out, I believe everybody knows what that scripture says," Pastor Godbee said with a chuckle. "But it *is* true. 'And we know that all things work together for good to them that love God, to them who are the called according to his purpose.' " Pastor Godbee quoted. "Oh yes! Won't God work things *out?!*"

"If you don't mind," Ethan said. "Would it be all right if I were to speak with this lovely lady . . . this butterfly in your flower garden, alone?"

"Oh now, butterfly is right," Pastor Godbee said. "This one here truly transformed from a worm to a butterfly today, that's for God's Heaven sure. She might have started out as a worm, and I'm going to tell you, when things began this morning, she was definitely looking like a fuzzy, creepy crawling worm—a caterpillar in everybody's sight, if you will. Before we knew anything, there she was tied up, wrapped up, tangled all up in a cocoon, not even of her own making."

"Yes," Ethan said. "When we find ourselves in a cocoon, whether from our making or not, it's definitely not a pleasant feeling. Our own digestive juices begin to eat away at us. Then there's the struggle as changes begin to take place. You don't know what's happening, but somehow or other, you're developing wings; you're in the midst of a metamorphosis . . . a transformation, if you will. The scripture says, 'And be not conformed to this world: but be ye transformed by the renewing of your mind. . . .' "

"Yes! Romans 12:2," Pastor Godbee said, taking it over, " '. . . that ye may prove what is that good, and acceptable, and perfect, will of God.' Glory to God Almighty!"

"Oh yes," Ethan said, a bit more toned down than Pastor Godbee. "Being transformed. But those wings you've miraculously sprouted are wet and still soft. They've not firmed up or dried yet. You find yourself beating against the cocoon walls with those newly sprouted things, trying with all that you have to make your way out."

"Come on now, preacher," Pastor Godbee said. "You're preaching to the *preacher* now."

"You're struggling hard and beating with all that you have within you to get out." Ethan began to squirm as he demonstrated a wrapped-up, tied-up struggle. "You can't help but wonder what's going on. Why what is happening is happening to you. You feel like you're all alone and that no matter how hard you try, there seems to be no way to escape," Ethan said. "You're praying for a little outside help, but help doesn't appear to be anywhere around. Believe it or not, the last thing you need, at that stage, is someone trying to help you out. Not right then . . . not during that period of the developmental struggle."

"And you *know* most of us are praying for somebody to come help us get out," Pastor Godbee said. "Bless God, this is a good Word right here! This is blessing me!"

"Yes, we might want to be helped at that point," Ethan said. "But what we think will help us is the very thing that, in truth, would end up crippling us. Because you see, those wings we sprouted aren't yet strong enough to do what they need to do. Being wrapped up in that cocoon, protected, even though we don't realize it, while we're trying to beat our way out, is causing our wings to become stronger as they dry and harden. In other words: what may look like a bad thing from one perspective is the very thing, in the end, that's going to strengthen you . . . make you stronger. It will be that thing that will allow you to fly. And not just fly, but fly high. Because once your wings are strong enough, once you're ready, in God's sight, you'll easily be able to break free from what was holding you back. And when you fly—"

"Glory!" Pastor Godbee began to flap his arms majestically as though they were wings and he'd suddenly taken flight. "Look-a there, look-a there! That's what folks are going to be saying when we take flight. Look-a there, look-a there!"

"Yes," Ethan said, looking over at me now. "So no matter what we may be going through, we just have to know that what Satan may mean for our bad, God will use it for our good."

"Amen!" Pastor Godbee said, nodding his head, then moving it around like a bobble head gone wild. "Glo-rrry!" he yelled out.

"Amen," I said, although more quietly than a now-dancing and shouting Pastor Godbee, who was having a praise session all by himself.

Chapter 52

Now unto him that is able to keep you from falling,
and to present you faultless before the presence of
his glory with exceeding joy.

—Jude 24

Pastor Godbee had gathered up his things to go home. "You can just lock it and pull the door closed when you're ready to leave," Pastor Godbee said to Ethan. "It locks from the inside. The man that locks up after everyone is gone will check it again before he leaves just to be sure."

Ethan nodded. Pastor Godbee left, closing the door behind him.

Ethan stood there looking at me with a soft smile on his face before finally reaching over and hugging me. "Are you all right?" he asked.

I pulled back from his embrace and forced a smile, then nodded. "I'm okay."

"I'm sorry for what you must have gone through today."

I hunched my shoulders. "It wasn't any of your doing. It is what it is." I took a few steps away from him.

"Yeah, but I can't help but feel like this was partly my fault," Ethan said. "I was the one who chose that place. I was the one who asked you to meet me there."

"And I was the one who made the decision to go," I said. "So don't beat yourself up about it."

He took my hand, led me over to the couch in the office, pulled me down, and we sat next to each other. He glanced at his watch. "I can't stay long. My wife and family are waiting for me at the restaurant. Then I have to leave from there and make my way to another church to preach a three-o'clock church anniversary program. I already know I'm going to be late for the program, but I'll be there before it's time for me to deliver the message. I'll just let that pastor know I'll be running late."

"Busy, busy," I said, trying not to let on that hearing this didn't make me feel good at all.

He held on to my hand. "So this lady had her husband followed, the person she hired took pictures, and then she accused you and him of having an affair, right in the middle of service today?" Ethan said, frowning. "Is that *actually* what happened?"

"That pretty much sums it up."

"That is something," Ethan said. "I've seen a lot of things in my time as a preacher, but that is *truly* something else right there."

"So you and Pastor Godbee know each other?" I said, changing the subject.

Ethan's eyes lovingly roamed over my face as he looked down at me. He then took his hand and slowly moved a strand of hair away from near my eye. I sat up straighter, once again feeling the effects of his touch. He put his hand down, then nodded. "Yes. Terrell Godbee is an awesome young minister of the Word. He's like a young Timothy to me, and I suppose I'm like an old Paul to him. I can see him doing great things for the Kingdom of God."

"I couldn't believe it when you walked in. I didn't know what was going on. For a second there, I wondered if there was a photo of you, and he had you come—"

"No. At least, not that I know of. He texted me and told me that something was going on over here that he could really use my spiritual help and advice on. When we talked, he told me he was going to see about getting all of you in his office to talk. I told him I'd be here as soon as I could get away," Ethan said. He then tilted his head to the side. "I had no idea this is where you attended church. And I certainly didn't know I would see you sitting here when I came in."

"It makes you wonder what's going on, doesn't it?" I said.

"Yes." He took my hand. "Now you know I don't *want* to, but I *do* have to go. I don't want to keep everyone waiting on me. I know you have things you're dealing with right now. And I really don't want to leave you either. But you know how things are with me and when it comes to me."

I forced a smile. *Yeah, I know how things are with you, especially when it comes to me, and you have to choose.*

"What do you want to do?" Ethan said when I didn't say anything. "What can I do to help make things better?"

I looked at him, then really deep into his eyes. I knew how much he blessed the people of God. I knew how much he loved what he was doing. There was no way I could tell him what I really wanted. I loved him; that much we both knew. Lying about it wouldn't keep it a secret from God, Who happens to know all things. But I also knew that there was no way Ethan and I would ever be together. Not at this time anyway. Probably not anytime soon either. He was married and he wasn't going to leave his wife or his position in the church. Not for me. I completely got that now.

Whenever the choice had presented itself to him, he had *never* chosen me. Not when it came down to choosing between me and his girlfriend in the early years. Not now with that same girlfriend who had become his wife. And most definitely (and understandably) not when it came to choosing between me and what he was doing for the Lord by way of being a minister in the church. His love for God was greater than his love for me. And in truth, I wouldn't have wanted him to be any other way. I think that's mostly why I love him so much. He, first and foremost, honestly and truly loves God.

Had Ethan done things that weren't pleasing to God? Yes. He's a man of God, not God. Does he really love me? Truthfully, I believe so. But we weren't going to be together, not the way I desired. I wished things had gone differently when we were younger and could have chosen a different path than we had. But this is where we were now. And as much as I loved Ethan Duane "Spears . . . Spear Carrier" Roberts, I knew that he and I could not continue seeing each other the way we had done over these past ten years. It just hurt too much.

I stood up. "I'm going home now," I said. "And you need to get on to your family."

Ethan stood up as well. He looked into my eyes, then nodded. "So I guess what you're saying without saying it is good-bye."

I smiled. "Somehow, good-bye never really seems to work for us. I guess I'm just saying so long. For now, anyway. But who can say what God has planned for us down the road? You and I may love each other more than anyone will ever probably know. And what we did or didn't do, honestly, is between me, you, and God. And as much as anyone might want to know what all has taken place between us, even down to this past Friday night in that lovely hotel room, suffice it to say, it's something no one other than us may likely *ever* know. But I *do* know that we both love God with all of our hearts, mind, and soul." I felt a tear begin a journey down my face. Then another, and another one.

Ethan reached up and gently wiped both sides of my face with his thumbs where the tears were making tracks, leading the way for more to follow. "I understand," he said. "But if you ever need me, will you at least call?"

I chuckled a little. "No. I will not," I said, then went to the desk and gathered up the photos, sticking them back into the large gold envelope. "And you won't be calling me. If it is God's will for us to be together, then God will have to be the one, from this day forward, to make it happen. But it will have to be the right way. For me and from here on out, I'm not settling for anything less."

Ethan nodded. "I respect that," he said.

"And as we leave this place, but not from God's presence, I'll say to you as it was recorded in Genesis 31:49," I said, forcing a smile. " 'The Lord watch between me and thee, when we are absent one from another.' I don't know how it is, and I'm not exactly sure when or how it happened, but somehow our souls are tied together. I can see that so clearly now. And as bad as it may sound, I believe, should either of us ever *truly* need the other, God will let us know."

Ethan slowly shook his head. "What you call 'forever soul ties,' huh?"

I nodded. "Forever soul ties. Would you believe that's what Pastor Godbee preached on today? God is something! Well, it appears that as long as you and I are on this earth, for whatever the reason . . . whatever the purpose that neither of us may quite understand—I know I certainly don't. Even at this juncture, as we walk away, our souls are somehow knitted together."

He leaned down, his face right there at mine. "So what *exactly* are you saying? That this really is it for us? It's the end of the line for you and me?"

I shrugged. "I suppose it is."

He nodded. "Then may I kiss you one last time before we part?" he asked, grabbing and embracing me tightly.

I wiped at my tears, then shook my head as I pushed his body away. It was one of the hardest things I'd had to do in a long time, but I knew in my heart it was the right thing to do. I deserve the best God has for me. No piecemeal, no half-stepping, no leftovers, no crumbs. But I had to love me enough to do what was right for me. And I had to love God enough not to compromise myself or my values.

I walked out of the door as he stood there. When I turned around one last time, he blew me a kiss, then gave me a hands-off hug by hugging himself. I smiled. And as I walked down the hallway, slowly at first, then faster, I found myself saying, "The Lord watch between me and thee, when we are absent one from another."

"Hey!" Ethan said. "Hold up!"

I stopped and turned around completely as he walked quickly to catch up.

When he reached me, he scratched his right brow, then spoke. "I don't want you walking to your car alone," he said. "I guess maybe some habits are just too hard for me to break. Since everybody else is gone, I want to make sure you get to your car okay. Also, I have something in my car for you."

I started laughing.

"What?" he said with a puzzled look. "What's so funny?"

"Oh, I was just thinking how a desire to walk me to my car was what got me in the mess I found myself in today. Deacon

Price's insistence to see me to my car safely got me caught up in those pictures."

Ethan nodded, then flashed me a reassuring grin. We continued outside. "So I take it your husband wasn't at church with you today," he said as we walked together.

"Nope. He doesn't care much for 'organized services.' He believes he can love God without having to sit in a pew every time the church doors open. Today was one day, I suppose, that I was glad he wasn't here to see just how bad Christians can cut up when we want to."

"Do you think he's heard about what happened today?"

"Most likely." I flashed a quick smile. "I'm sure somebody's told him by now."

"So what are you planning on telling him?" Ethan asked just as we reached my car.

I stopped and turned to him as I unlocked the door. "If he should ask, I'll tell him the truth."

"Which will be . . . ?"

"That Barbara Price showed up at church today with pictures of me and her husband together. That she publicly accused me and him of having an affair, but that her accusations were false, without merit, and *so* not the case."

"And if your husband happens to ask you what you were doing at that hotel in the first place? What will you tell him *then?*"

"I will tell him that I was having a wonderful dinner, being treated as though I was loved, and equally, like I truly mattered. And that maybe *he* should try doing that for me sometimes, himself."

Ethan started laughing. "You know you're crazy, don't you?" I knew he was merely teasing me.

I smiled, opened my door, threw my pocketbook and the envelope with the photos inside onto the passenger's seat, and slid into my seat. "I know that there are some crazy even a pill can't cure," I said.

"Oh, wait a minute! Don't leave just yet. I need to run to my car and get what I told you I have for you."

"Ethan, I don't know about a gift. . . ."

"Just sit right there. I'll be right back." He hurried to his car, a few rows down from mine, and rushed back.

Leaning down and inside my opened car door, he held out a square, beautifully wrapped gold package. "I had planned on giving this to you the next time I saw you," he said. "I just didn't realize that the next time would be today, or that the next time might possibly be my last time." He handed the box to me. "For you."

I took it. "You want me to open it now?"

He smiled. "Please. I'm telling you: when you see this, you're not going to believe it." He shook his head as he continued to smile. "I promise; you're not."

I carefully tore off the gorgeous gold wrapping from the box and lifted the white, square top. Inside was one half of a gold coin necklace, a Mizpah people call it, with the scripture I'd just quoted to him in Pastor Godbee's office of the covenant made between Laban and Jacob in Genesis 31:49: "The Lord watch between me and thee, when we are absent one from another."

I pressed the half-coin pendant against my heart and began to cry. He moved toward me; I waved him back, then waved for him to move back even farther. I couldn't let him touch me. I couldn't. If I did, I would never be able to break away. I quickly grabbed the handle and closed the door, effectively putting a barrier between us. I then cranked my car, blew him a kiss through my window as I pressed that half of a complete coin to my heart, then drove away.

If Ethan and I were ever to be, it would have to be God's way, and *only* God's way.

That is . . . should there ever be a next time.

Chapter 53

But if ye do not forgive, neither will your Father which is in heaven forgive your trespasses.
—Mark 11:26

A s I pulled into my driveway, Zeke stepped out of the front door. Evelyn Payne was with him. I didn't know *what* that was all about, since Evelyn had never been to my house, not *ever*. In fact, I didn't even know she knew where I lived. So instead of parking in the garage the way I normally did, I parked outside. I didn't know: I might just have to make a quick getaway and not need to wait for the garage door to let me out. I just knew Evelyn had better not be at my house telling Zeke what had happened at church today. I knew she had better not. I grabbed the envelope with the photos, stepped out of my car, and walked up to them.

Evelyn was extremely nervous. She immediately glanced down at the envelope I held in my hand.

"I'm sorry," Evelyn said. "I'm *so* sorry."

"Oh, you're sorry?" I said, not having a clue what she was apologizing for. But having learned a long time ago it was best to keep your mouth shut when someone was telling you something that may end up benefiting you, I didn't volunteer any evidence of my lack of knowledge.

"Listen, I can explain everything," Zeke said. I saw him also glance down at the envelope. Apparently this envelope meant something to the both of them. I understood why it would to

Evelyn, since she was in one of the photos and Barbara had called her out. But Zeke was a mystery at this point.

I shrugged, hoping my actions would encourage them to continue talking. I decided to go into the house. If something was going to go down, I didn't want the neighborhood to witness it, especially not "Gladys Kravitz" from across the street. Okay, that's not Ms. Corrine's real name, but she reminded me so much of that nosy neighbor on the classic television show *Bewitched*.

Zeke and Evelyn followed me into the house. I quickly took out my cell phone and made sure it was on, just in case I needed to call 911 in a hurry and couldn't get to my regular phone.

"Are those the photos Barbara Price had at church?" Evelyn asked.

I glanced down at the envelope and with a twinge of attitude said, "Ye*p*."

Evelyn sighed. "You know that woman is crazy. She's crazy, I'm telling you. If you ask me, I'd say she needs to be committed. I can't believe she would do something like that right in the middle of a church service, of all places. That woman has no respect for the Lord's house, no respect at all."

"She was definitely in rare form today," I said. "That's for sure. But then, you did leave early, before she got going good."

"I take it you've looked at those photos?" Evelyn's voice was shaking.

"Yeah. Me and Pastor Godbee both have. Of course, it was Barbara who insisted that Pastor Godbee take a look at them. He didn't really want to, but she wouldn't stop until he'd seen them."

Visibly upset now, Evelyn began to shake her head. "I shouldn't have left like I did. I should have just stayed. I kept telling myself I should stay right there. I just couldn't believe she had pictures." There was nervousness and uneasiness with her.

"Yep. You're definitely in here." I looked at Evelyn first. And because I felt there was more going on, I looked at Zeke, who was also uncharacteristically nervous and uncomfortable.

"Baby, listen: it's not at all what it looks like," Zeke said. "Evelyn and I are merely friends. That's all . . . just friends. She's been trying to get me to come back to the Lord."

"Is that right?" I said, still not having a clue what he was talking about but believing if I let him keep on, he'd spill everything. The "we're just friends" statement was a dead giveaway this might not turn out well.

"Yes, we're just friends," Evelyn said, glancing between me and Zeke as though the two of them were trying to exchange coded messages. "He's a good man, your husband is. He's been quite helpful to me since my husband passed away, you just don't know. He, as well as Deacon Price; Pastor Hutchings, when he was still our pastor; a lot of people. But your husband has been a true blessing here lately."

"Oh, he has, has he?" I reached deep to force this smile. "Yeah. That's my Zeke. Always trying to see what he can do to help somebody else." What I was hearing was *past* shocking. But I refused to let on that any of this was news to me.

"I don't know exactly what those photos in there show," Evelyn said, nodding toward the envelope. "But I'm not an adulterer like Barbara accused me of today. She thinks somebody wants her husband, your husband, everybody's husband. But don't nobody want Willie."

"Of course," I said as I made a show of looking at the envelope, wiggling it a bit as I watched both her and Zeke's attentive reactions. "Who would want Willie when there are *so* many others to choose from?"

"May I see those?" Evelyn said.

I held up the envelope again. "You mean these photos here?" I then remembered that there were also photos of me and Willie in there that she obviously hadn't been told about yet. And she'd rushed out before Barbara began accusing me.

"Yes," Evelyn said.

I let my hand drop back down. "I tell you what: why don't you just tell me the truth and let's stop playing games?" I said. "Okay?"

"You mean about why we were there?" Zeke said, jumping in at that point.

Now that took me back a bit. Zeke was confessing that he was there at the hotel on the same night I was. If I hadn't been trying to keep my cool, I would have covered my mouth from this revelation. Zeke and I were in the same building on the same day. I'm not sure when he was there, but what if we had run into each other? *Gracious a-mighty!*

I kept my composure and tried not to allow too much of the shakiness I was now feeling enter into my voice. "So . . . you two are having an affair." I said it point blank, mainly (possibly what Barbara Price was doing) to smoke the truth out.

The two of them exchanged quick looks again. "Don't be silly. We're just friends, I told you," Zeke said with a nervous laugh.

"But you didn't address my statement." I directed my full attention to Zeke now. "The two of you and the truth this time." I shook the envelope a few times.

"You know, I really should be going," Evelyn said as she stood up hurriedly.

I stood up as well. "Why in such a rush? Why did you even come here to my house, of all places?"

She took a few steps back. "I was so upset with what happened at church today. I couldn't think straight. I was thinking you would be home shortly after church dismissed. Zeke just tried to help calm me down. That's all. He was trying to calm me down."

"Good old Zeke. You can always count on him to be around when you need him," I said as I looked at him. He knew I didn't mean that *at all.* "I'm sorry, but I still haven't gotten a straight answer yet. The affair . . . do you want to tell me about it or not?"

"I'm sorry," Evelyn said, then quickly exited my house through the front door. I didn't bother to pursue her. Turning back to Zeke, I nodded. "I guess that just leaves me and you," I said. "The way it should be anyway."

"Listen, I know this doesn't look good. But if you don't mind, can I *please* see the photographs." Zeke nodded at the envelope I still held.

I looked down at the envelope and thought about his request. "You know what: I don't think I'm going to let you see them." I then sprinted toward my office. Zeke followed after me. I headed straight to the shredder.

"What are you doing?" Zeke said as I began to feed the envelope with the photos into the shredder. "What are you doing?!"

"What does it look like I'm doing?" By this time, I was crying hard.

Zeke came over and hugged me. "I'm sorry I've hurt you like this. I'm sorry!"

I wanted to push him away, but I couldn't.

"I promise you, if you'll give me another chance, I'm going to do better. I'm going to do better by you. Listen to me: you're the love of my life," Zeke said, framing my tear-stained face between the palms of his hands. "Do you hear me? I don't want to lose you. Please forgive me," he said. "Please."

"I'm the love of your life, huh?" I laughed. "Oh, that's a joke!"

"I know I've not done right by you. I know that. But I'm asking you to forgive me. Please." He dropped to his knees as he held onto my hand. "Please forgive me."

It was during that time—when I was about to tell him where he could go, and how fast he could get there . . . as I heard Zeke begging me to forgive him—that I got it. I *got* it. I had my own things I needed to be forgiven for. And just as I wanted God to forgive me, I had to forgive, likewise. Whether I realized it or not, I was setting the watermark level to be used for my forgiveness. *Forgive us our trespasses as we forgive those who trespass against us.* Without even thinking what I was doing, I'd shredded the evidence, just as God shreds evidence of our forgiven sins. *If I do not forgive, neither will My Father which is in Heaven forgive me of my trespasses.*

I can't say where Zeke and I will go from this point. In a perfect world, from here on out, he would be everything I desired in life, and maybe I'd be a little more of what he desired. In some folks' world, I shouldn't have even considered going any further with him. I definitely shouldn't have given him another chance after he'd pretty much confessed to cheating on me with Evelyn. But we don't live in a perfect world; we live in a real world. And in the real world, you find there are times when you just have to make the best of each day you're given with what you have.

What I do know is that I deserve better than I've been getting. And at this point, I refuse to continue crawling on my belly and accepting less. Zeke is my husband. He's the man, years ago, that I pledged my heart to—for better or worse. But things are going to have to change in our household. Because if they don't, we're not going to make it. And this time around, it's not going to be all on me either.

And that's exactly what I told Zeke. He nodded and professed that he understood; only the passage of time will truly tell.

"Can we pray?" Zeke said after, hours later, we'd both had our full say.

I almost broke down in tears again when he said that; I'd waited so long to hear those words from him. I nodded yes.

He took both my hands, squeezed them, and began to pray. "Our Father. The God of Abraham, Isaac, and Jacob. Lord, I come to You first of all to confess that I am a sinner. Please come into my heart, Lord Jesus. Forgive me for all of the things I've done wrong. Please . . . save me. God, I believe that Jesus is Your only begotten Son. I believe that Jesus came to earth and died on the cross for my sins. I believe that Jesus rose from the dead on the third day. And I believe that right now, He's sitting on Your right hand. I believe all of this in my heart, and I'm confessing with my mouth, the Lord Jesus Christ, thereby transforming me from a sinner, to a sinner who is now saved by grace. Thank You, Lord. I thank You."

As Zeke prayed and tears fell from my eyes, I began to feel as though I was being completely transformed myself, from a caterpillar into a beautiful butterfly with magnificent wings that would now allow me to fly as high as I could see myself soaring.

Zeke told me to wait right there as he went outside. Upon his return, he brought with him a single red rose from my rose garden. One single flower. No one can appreciate what that one gesture, coming from Zeke, meant to me.

I laughed. It was a laughter that flowed from the joy of the Lord.

I was born a sinner.

That's the first thing you would have needed to know about me. The second thing you need to know is that I am saved by grace. No more a worm, but a child of the Most High God.

I am a sinner saved by grace.

Not only had Zeke changed, but somewhere along the way today, I suppose so had I.

No. I wasn't fooling myself. Life wasn't going to be easy. But at least now, I could look forward to the view my wings would afford me to see.

Still, I've learned: time truly has a way of telling that which was once untold.

Discussion Questions

1. Did the first chapter affect you in any way? If so, how?

2. What did you notice about the person telling the story when it came to her name?

3. What were your initial feelings about Ethan Roberts? Did those feelings/thoughts change at any point of the story?

4. Discuss the person Ethan called "Butterfly" and her relationship with her husband. With her children.

5. Discuss Ethan's relationship with his wife and children.

6. Should the person we know as Butterfly have left her job to pursue her own business at that stage in her life? Please discuss.

7. Was it a mistake for Ethan and Butterfly to have gone to lunch in the first place? What about meeting at the park? Given how the two felt, should they have eaten alone at her place of business? Discuss.

8. What do you believe Ethan and Butterfly could have done to improve their respective marriages? If you feel they did as much as possible, discuss your belief.

9. Zynique chose not to go to college. Do you believe she was wrong and should have? Should her parents have tried harder to get her to go?

10. Discuss your thoughts regarding Zanetta, Zion, Zynique, and Madame Perry.

11. Discuss Ethan and the situation surrounding his missing daughter. Was Ethan right to have called Butterfly when all of this was going on?

12. Was Zynique out of line in telling her father what she thought when it came to how he treated her mother? Why or why not?

13. What were your thoughts about Zeke being gone so much? If you think he was wrong, what do you think his wife should have done to change things?

14. Talk about the tie between Ethan and Butterfly.

15. Discuss both the restaurant and hotel incident.

16. Discuss what took place during the church service with Barbara Price and Pastor Godbee and later the meeting that transpired in Pastor Godbee's office. What were your thoughts when Pastor Godbee's mentor arrived? Discuss that and all that transpired afterward.

17. Do you feel that, in the end, Butterfly made the correct decision? Why or why not?

If you enjoyed *Forever Soul Ties,* don't miss
Redeeming Waters

Available now wherever books are sold

Here's an excerpt from *Redeeming Waters.* . . .

Chapter 1

*The waters wear the stones: thou washest away the
things which grow out of the dust of the earth; and
thou destroyest the hope of man.*

—Job 14:19

Brianna Bathsheba Wright Waters looked out of the window of their three-bedroom, one-and-a-half-bathroom
house at the rain. A "starter home" is what her twenty-three-
year-old (three years her senior) husband of eight months, Unzell Michael Waters, told her over two months ago when they
bought it.

"Baby, I promise you, things are going to get better for us
down the road," Unzell had said after they officially moved in.
"I know this is not what either of us envisioned we'd be doing
right about now. But I promise you, I'm *going* to get us into that
mansion we talked about. I am."

She'd married Unzell at age nineteen, a year and a half after
her high school graduation, as Unzell was finishing his final
year at the University of Michigan. Unlike most women she
knew, Brianna wanted to marry in December. The wintertime
was her favorite time of the year. She loved everything about
winter. It wasn't a dead period as far as she was concerned. To
her, that was the time of rest, renewal, anticipation, and mira-
cles taking place that the eyes weren't always privy to. Winter
was the time when flower bulbs, trees, and other plants could
establish themselves underground, developing better and
stronger roots. Winter was the time when various pests and

bugs were killed off; otherwise the world would be overrun with them. Brianna loved the rich colors she would be able to use in a winter wedding: deep reds and dark greens.

But she equally loved summertime. Summer was a reminder of life bursting forth in its fullness and full potential after all seemed dead not so long ago. Summer now reminded her of her days of playing carefree outside, *truly* without a care in the world.

So she and Unzell married the Saturday before Christmas. It was a beautiful ceremony; her parents had spared no expense. After all, this would be the only time they would be the parents of the bride. Her older brother, Mack, might settle down some-day. But even if he did, they would merely be the parents of the groom, which was a totally different expense, experience, and responsibility.

Unzell Waters was already pretty famous, so everybody and his brother wanted to be invited to the wedding ceremony. Un-zell was the star football player at the University of Michigan and a shoo-in for the NFL. As a running back, he'd broken all kinds of records, and the only question most had was whether he would be the number-one or number-two pick in the first round of the NFL draft the last Saturday in April. Unzell was on track to make millions—more millions than either he or Bri-anna could fathom *ever* being able to spend in *several* lifetimes.

Still Brianna's best friend, Alana Norwood had been her maid of honor. Alana had grown wilder than Brianna, but Bri-anna understood Alana . . . and Alana understood her.

"Girlfriend, I'm glad you're settling down so early, if that's what you want," Alana had said when Brianna first told her she and Unzell were getting married in a year. "But I plan on see-ing *all* that the world has to offer me before my life becomes dedicated to any one person like that."

Of course, when Alana learned *just* how famous Unzell was even *before* he was to go pro, then heard about the millions of dollars sports commentators were predicting he'd likely get when he signed—no matter which team he signed with—she said to Brianna, "God really *does* look after you! Of course, He's always looked after you. People on TV are talking eighty-six million dollars, over five years, just for one man to play . . . one man, to *play*. And you're going to be his wife? I know you used to say all the time that you were God's favorite. Well, I'm starting to believe maybe you really are."

"Alana, now you know I used to just *say* things like that. I don't *really* believe God has favorites," Brianna said. "The Bible tells us that God is no respecter of persons. We're all equal in His sight."

"Well, we may have the *opportunity* to be equal, but it's obvious that not all of us are walking in our opportunities. Not the way you do, anyway. So you're definitely ahead of a lot of us, not equal by any means. All I know is that you spoke that Word of Favor with a capital *F* over your life, and look what's happening with you so far."

The wedding was absolutely beautiful, every single detail and moment of it. But with the championship game being played the first week in January, Brianna and Unzell were only able to spend one day of a honeymoon before Unzell was off again to practice.

Michigan's team was the team to beat with number twenty-two, Unzell Waters, being one of the main obstacles standing against the other team having even a *semblance* of a chance. Brianna was at the game in Miami watching it along with her family. With two minutes remaining in the fourth quarter, Michigan was already a comfortable three touchdowns ahead. In Brianna's opinion, there really was no reason for Unzell to even be on the field. She, her grandfather Pearson Wright, and father Amos Wright were saying as much when that play happened—the play that would alter Unzell's career and life.

One of the other team's players grabbed Unzell by the leg as he ran full speed and yanked him down, pulling his leg totally out of joint. With him being down, everybody on the other team piled on him. Unzell was badly hurt. Instantly, his prospective stock for the NFL plummeted. Then came the doctor's prognosis. Even with the two necessary surgeries, Unzell would never be able to play football at that level again.

Brianna assured him things would be all right. "God still has you, Unzell."

"Yeah, but if God had me in the first place, then why would He allow something like this to happen to me . . . happen to us?" Unzell said as he lay in that hospital bed. "God knows both of us. He knows us, Brianna. He knows our hearts. God knows we would have done right when it came to me being in the NFL. So why? Why did this happen? And if God is a healer, then why can't He heal my leg completely? Why can't He make me whole again?"

"I believe that God *can* heal your leg, Unzell," Brianna said. "But right now we have to deal with reality. And from all that the doctors are saying, football is out for you, at least for now. So you and I need a new direction, that's all. We're going to be all right though." She lovingly took hold of his hand, then squeezed it. "We are." She smiled.

"So you're not going to leave me?"

Brianna frowned as she first jerked her head back, then primped her lips before forcing a smile. "Leave *you*? Where did *that* come from?"

"Face it; I'm not going to be making millions now. In fact, I'll be doing well just to find a job, any job at all, in this economy."

"First of all, *Mister* Waters, I did not marry you for your money or your potential money. I've known you since we were in high school. You were in the twelfth grade; I was in the ninth. You didn't have any money then and I fell in love with you. So if you think I married you for your money, then maybe I *should* leave you." Brianna put her hand on her hip.

"I know, Bree-Bath-she," he said, calling her by the pet name he sometimes called her. "But do you know how many women wanted me because they saw dollar signs?"

"Yeah, I know. I'm not stupid. I even think you thought about getting with a few of them. In fact, who knows, maybe you did. But still, I married you for you. And I married you for better or worse; for richer or poorer."

"Come on, Brianna. Nobody really means that part when

they say it. Who truly wants to be with someone poor? Sure, we may feel that's where we are at the time, but all of us believe our lives are going to get to the better and the richer at some point—sooner rather than later—not worse or poorer."

"Well, if me staying with you now after you've lost millions of dollars—that if I'm not mistaken, you never really had any-way—means I meant what I was vowing when I said those words, then please know: I meant them when I said them. Okay, so those in the know were saying you'd likely get a con-tract worth eighty-six million dollars over five years with a guar-anteed fifty million and now it looks like you won't. So be it. I'm just glad you're okay. You could have been paralyzed on that play. You and I will do what we need, to be all right. Be-sides, you're graduating in May. You'll get your Electrical Com-puter Engineering degree. Do like most folks and either get a job or start your own business. Regardless, Unzell, I'm here to stay. So deal with it." Brianna flicked her hand.

Unzell smiled, then looked down at his hand. "God has cer-tainly blessed me richly." He looked up. "God gave me you."

"Oh," Brianna said, all mushy as she kissed him. "That was *so* sweet."

Brianna couldn't help but think about how far she and Un-zell had come since that fateful day. Following Unzell's two surgeries and the rehabilitation period, she'd suspended at-tending college and gotten a job as a secretary, living with her parents while he finished his final months of college in Ann Arbor. After Unzell graduated, he moved back to Montgomery, Alabama. He was relentless about getting a job, even when it felt like no one was hiring. He was diligent, beating the pave-ment and searching the Internet. In four weeks, he landed a job as an assistant stage manager setting up stages for music concerts, but was told if he wanted to excel in this business, he needed to be in Atlanta.

So that's what he and Brianna did: moved to Georgia.

It didn't hurt when Alana told Brianna that she was also mov-ing to Atlanta to pursue her dream of becoming a video girl. At least now, Brianna and Alana would each have a friend in their new city. Brianna especially needed someone after quickly learning that in his position, Unzell could be gone for weeks, sometimes even months at a time.

Brianna continued to stare out of the window. She suddenly began to smile.

"And what are *you* smiling about?" Unzell said, jarring her back to the present.

Spinning around, she kissed him when he came near. "I didn't hear you come in."

He embraced her. "You were gazing out of the window. It looked like you were in deep thought; I didn't want to disturb you. Then you broke into that incredibly enchanting smile of yours, and I couldn't hold myself back any longer. Did you just think of a joke or something that made you happy?"

"Look," she said, pointing outside.

He looked out of the window and shrugged. "And what exactly am I looking for? All I see is rain, the sun shining, and trees and other things getting drenched."

"Don't you know what that's supposed to mean? Rain while the sun is shining."

He laughed. "Here we go again. Another something you learned when you were growing up? Like not stepping on a crack so you won't break your mother's back. Not walking under a ladder or splitting a pole because it will bring bad luck. Not sweeping someone's feet or you'll sweep them or someone else out of your life."

"No. Not exactly like *those* things, which are merely superstitions. This is different. I'm not saying that I believe it, but they say that when it's raining and the sun is shining, the devil is beating his wife."

"Yeah, right." Unzell smirked. "Actually, the scientific term for it is 'sunshower.'"

"Scientific term, huh? Well, people also say that if you stick a pin in the ground and listen, you can hear her screams."

"Oh. So do you want to go outside and do that so we can put that old wives' tale to the test?" Unzell's eyes danced as he spoke. "I'm game to play in the rain if you are."

"Nope. Alana and I tested it out when we were younger."

He laughed. "And the verdict was?"

"I didn't hear a thing. Of course, Alana claimed that she did. She said the scream was faint. But honestly? I think she heard something because she wanted to believe it was true. Then she said we'd used the wrong kind of pin and that's why it didn't work right."

"Alana is something else, that's for sure. So how is she these days?"

"Still trying to get a contract as a video girl or video whatever they're called."

"I wouldn't ever count Alana out. Before you know it, she'll be over here forcing us to watch her DVD, showing how she was 'doing her thing.' " He made a quick pumping dance move followed by the long-outdated Cabbage Patch.

Unzell wrapped his arms around Brianna. She fully submitted, lying back into him, then rubbing one of his hard, muscular arms that gently engulfed her.

"The devil beating his wife," he said with a sinister giggle as they both looked out of the window. "Well, now, I think I've heard just about everything."

Brianna broke away from his embrace and turned to face him, playfully hitting his arm. "Just don't *you* ever try that devil move on *me*."

He grabbed her and lovingly locked her again into his arms, gazing deeply into her brown eyes as they faced each other. "Never. I promise you I will *leave* before I *ever* raise a hand to you." He hugged her. "I would never abuse a blessing of God; I'm too afraid of what God would do to me if I did." He gently pushed her slightly away from him to look into her eyes again. "Besides, I love you too much. We're one body now. So whatever I do to you, I'll be doing to myself. And I would *never* lay a negative hand or word, for that matter, on myself. Therefore, I won't ever do anything like that to you."

"See, that's why I love you so much." She cocked her head to one side. "You really get this whole concept of loving your wife the way Christ loves the church."

"I wouldn't want our life together to be any other way. Not any other way." He pulled her to him and squeezed her as he locked her in his arms, causing her to giggle out loud. He stopped, cupped her face, and kissed her with an overflow of passion.